# MURDER BY NUMBERS

In Silicon Valley, Death Has An Algorithm.

R.S. VAISBORT

PUBLISHER'S NOTE
This is a work of fiction. Names, characters, places, and incidents either are the product of the author's imagination or are used fictitiously, and any resemblance to actual persons, living or dead, business establishments, events or locales is entirely coincidental.

ISBN-10: 150074011X
ISBN-13: 9781500740115

*For my family, friends and colleagues,*
*for their friendship, encouragement, trust, and guidance.*
*And, with the greatest love and gratitude,*
*for my wife, Audra, and my children, Dante and Navarro.*

"THE PROBLEM WITH PUTTING TWO AND TWO TOGETHER IS THAT SOMETIMES YOU GET FOUR, AND SOMETIMES YOU GET TWENTY-TWO."

— Dashiell Hammett, *The Thin Man*

# Chapter 1

February, 2001
The San Francisco Bay Area

Darren Park kept one eye on the road while he glanced at the dashboard clock with the other. Early evening filtered through the rain-splattered windows. "Jesus," he yawned. Only six p.m., and he was ready for bed.

He'd felt pretty good since arriving home from Korea ten hours earlier. He'd hit the ground running and hadn't stopped. In fact, he'd felt particularly good when he left the office. He hadn't thought about coffee then. It was all about getting on the road, beating traffic, and getting to dinner. But jet lag was setting in. An oversight he was now regretting.

Darren looked down at the empty cup holder forlornly. "Where's that grande latte when you need it?" He craved a java fix. "Those damn Starbucks are everywhere, except where you really need them." He stared at the dark road stretching ahead.

He rubbed his eyes. Darren needed caffeine. He'd just have to run on empty until he got to Half Moon Bay – another half hour at least.

"Goddamn Bay Area weather," he muttered, leaning forward and peering through the rain hitting the windshield. He drove slower than he cared to, but he still made good time. "My Clark Kent to Superman move was pretty slick," he thought. A faint smile crossed his face.

Instead of going home to change his clothes, he'd gone from jeans and a tee shirt to his best suit while sitting in the front seat of his car. All this while parked in a remote corner of Synergy's parking lot. It hadn't been particularly comfortable or easy. But it beat going all the way home. And he sure as hell wasn't going to wear a suit to work all day. Suits, ties and technology companies didn't mix. Wearing one would inevitably provoke a thousand questions. He could just hear the comments: "Job interview, Darren?" "Going to a funeral, dude?" Questions he didn't feel like dealing with. Changing clothes in the car was a smart move.

But he wasn't sure he'd gotten everything together quite right. He tugged at his shirtfront, fingering each button. Somehow he'd managed to match the proper button to the proper buttonhole. He couldn't afford to be wrong and walk in looking like a slob…or an amateur. Not tonight. He turned on the car's interior dome light and flipped down the vanity mirror to double check.

"You *are* looking good Mr. Park," he said with a smile. He looked sharp: dark gray wool jacket and slacks with a sky blue dress shirt. And, of course, the wristwatch. His favorite – a Rolex Daytona.

The watch said it all. Style. Success. Edge. If it were up to him, he'd wear it to work every day. That would make a statement. A jeans-and-tee-shirt-wearing Silicon Valley drone sporting a five-thousand-dollar watch for all to see. But for now it would have to make a statement on rare occasions well outside the office, when worn with a stylish business suit. Occasions like the present.

He caught another look at himself in the rearview mirror as he flipped off the dome light. His hair was perfect. He smiled again. For the first time in his life, he was profoundly pleased with himself. He hit the play button on the CD player. A mindless monotony of electronic house music poured through the car's six-speaker sound system. He tapped his hands on the steering wheel in an involuntary rhythm. He fought the jet lag and psyched himself up for his meeting. Another thirty minutes, forty on the outside, and he'd be there.

Darren silently calculated the time he would spend at the dinner meeting. It was an important one, but the way he had it figured, he'd be home in bed by nine, nine-thirty. With luck, early enough to catch tonight's episode of *The Sopranos*.

He was about to check his voicemail messages when he noticed the headlights in his rearview mirror. He picked up the cell phone, paused a second, and put it back down. "Screw it," he decided. "If anyone called, they can wait 'til tomorrow for a response."

Tonight was not the night to answer e-mail or make phone calls, he thought, and went back to his post-dinner planning. Watch a little television…or veg out on the PlayStation? PS2 it would be. He had become addicted to playing that thing. He knew buying it was a mistake.

The headlights flashed again in his rearview. The car was approaching damned fast for a night like this. And the lights were damned bright.

Darren waved his hand in front of the mirror. "Turn off your stupid high beams!"

A moment later, he realized that the approaching headlights weren't high beams. They were just the normal driving headlights of an oversized SUV. "Tanks," he muttered. "Should be outlawed… along with the housewives who drive them!" He silently ranted about the foolishness of these behemoths on suburban roads. He bemoaned the fact that his BMW M3 could get lost in a parking lot filled with the oversized vehicles.

Darren was acutely aware of cars. He always had been. He could identify the make, model, and year of just about every vehicle on the road. Which was how he knew the approaching headlights belonged to a GM Suburban. "The Brontosaurus of the SUV universe," he said, shaking his head. Its headlights rode a good two feet higher on the road than those of his road-hugging sports car.

"Son-of-a-bitch better slow down, or he'll run right over me without ever knowing it," Darren whispered. The SUV approached rapidly and braked hard to a following distance of twenty feet. Darren unconsciously pressed the accelerator to gain a little distance.

Despite his increase in speed, the Suburban continued to bear down on him. With this guy riding his bumper, Darren worried that he had a drunk driver behind him. He added some speed. Again, the Suburban matched it.

"All right, all right," Darren said out loud. "I know you're in a fucking hurry, but there's nothing I can do about it."

The two-lane mountain road did not allow for the possibility of passing. At least not along this curving section. Darren breathed slowly, trying not to allow another irritating Bay Area driver ruin what had been a mellow and enjoyable drive. "That's right, kid," he said to himself. "Breathe in, breathe out ..." He glanced at the speedometer. He was going over the speed limit, but not by much. The weather sucked and the road was slick.

"Bastard," he muttered as the SUV's headlights flooded the interior of his car. Darren pressed down a little harder on the accelerator. "Happy now, asshole?"

The SUV stayed on top of him. Darren rounded the curves at fifty miles an hour, with the Suburban riding his bumper. He considered slowing down just to bust the other driver's chops – but decided against it. After all, who knew what the asshole was capable of? Getting pissed off at this guy would only serve to ruin the perfectly good evening he had been looking forward to.

"Just one more curve," he thought to himself. He'd come to know this roadway well. Sure enough, as he came around the last curve, he entered a straightaway. He eased to the right, allowing the Suburban to shoot past him.

"Fuck you," Darren said, glancing up as it sped by. He was denied, though, of any chance to look the asshole driver in the eye. The windows were tinted darker than the rainy night sky over Highway 92. A limousine tint. He flipped his middle finger at the taillights quickly pulling away.

He settled back to enjoy his drive. "Breathe in, breathe out," he meditated silently, raising the volume on the stereo and resuming his incessant tapping on the steering wheel. A short distance later, the highway reached its crest and began its downhill ride toward Half Moon Bay. Along his passenger side, a steep rock face rose up and became lost in the rain. Across the oncoming lane, the highway dropped off into a sheer canyon filled with oak trees. In the distance ahead, Darren could see the dull yellow haze of the town's sodium streetlights. He felt another grumbling in his stomach. Dinner couldn't come soon enough.

What he needed now was to mentally prepare for his impending meeting. Things were going well with these people. He didn't need to hit a home run, but he couldn't screw this up either. "Stay calm. Good eye contact. Don't talk too much," he reminded himself. His stomach grumbled with hunger and nervousness. Every one of these meetings was of vital importance.

"Keep charming them with your personality. Impress them with your attention to detail," Darren counseled himself.

Attention to detail that included wearing his Rolex.

He kept time with the music and his eyes fixed on the road ahead. "*What the…?*" There were red taillights up ahead and, if he wasn't mistaken, they belonged to the Suburban. "Now what's the problem?"

Darren slowed down, but even so he quickly reached the slow-moving Suburban. "This guy *must* be on something," Darren thought. He was now driving less than thirty miles an hour and was completely boxed in by the Suburban.

"I do *not* have the time for this," Darren said, exasperated. At this speed, he would be late for his dinner meeting. That did not play well with his stomach and would not play well with his dining companions. They were sticklers for punctuality.

Darren narrowed his eyes in anger. He couldn't risk everything being thrown off.

Darren was fully aware of the futility of tailgating the Suburban. His little BMW was little more than a fly on the ass of GM's huge dinosaur.

"Enough of this shit," he thought. He didn't have a powerful sports car for nothing. He gunned the accelerator and downshifted, planning to dart around the Suburban. He eased over enough to see that there was no oncoming traffic. He entered the oncoming traffic lane and sped forward. As his speedometer raced higher and higher, the road – and dinner – opened up gratifyingly before him. He could almost taste it. "What should it be tonight? Steak or lobster?"

His front bumper was even with the Suburban's driver's side rear panel when, without warning, the Suburban veered into Darren's lane.

"What the fuck!" Darren yelled.

Before he could slam on his brakes, the Suburban's back bumper smashed against his right front tire.

"No!" screamed Darren.

He instinctively turned his steering wheel away from the impact. But now, as the impact threw him toward the guardrail, he turned it violently back toward the Suburban. To no avail. The power of the Suburban threw Darren's little sports car too hard. The Beemer hit the barrier at full speed.

The loud, metallic sound of the guardrail tearing at the side of the BMW drowned out the noise of the rain and the music blasting through the speakers. It drowned out Darren's piercing shriek that came from some place he didn't know he had.

The BMW scraped against the harsh metal of the guardrail for a few feet until it hit a weak post. The guardrail gave way and the car broke through, careening down the steep mountainside into the dense oaks below.

The Suburban picked up speed and eased back into its lane. It continued down Highway 92 in the direction of the storm-drenched Pacific, its red taillights quickly disappearing behind the heavy curtain of rain.

# Chapter 2

Detective Holland, a stocky veteran of the San Jose Police Department, made his way through the maze of desks until he came to the desk of an attractive, if tired and overworked, young woman. She didn't notice him at the corner of her desk. She was concentrating on her computer monitor.

Holland rapped his knuckles softly on her desk.

Detective Kaitlin Hall looked up. "Hey, Ed," she said. "What's up?"

"You're supposed to be on the phones tonight, remember?"

"Yeah, I remember," she said unenthusiastically.

"Well, you've got a call holding on line two."

She made a face. "Why didn't they just put it through?"

Ed chuckled mildly. "They did. You were too busy to bother picking it up."

Kaitlin turned away and sheepishly punched the second line on her telephone, the one with the angry, blinking light. "High Tech Detail, Detective Hall."

The voice on the other end of the line crackled through the static of a cell phone, barely audible. "Sergeant Collins, California Highway Patrol," the voice said, identifying itself.

Kaitlin frowned. "Pathetic analog," she thought to herself. She had a love-hate relationship with cell phones.

"We've got a fatality you might be interested in," Collins stated matter-of-factly.

"I'm listening," she said.

"A guy went off the side of Highway 92 last night. About ten miles from Half Moon Bay. We just recovered the car this afternoon – "

"That's interesting? What's it got to do with us?"

"Victim's name is Darren Alan Park," Sergeant Collins went on, a deaf ear to her abrupt manner. "DOB 11/15/72…"

As Collins spoke, Kaitlin tapped her keyboard and opened a new window on her monitor. She typed the name into the San Jose Police Department's crime database. No matches. "I'm not seeing anything here on a Darren Park," she reported to the sergeant.

"I didn't expect you would," Sergeant Collins said. "Victim had a picture ID badge that identified him as a Systems Administrator at a place called…" there was a pause as Sergeant Collins referred back to his notes, "… place called Synergy Secure Computing which is in your jurisdiction," he added, erasing any doubt she'd had about receiving the call.

The victim was a techie at a high-profile company.

"Got it. Thanks. Hold on a sec – "

"No problem."

Kaitlin hit speaker phone. She put her hands against the edge of her desk and pushed away, lengthening her arms until her elbows locked. She rolled her shoulders and slowly stretched her neck and back muscles. Her muscles were tight and her bones ached. "Shit," she sighed to herself.

She was only thirty years old but the job sometimes made her feel fifty. Even her regular five-mile runs, which kept her in pretty good shape, did little to ease the strains of being a detective.

On any given day, Kaitlin was parked at a desk staring at a computer monitor for most waking hours. Add to that only a handful of hours she managed to sleep at night and the result was painfully obvious. She had no life.

Still, being a detective had benefits. Although she suffered more lower back pain and eye strain than the years she'd spent in a patrol car, the odds of getting shot were measurably reduced. San Jose was rough and getting worse.

"Okay," she sighed, stretching her hands toward the fluorescent lights lining the ceiling, "What's up with Darren Park?" She leaned forward, turning her attention to her computer.

The job of Systems Administrator was a mission critical position at any company. And as computer systems administrator at Synergy Secure Computing in Mountain View, the late Darren Park had access to every significant computer system and file throughout Synergy's operations.

Darren Park wasn't just a techie. He was a techie with full network privileges. He was a player.

The death of a systems administrator was worth probing. As Kaitlin knew too well from the hours she and five other detectives in the unit spent interviewing systems administrators, they were invariably goal-oriented. They pushed themselves hard. They didn't like to die before conquering the world.

Still, crimes involving systems administrators tended to involve straightforward matters of computer intrusion and hacking, internal fraud, trade secret theft, software counterfeiting and computer theft. The High Tech Detail was not a blood-and-guts detail. It was a silicon-chip-and-Internet-router detail. One typically focused on intelligence and greed, not brutality. Kaitlin and her colleagues used their understanding of cutting-edge technology to stay one step ahead of the criminals who never ceased in their efforts to plunder ground zero of the world's technology capital, Silicon Valley.

The team was made up mainly of old school detectives who had learned the ins and outs of technology crime "on their feet" – by working the beat in Silicon Valley. The other detectives had been culled from the ranks or recruited from outside the department based on their extensive technical backgrounds. The recruits learned police work by going through the academy and working as street cops. Then they learned how to be detectives by working with the old-timers.

Kaitlin was the baby of the team. A member for only six months, they handed her the least interesting of techno-crimes; petty and grand theft of computer equipment. Bottom of the barrel stuff. Hardly challenging work. Most of her time consisted of gathering evidence on the bands of criminals that did things the old-fashioned way – stealing computer components off the backs of delivery trucks. Or, in a nod to efficiency, sometimes stealing the whole damned delivery truck.

"And I nearly killed myself getting a Ph.D. in computer science *for this*?" Kaitlin lamented several times during the past six months. Absolute drudgery. She wondered if maybe her family and friends had been right when they tried to convince her to remain an academic.

"What kind of career is police work for a pretty genius like you?" her father wanted to know.

At the time, she had taken it as a sentimental, rhetorical question. Now, she wasn't so sure. With her neck and back strained and her ass numb, detective work didn't seem so intriguing.

But now she had Darren Park to consider, and something that told her this would be more interesting than a truckload of missing monitors. She entered the search words "Synergy Secure Computing" into her computer and found that Synergy was a developer of powerful encryption software.

"Well, what do you know?" she whispered to herself.

The significance of Synergy's product offering was immediately evident. Encryption software is the holy grail of every network in the world. Synergy clearly had potential as a target for technology crime.

As Kaitlin continued to research the company, it quickly became plain that, more than most other companies in the encryption business, Synergy had extraordinarily valuable intellectual property in the form of encryption algorithms – mathematical formulas – that functioned as combination padlocks on computer messages and files that people wanted kept secret. It didn't require a big leap to conjure up a scenario where a systems administrator could use his access for personal gain.

Of the companies in Silicon Valley most vulnerable to industrial espionage, Synergy was easily in the top ten. The Chinese government, along with Islamic fundamentalists, Basque terrorists, and a number of rogue states and rebel factions had all gone high-tech. Encryption software could conceal their communications and, therefore, their activities. In fact, Kaitlin recalled that the FBI had recently disclosed evidence that its most-wanted terrorist, Osama bin Laden, had initiated an "e-Jihad" – an electronic Holy war – using encrypted excerpts from the Koran distributed over the Internet.

If Synergy was attractive to bad guys, that made the late Darren Park equally attractive. And all the more interesting to Kaitlin Hall. Nevertheless, she reminded herself not to jump to conclusions: a habit of smart people, but not smart scientists. Finding a basic fact sheet on Synergy, she hit the print key.

After several minutes of listening to nothing more than the clicking of Kaitlin's keyboard, her occasional sighs, and now the printer sputtering out pages, Sergeant Collins had grown impatient. "Detective Hall? You still there?"

Kaitlin glanced at the phone. Lost in her thinking about Synergy, she'd pretty much forgotten about Collins. "Yes, I'm still here." She copied the information onto disk and then packed it, along with the hard copy, into her laptop case, which was more college backpack than a professional's accessory. "I'm leaving now," she told the sergeant. "Depending on traffic, I'll be there within an hour."

Depending on traffic. Kaitlin knew that her trip toward Half Moon Bay on Highway 92 could take two hours, especially factoring in weather conditions. Although the Valley's recent economic downturn *had* eased congestion, the traffic in and around America's 11th largest city was still a nightmare.

Kaitlin looked out the window of the squad room located on the first floor. Night had fallen and a heavy rain was illuminated in the bright overhead lights of the parking lot. She frowned. As pleasant as the climate was in summer, winter in the Bay Area could be equally dismal.

Just before Kaitlin hung up, she asked, "Sergeant, what kind of car was Park driving?"

"A Beemer."

She rolled her eyes. "Should have guessed," she thought to herself. "How about computer equipment or software? Find anything in the vehicle?"

"Nope," he said.

"A backpack?"

"Nothing like that," he said, looking down at his notepad. "There was a set of golf clubs in the trunk. A cell phone and a Palm PDA. Nothing else in the way of personal effects."

She smiled. The personal digital assistant was a major score. She knew that PDAs had a lot to tell and never lied. "Thanks, Sergeant. I'll be there soon."

As she hung up and gathered her things, she took a look around the small squad room. Detective Holland was nowhere to be seen. Three desks down from hers, Rob Newmeyer was the only other detective in the office. Everyone else was at dinner or off shift with their families or something. In other words, having a life. Not Rob though, bless his heart. He was engaged in a very intense phone conversation.

Rob was the next most junior detective in the squad and that, along with their mutual interest in all things tech, helped the two of them forge an exceptional bond.

Other than Rob in the squad room, there was only Captain Torres in his office. "Man, oh man," she thought to herself. Captain Enrique Torres was a man who seemed to have it all. Handsome. Well-educated. Articulate. Hispanic. That was an impressive combination in San Jose, the *de facto* capital of Silicon Valley. Responsibility for the High Tech Crimes Unit was only a resume builder for Torres. He had bigger game to hunt. His future pointed to the mayor's office, or maybe the governor's mansion.

All of that was mere commentary to Kaitlin. At the moment, her concern was getting past Torres' door without being spotted. The last thing she wanted was to recount Sergeant Collins' call and explain why she was headed all the way to Half Moon Bay to investigate a traffic accident that had not been assigned to her.

She'd be damned if the first interesting thing that came across her desk was taken away.

Luck was on her side. Torres was in a familiar position: His back to his interior window, his oversized leather chair rocked back, his feet up on his credenza, and the telephone glued to his ear. Kaitlin had never met a man who could work a telephone like Torres. He was the king of the schmoozers. He worked the phone within the department, with the press, and with dozens of Silicon Valley business leaders he'd cultivated relationships with over the past three years.

If he did decide to run for higher office, he wouldn't be without some heavy-hitting supporters.

Kaitlin took her Gore-Tex rain shell off the wooden coat rack and slipped out the office door. Torres never moved. Quietly, Kaitlin eased the door to the stairway closed. She skipped down the concrete steps, her footsteps so light that they barely echoed in the hollow stairway.

Kaitlin darted from the main entrance of the SJPD into the parking lot. She pulled out of the lot onto West Mission Street, bound for I-280 north to always foggy Half Moon Bay.

As she approached the onramp, she could see a long, red line of brake lights up the freeway, even though it was well past rush hour. During the past ten years while the technology industry boomed, Silicon Valley's population had grown exponentially, yet its infrastructure had not. As a result, traffic was often named as the single greatest threat to Silicon Valley's continued economic growth, and the suburban lifestyle it had spawned. But then the plunge in stock prices took peoples' minds off the traffic problem.

Kaitlin didn't care. She owned few stocks and generally didn't mind traffic. It was free time. Time without a computer monitor in front of her. Time to think.

# Chapter 3

Darren Park's BMW had hurtled some two hundred and fifty feet from the roadway, most of that distance downhill and through a densely wooded ravine. Even the BMW's solid steel cage was of no use to Darren. The car was crushed on all sides.

Kaitlin had no trouble finding the scene of the accident. When she arrived, magnesium flares sizzled on the wet roadway. A sheriff's deputy, wearing a long, yellow poncho fitted with reflecting stripes, waved the morbid and curious along with sweeps of his flashlight. Kaitlin opened her window and lifted her teardrop red light to the roof of her car. Quickly closing her window again, she switched on the flashing red light and pulled over to the shoulder, near to where another officer was surveying the scene and making notes using a waterproof clipboard.

Kaitlin twisted and turned to put on her rain poncho and pushed open her door, only to be hit by intense wind and rain. "Shit," she muttered, not for the last time wondering if her family had been right in trying to dissuade her from going into police work.

She approached the officer surveying the scene. "Sergeant Collins?"

"Yep," he said, surprisingly cheerful for a man standing in the ice cold rain, surveying a fatal car accident.

"Detective Hall," she said, identifying herself. "We spoke earlier."

"Right," he said. "Good to meet you."

"Thanks for the call." She stepped gingerly into the thick mud of the shoulder and looked over in the direction of the torn and twisted guardrail. "What've you got?"

"Car over the side," he said in perfect cop understatement. He pointed his flashlight down the embankment. In the stream of light, she was able to see the broken tree limbs that marked the car's descent halfway down the ravine.

"Ugly," she noted.

He nodded. Then he swung his flashlight toward the far end of the shoulder where a heavy-duty police tow was dragging what was left of the Beemer back up to the road.

Kaitlin frowned. Her stomach tightened as she imagined what Darren Park might look like inside the vehicle.

"How about that…?" Collins said, his voice still cheerful.

"What?" Kaitlin asked.

He nodded in the direction of the car. "It didn't catch fire. Just about every canyon jumper flames out."

She couldn't help but think that Collins was a little disappointed by this anomaly. She shivered involuntarily then walked toward the wrecked car as it was settled on the roadway. Her own street experience allowed her to read some details from the car. The convex impression in the windshield marked the spot where Darren's head hit it. If that hadn't been the cause of death, it would be a damned close second.

She leaned down and looked into the window. The black leather interior was strewn with mud and vegetation. But otherwise, to her relief, empty. However, in the glow of Collins' flashlight, which he shined over her right shoulder, several dark streaks were clearly visible. Blood stained the dashboard and driver's side floor mat. She recoiled. This had been a gruesome death.

"Okay, I've seen enough of the vehicle," Kaitlin said, straightening up.

Collins nodded and then shifted the direction of his flashlight toward his squad car. Without a word, he walked her over and showed her Darren Park's personal effects, all neatly bagged and tagged.

"At this point, I'm not thinking of this as evidence," he noted. "Just things to return to the victim's family. But if things aren't done right from the get-go..." He left off the thought. They both appreciated the significance of his professionalism.

Kaitlin slid halfway into the back seat of Collins' squad car. "Any sign of foul play?" she asked as she poked through the evidence bag with the tip of her pen.

"None we can determine. No witnesses so far." He glanced over at the Beemer. "Of course, the car's so banged up, it'd be almost impossible to determine if it had hit anything before going through the guardrail." Just then his radio squawked to life. He shifted his attention to answer, but not before furtively checking out Kaitlin and her long legs stretching halfway out of the squad car's back seat.

Although she focused her attention on the contents of the evidence bag, she was aware of his gaze. She accepted it with a certain dispassion, a scientific acknowledgement. When she'd been a computer scientist, she'd been surrounded by men. But the men in the Berkeley and Stanford scientific community were, for the most part, techies who were more interested in microprocessors and Boolean logic than a flesh-and-blood woman.

Cops, as she quickly learned at the academy, were a different breed. They were quite comfortable in their appreciation of and their desire for a woman. Any woman. All women.

Although she had never done much of anything to accentuate her natural attractiveness, Kaitlin was immediately a focal point of interest. She was uncomfortable with the attention at first. But now, she was unfazed. It was simply a curious and not very well understood fact of life. It was like the weather. Unpredictable, unchangeable, and not worth worrying about. As far as she was concerned, men could check her out to their hearts' content.

The first thing Kaitlin examined were the contents of Darren's wallet. Sixty-three dollars in cash. A California driver's license. An American Express card – green not gold. A Blockbuster Video card. An HMO insurance card. No personal photographs. Not one.

But nothing out of the ordinary.

She released the wallet and picked up Darren's passport. Carrying a passport in Silicon Valley wasn't unusual. Regular overseas travel was the norm rather than the exception for many executives and techies. Tech was a global business, now more than ever. Kaitlin studied Darren's passport photo. He had Asian features, close-cropped black hair and intense, dark eyes. The photograph itself was unflattering. No surprise there. But even the unflattering photograph made it clear that he'd been a good-looking guy. "Well, not bad-looking anyway," Kaitlin corrected herself dispassionately.

As she flipped through the passport, she saw various visa stamps that indicated timeworn travels of an American college student. Mexico. England. France. Various entries for Asia. As she continued through the pages, a bright blue visa stamp caught her attention. An entry and exit stamp from the Republic of South Korea. Perhaps a family visit, she wondered. The exit stamp was dated January 23rd. "*Yesterday*," she noted. And the entry stamp was only two days prior. "That's a pretty long trip for such a short visit, family or not," she thought.

In the context of Darren Park's recent Korea trip, the other stamps from the Far East took on greater significance. She flipped back through the passport with a new perspective – Japan, Hong Kong, Singapore. All within the past twelve months. And all two-day round trips.

Darren Park had definitely been racking up the frequent flyer points. She dropped the passport back into the evidence pouch, still processing what, if anything, all that travel was about.

She pulled a cell phone out of the bag. The battery was just about dead. Kaitlin moved quickly. In seconds, she determined that the phone would easily reveal Darren's programmed phone numbers and recently received calls. This information would be important if – and she mentally emphasized *if* – there was any reason to open an investigation from what was most likely a simple, though tragic, car accident.

"Come to mama," Kaitlin whispered as she lifted the crown jewel of evidence from the bag – Darren Park's Palm V. The information contained in Darren's PDA could open many avenues for investigation. So-called personal digital assistants, like the Palm device, were used religiously by nearly everyone in Silicon Valley. The advantage for Kaitlin was that, unlike a human personal assistant, the Palm would never lie to cover its owner's ass.

Suddenly, Collins' flashlight was shining on her once again. He watched her intently as she poked at the PDA, using its little plastic stylus. He leaned closer, puzzled. "What the heck are you looking for?"

"I'm not looking for anything." Kaitlin said, distracted.

Collins shrugged. He pointed his flashlight and swept the beam over the road surface from left to right one last time. "I couldn't find any skid marks. That usually means the driver fell asleep and went off the road." He looked up and gazed at Highway 92. "Or maybe he just lost control. Conditions like this…" he observed. He turned back to Kaitlin. "You know how those Beemer drivers are."

"Yeah, I do," she conceded.

There were two varieties of Beemer drivers in the Bay Area. One comprised of young, newly wealthy techies driving from their small, overpriced apartments to their eighty-hour-a-week high-tech jobs. The other comprised of yuppies – older, distinguished lawyers, accountants, venture capitalists, and bankers – many having made small fortunes by exploiting the talents of the first variety of Beemer drivers.

"A symbiotic Beemer relationship," she mused to herself, being quite familiar with the dynamic.

Kaitlin was one of a small handful of people who had brains and talent to ride the high tech wave but chose not to. While her friends were creating and cashing in on the new technology, she had cloistered herself first in the world of academia, then in the world of law enforcement. Which was why she now found herself, thirty years old, beautiful but world-weary, on the periphery of Silicon Valley's economic-technology continuum.

Socially and financially, her decisions left her out in the cold. As a cop investigating high-tech crimes, those decisions put her right where she needed to be. She had knowledge and insight without the restrictions of being an insider. Which was to say, Kaitlin had neither a Beemer nor a Palm V.

"Well, that's suboptimal," she sighed.

"What's the problem?" Collins asked, not completely sure what the word "suboptimal" meant.

She looked up from the Palm's screen. "Password protected," she said. That meant it would require a good bit of work on the part of the small, but proficient, staff of forensic engineers to crack Darren's device.

Collins nodded as if this information carried a lot of weight with him. But before he could say anything, his cell phone rang. He turned away for a moment to take the call. When he got off the phone, he turned back to Kaitlin.

"That was San Mateo morgue," he said. "Family just ID'd the body. We're just about done here, so I'll be heading down to talk to them." He drew a breath. Any joy that had been in his voice was now drained by the task of speaking to the victim's family. "Anything you want me to ask them?"

There were easily a dozen questions she wanted to know the answers to, but she realized that she needed to be selective. Collins would be speaking to a grieving family. "Ask them if they might know the password to this gadget," she said, holding up the Palm V in her hand. "It might be the name of a family pet. Mother's maiden name. That sort of thing." She gently replaced the device into the evidence bag and zipped it shut. "And let them know that I'll be in touch with them in a day or two to discuss the accident."

"You got it," he said, still wondering why she was so interested in a car wreck.

Kaitlin slipped her rain hood over her head and darted from the back seat of Collins' squad car and into the rain. "Oh, one more thing," she called back to Collins as she trod through the mud. "Please give them my condolences."

She opened her car door and slid in behind the wheel. She took several deep breaths. As much as she tried to deal with death as a scientist, which was to say clinically, or dispassionately as a cop, the immediacy of death always startled and disturbed her.

After three years as a cop, her skin was a good deal thicker but her sensitivity was still intact. So much for her young girl fantasy of growing up to be like Angie Dickinson in *Policewoman*. Tough as nails was just not her style.

Back on the road, she called to check in with Newmeyer in the office.

"You're where?" he exclaimed when she told him where she was calling from. He winced and instinctively cocked his head to look sideways in the direction of Captain Torres' office.

"Yes, yes, I *know* I'm supposed to be working on the Comtak case," she admitted. "But, come on, that shouldn't be our case. That's just stolen property that *happens* to be computer monitors. It could have been carrots stolen from those trucks."

"Expensive carrots," he countered.

She didn't reply.

"Look, 'Ours is not to reason why…'" Rob counseled her. "Bottom line, it *is* our case." At least, it's *my* case, he thought to himself. "Come on, Kaitlin, you don't have to find any justice in it, you just have to do it. Promise me you'll head to Sunnyvale tomorrow morning," he pleaded gently.

She remained silent.

"Kaitlin?"

"Oh, all right," she agreed reluctantly. "Sunnyvale it is."

Rob seemed pleased. His cajoling had worked. Kaitlin was pleased. Because after a minute, she realized that a trip to Sunnyvale on the Comtak case would readily allow for a short, convenient detour to Synergy Secure Computing in neighboring Mountain View.

# Chapter 4

By the time Kaitlin arrived at Synergy the following morning, news of Darren's death had circulated throughout the company. Synergy was a relatively small operation. With fewer than two hundred full-time employees, Synergy was more like an extended family than a corporation. As such, nearly everyone in the company knew Darren, including the President and CEO, Pradeep Gupta.

As befitting a company with genuine security concerns, Synergy had a number of layers of internal security that Kaitlin had to go through. She signed the visitor's log at the reception desk, where she took in the list of others who had arrived earlier in the day: a few visiting engineers from big name tech companies, a catering service (catered meals were prevalent incentives and a not-so-subtle way to keep employees working at all hours), and a host of others with names she couldn't place. She clipped on her visitor's badge and was ushered into the CEO's office, a relatively modest space taken up with journals, magazines, and computer equipment.

The night before, Kaitlin had done her research on Synergy and on Pradeep Gupta. Gupta was a computer engineer by training and a high honors graduate from India's prestigious Institute of Technology. He had immigrated to the United States only ten years earlier, on the cusp of a huge wave of talented, but less entrepreneurial, engineers that landed in Silicon Valley to take advantage of the technology boom.

Gupta had expanded his range of opportunities by obtaining an MBA from Stanford. He then launched his own company and developed a powerful suite of encryption software that was the best in the industry.

It was hard to overestimate the value of encryption software to the continued growth of the technological revolution. With the explosion of Internet use, privacy and protection had become the next great challenge for cutting-edge technology. It would be another decade before everyone realized the massive threat to data privacy. And that the battlegrounds of future wars would be digital. In these wars, encryption would be both the missile and the defensive armor.

From banking to love letters, there were many legitimate and practical uses for encryption software. However, there were just as many illegitimate uses. And it was for those reasons that the government maintained strict export controls on software. Kaitlin knew the US and allied intelligence community was appropriately concerned about the ability of a terrorist group, rogue nation, or enemy to communicate in complete secrecy.

As a result of these controls, only the weakest encryption software was available for export without approval by the

Commerce Department – and it did not grant approval often or easily. So, despite the incredible international demand, encryption software developed in the United States had only one market: the internal market and highly trusted U.S. businesses. Where encryption usage could be monitored and contained within the purview of U.S. law.

Synergy, along with its fellow American competitors, had argued for easing of export regulations for years. Their argument was simple and straightforward – if they were prevented from selling encryption software, the bad guys would either rip it off or buy it someplace else. The French and the Russians were very happy to oblige. All that was being hurt by the encryption export controls were American economic interests. It made people like Pradeep Gupta angry and resolved to challenge the status quo. But the CIA, NSA and others didn't have to worry about economic trade-offs.

Against a backdrop of the dot-com boom, this high-stakes, military-technology dynamic created a witches' brew of desire. Companies like Synergy were targets for all sorts of interesting offers from foreign governments. And those offers could be quite alluring. Which brought to mind Darren Park's recent travels to the Far East.

As she trod down Synergy's sterile hallway with her escort, the struggle between her imagination and her police training objectivity was in full swing. Exiting the corridor and navigating a sea of cubicles, a handful of private offices and conference rooms came into view. Kaitlin quickly found herself at the doorway of Pradeep Gupta's office.

"Hello, hello," Gupta called from his desk.

At first she couldn't see him ensconced behind a bank of enormous computer monitors.

"Come in, come in," he urged her. A hand reached up above one of the monitors and beckoned her forward.

As she approached, Gupta stood up and smiled softly at her. He gestured to a chair for her to sit. "You are here regarding poor Darren," he said.

She nodded her head. "Yes. I'm sorry to bother you..." She knew before the words finished coming out of her mouth that she wasn't supposed to say things like that. Detectives didn't need to be apologetic.

"It's no bother," Gupta said. "He was a wonderful, young man," he said, haltingly. "I just sent an e-mail to the entire company, letting them know," he added somberly. "So sad, so sad..."

"Could I ask you a few questions?" Kaitlin asked.

"Please," he said, inviting her to begin as he sat down.

Kaitlin shifted her chair so she was looking directly at Gupta through a break in the computer monitors. "Mr. Park was your systems administrator?"

"Yes. A fine one too. He'd been here nearly four years." He sighed. "It will be difficult to replace him. Even in today's market..."

Gupta, in a seamless shift from Darren Park's death to the difficulty in replacing him, had answered Kaitlin's next question of whether Darren Park was a good employee.

"I assume, as a systems administrator, Mr. Park had supervisor access to Synergy's computer network," Kaitlin asked, getting to the point perhaps too quickly.

"Yes, of course," Gupta said.

"Who else had those privileges?"

"Why, I did, of course," Gupta said. "And our IT Director. As you can imagine, given the nature of our work, access to our network is closely guarded."

"You're not aware of any recent security breaches then?"

Gupta shook his head violently. "Absolutely not!" he insisted, with more energy than the response required. He quickly regained his composure. "I'm very sorry," he said. "I didn't mean to sound so defensive, but our company is at a critical juncture. You cannot imagine how painful Darren's death is to me and to Synergy. However, any questions that his death might raise about our security... If my answers are misconstrued or misstated – it could be very damaging. I answer to a Board of Directors, you know. And the Commerce Department watches us very closely."

"I understand," Kaitlin said, trying to reassure him. "I have no intention of having any information you give me misrepresented by anyone."

"Thank you."

It was clear to Kaitlin that Gupta had more on his mind than the typical techie. Gupta had bigger concerns than a new Beemer or Rolex watch. A Beemer was simply a new hire bonus for a talented mid-level employee. His company was on the verge of going big, and possibly going public.

In order to make the quantum leap to the next stage, Gupta had to nurture and protect his investment in Synergy – toward an IPO or acquisition by a much larger company.

In either case, his plans concerned a personal gain of hundreds of millions of dollars. But after the bust of the dot-com boom, tough times had quickly descended on Silicon Valley, and no company's fortune was guaranteed. Only the smart, nimble, and well-positioned survived. Gupta was intent on more than surviving. The money he hoped to make was a lot of money by U.S. standards – but it was an obscene fortune according to India's.

"Tell me about Darren's relationships with his co-workers," Kaitlin asked, sensing the benefit of backing off her prior line of questioning.

Gupta paused. Despite the openness of his broad face, he was an extremely smart man. And cautious. Everything he did was a move on a chess board, a strategy that moved him toward a win, or toward a loss. He weighed the significance of Kaitlin's request, as well as the consequences of whatever answer he might give.

"I… I don't understand the nature of your questions. Darren was in a car accident. You sound as if there was more to it than that."

Kaitlin nimbly deflected. "Mr. Gupta, there is absolutely no evidence to suggest that Mr. Park's accident was anything more than that, a tragic accident," she said in a soothing voice. "However, any fatality demands that we follow protocol. That said…due to the sensitive nature of Synergy's business, and *because* Mr. Park had complete access to your network, we need to make certain that there is nothing beyond the obvious."

"I see, I see," Gupta sighed. "Yes, I understand. Of course. That makes perfect sense. I don't mind telling you, Darren's death has put me a little on edge. Very sad." He shook his head. For a guy who'd unflinchingly quarterbacked massive business successes, he seemed genuinely sidelined by the incident.

"As for Darren's relationship with his co-workers, well, Darren was a very popular employee. He was talented and hardworking, so he fit in well within our company's culture." He paused for a millisecond and continued. "He didn't have, uh, what it takes," he went on, "intellectually that is, to be a programmer. But that never led to conflict with Darren and the others."

Kaitlin got the gist. Lines were clearly drawn in Silicon Valley. Hierarchies firmly in place. Programmers were at the top. They had the talent, determination, and stamina that fueled Silicon Valley's technology engine. As a result, until the recent downturn in the economy, they were idolized like rock stars. Even now a star programmer could name his own price.

Technicians, even talented ones – as Darren Park appeared to have been – were relegated to "support staff" status. Even though the dot-com crash had leveled the playing field, technicians still had the responsibility of keeping programmers happy.

"If I'm not mistaken, Darren came from a family with money," Gupta said. "He wasn't hungry the way many others are. Also, I believe he had a serious girlfriend. Those two things set him apart. Still, he will be very hard to replace," Gupta mused, touching again on that point.

Kaitlin crossed her legs and shifted her notepad across her lap to jot down a note. As she did, she noticed Gupta's eyes lock on her exposed calf and lower thigh. She might not have placed much stock in her good looks, but she was not blind to its advantage. "I'm sorry to take up so much of your valuable time…" To her credit, she stopped short of batting her eyelashes.

"It's no problem at all," Gupta said with a slight smile. "Really."

"I only have one other question," she said. "Did Mr. Park travel often on business?"

Gupta shook his head. "No. This is our only office. Darren had no company business outside this building."

Having seen Darren Park's passport, Kaitlin was surprised but kept a poker face.

"I see. Had he taken any recent vacations…or personal time off?"

"I don't believe so, but I can answer that for you in a second," Gupta said. He swiveled around in his chair. He keyed in some information into one of the computers at his desk. "According to our records, other than a handful of sick days over the past several months, he hasn't taken a vacation in close to a year." Gupta sighed. "Now that's a pity."

"What's that, Mr. Gupta?"

"He died with over six weeks of accrued vacation time."

"Yes, that is a pity," she said. She realized that it was a harsh price young people paid for their dedication. Darren Park died without ever enjoying the vacation time he had earned. She wondered what that said about him. On further reflection, she realized that she hadn't taken a vacation in *two* years, and she wondered what that said about *her*.

Gupta's assistant buzzed over the intercom. "Pradeep, your 10 a.m. with Harriman & Co. is starting in conference room A," her tone half-nag and half-request. Gupta rose to his feet, extended his hand and eked out a small smile. He excused himself with the same courtesy as when he had greeted her.

The long hallway that had led to Gupta's office seemed twice as long heading back to the lobby. Her mind buzzed. Finally, Kaitlin's visitor badge was collected, and she emerged through glass doors into the parking lot in a reverie.

She left Synergy convinced that there was much more to Darren Park's death than falling asleep at the wheel.

# Chapter 5

"Detective Hall, I know that *you know* that I don't like to look foolish…"

Kaitlin tapped the tip of her shoe on the carpet. She had the distinct feeling of being called into the principal's office. A feeling that she had gotten used to at school *and* work. The difference being that Captain Torres was much more intelligent than any of Kaitlin's school principals. He knew when to speak calmly and kindly…while handing you your heart on a plate. And when to show his anger. This was one of the anger times.

"What the hell made you drive out to Half Moon Bay to investigate a *traffic fatality*, for Chrissakes?"

Kaitlin stood dutifully before Captain Torres. "I answered a call from the Highway Patrol, sir. They specifically referred the call to our detail. I was the only one in the squad room at the time…" she said, praying that Rob Newmeyer's presence had not been noted. "They were in the process of removing the vehicle from the accident site. If I didn't get out there for an examination, the opportunity would have been lost."

She made a conscious decision not to mention her visit to Synergy that morning.

Captain Torres let out a slow breath, as though *he* had been holding his breath, not Kaitlin. "What disturbs me, Detective, is that I learned about your activities from an outside source. This makes me look like a fool, Detective, and I believe I have been quite clear regarding my feelings about that."

"Yes, sir, you have been very clear about not wanting to be made to look like a fool."

Torres eyed her suspiciously, not sure if she was joking with him or simply agreeing with him.

Despite Torres' dressing down and despite the color that had risen on the back of her neck, she had not given leave of her intelligence. Captain Torres' remark about learning of her activities from *outside* the detail struck an odd note. Why would anyone mention her visit to the accident scene to Captain Torres? Who even knew about it? Only Newmeyer. But he was *inside* the Detail.

She cleared her throat. She'd had enough of Torres' chastising. Now she wanted answers to her questions. Before she mustered up the courage, there was a loud knuckle rap on the glass window to the office. Both she and Captain Torres looked up to see Special Agent Alex Renfro of the FBI looking in at them.

This meeting had suddenly gotten stranger.

Kaitlin knew Renfro too well. A few years earlier, she had applied to the FBI. Renfro had been one of her three interviewers.

Her application was rejected shortly thereafter.

It was the year before *that* that she and Renfro had first crossed paths at the DEF CON convention in Las Vegas. DEF CON was the premier hacker convention – attended by the worldwide elite of hackers and computer security experts. Attendance was conservatively ninety-five percent male. From Kaitlin's perspective, they weren't much to look at. As for the few women attendees, ninety-five percent would not have earned a second glance at *any* gathering.

But these were hackers, male and female computer geeks of the first order. Sex was not a consideration, unless it was virtual sex over the Internet. In which case they were plenty interested, attested to by the fact that the only people making serious money on the Internet were those distributing pornography.

Kaitlin toured the Strip alone, stopping at a number of less desirable locales. Kaitlin's memory of their encounter was vivid.

"Hey, Hall!"

The sound of her name was disorienting enough. Turning and seeing Renfro calling it out was stranger. However, the convention had left her aching for some semblance of social interaction, so she accepted a few drinks with Renfro and his FBI buddies. Well, as they say, one thing led to another, and Kaitlin woke up the next morning in Renfro's hotel room, his right hand firmly gripping her naked thigh.

She gently lifted his hand from her leg and got dressed.

"What's up?" he asked sleepily as she finished buttoning her blouse.

"Got a plane to catch," she said.

"Ah."

She returned to the Bay Area. Neither she nor Renfro made any effort to call each other or get together. Not that Kaitlin lost any sleep over it. She was a healthy young woman and deserved a roll in the hay as much as anyone else.

Still it was awkward to endure sudden flashbacks to that lame Vegas hotel room and that catastrophic FBI interview right there in her supervisor's office.

Torres wasn't excited either. "What the hell?" Torres said under his breath when he saw Renfro. His face, however, was a mask of gracious welcome. Kaitlin knew without a doubt that Torres would easily ascend the law enforcement ladder.

He gave her a quick look of approbation and said, "Detective, we'll continue this discussion later." Then he waved Renfro into his office. "Special Agent Renfro, please come in."

Renfro stepped into the office as Kaitlin turned to leave.

"Agent Renfro, I believe you know Detective Hall."

Renfro nodded at Kaitlin. "Yes, I do indeed. Good to see you again, Detective."

Kaitlin took in Renfro from head to toe. He was a good-looking man, no doubt about it. Alcohol alone hadn't gotten her into his hotel room. Tall with dark hair and a solid physique: she could have done a hell of a lot worse, she mused.

She smiled without saying a word to Renfro. But with an intuitive sense of timing, she turned and faced Torres. "Captain, thank you for your advice on the Park case. As usual, you are one hundred percent right. I'll get you a full status report by the end of the week."

Only the most astute observer would have noticed the anger in Torres' expression. "Thank you, Detective," he said, nodding curtly and sucking back the words he really wanted to unleash. "I look forward to your report."

Kaitlin smiled at the two men and then slipped out of the room into the bright fluorescent light of the squad room.

# Chapter 6

Kaitlin, to her dismay, was in a philosophical mood when she arrived home that evening. And, as usual, her life was the primary subject of her philosophical musings. Her prospects. Her refrigerator's contents. Her handling of the chance meeting with Renfro in Torres' office. Her odds of getting off her ass and becoming a mover and shaker like Torres or just a lifetime plodder.

She frowned. She might have to pay for her little ploy with Torres.

But, curiously and uncharacteristically, she didn't care. Maybe it was the combination of Renfro's showing up and Torres' dressing her down. Or maybe the memory of that lost night in Vegas. Or the easily recalled sensation of Renfro's hands on her body.

Whatever.

Before leaving the office for the evening, Kaitlin had checked her voicemail and e-mail. There was a voicemail from an investigator on the burglary detail with information regarding Comtak's stolen computer monitors. Yawn. Her e-mail messages were similarly uninspiring. Save for one unsurprisingly bizarre message from Slim Yamazaki.

"Slim, Slim, Slim," she sighed, as her eyes scanned the two-line e-mail: *THERE IS A NUMBER LARGER THAN ONE, BUT LESS THAN TWO. IT DESCRIBES MY THOUGHTS. OR, AT LEAST IT ONCE DID. WHAT IS YOUR NUMBER?*

Slim was Kaitlin's mentor at Berkeley before he dropped out of the computer science Ph.D. program. Not many undergrads had the opportunity to learn from someone like Slim. His brilliance inspired her to continue in her own studies, entering the Ph.D. program at Stanford. In reality, he had inspired her with his brilliance *and* his disdain for the limits of academia. Slim was more hacker than student. But his brilliance was sterling and without equal.

After he left the program, Kaitlin remained in touch. Slim's psychological make-up never failed to fascinate her. One part genius. Two parts traditional Japanese culture and sensibility. One part Ultimate Frisbee fanatic. One part hardcore Berkeley radical activist.

That was a lot of parts to pack into Slim's wiry, athletic frame but somehow he did it. Slim's complexity was one of his most attractive features, and any time she got an e-mail from him, it made her happy.

But what did his message mean?

She pondered that question on the drive home and later as she rummaged through the minimal offerings in her refrigerator. It could simply mean that he had lost or forgotten Kaitlin's phone number. He'd done that on more than one occasion. A true genius can't be bothered to remember a phone number.

Or it could mean something more.

Despite the fact that she was sure he would never answer, she dialed Slim's number. She glanced at her watch. Six o'clock. Middle of the night for a true hacker.

Hackers, crackers, and other computer nerds were nocturnal creatures. Which explained their pasty complexions and the dark rings under their eyes.

Kaitlin let the phone ring. After five rings, a canned computer greeting stated, "Please leave me a message." So she did.

Short, sweet, and to the point, Kaitlin said, "There is a number which describes me. It is 408-555-9259." As she was about to hang up, she heard the beep of her call waiting service. She clicked the phone's "flash" button and answered the incoming call. But not without trepidation. It could be Captain Torres getting back to her about the Darren Park ploy.

"Hello?"

"Detective Hall?" It wasn't Torres.

"Speaking."

"This is Officer Palance in the crime lab. I have good news for you."

"What's the word?"

"We've got a password for you..." Palance's voice was filled with earned pride. It had taken the lab less than an hour to crack the password. Actually, Darren Park's password turned out to be straightforward. His last name spelled backwards: K-R-A-P.

A tad juvenile and, therefore, fairly predictable for a techie. But certainly not a suitable password when it came to security. Kaitlin shook her head. She was sure that the systems administrator for Synergy would have had a more complex password. One that might have stymied the crime lab for more than sixty minutes.

Kaitlin looked forward to delving into Darren Park's soul. Several uninterrupted hours of plumbing the depths of his Palm should turn up a number of nuggets about his likes, dislikes, and behavior. It never ceased to amaze Kaitlin how much you could learn from someone's calendar, phone and address book, e-mail messages, and mileage log.

Between the Palm Pilot and her scheduled meeting the next morning with Darren Park's girlfriend, Rachel Weinstein, Kaitlin figured that she was on the cusp of knowing Mr. Park better in death than most people knew him in life.

"Cool," she said to Palance. "You guys are the best."

She could almost hear him smiling on the other end of the line.

After Kaitlin changed into a comfortable pair of sweats, she curled up on the couch and turned on the TV, hoping to watch an episode of *Law & Order*. She was a cop twenty-four hours a day, then she watched more cops on TV. She winced at the pathetic irony.

# Chapter 7

Palo Alto. To Kaitlin, that didn't mean neat suburban houses, apartment buildings, or big shopping centers. To her, Palo Alto meant one thing: Stanford University. Kaitlin didn't take into account how she would feel returning. During the drive from her apartment to Stanford's campus, she experienced a range of emotions – nostalgia to something akin to what a prisoner feels when returning to his former jail cell.

The heavy cloud cover that burdened the Bay Area for the previous two weeks had finally lifted. Sunlight glistened on the still-wet streets. The manicured lawns of Palo Alto glowed a luminous green.

She drove down Palm, around the Oval, parking near the Science and Engineering Quad. She drew a deep breath as she walked across to the Allen Center for Integrated Systems, where she had arranged to meet Rachel.

Kaitlin hesitated before opening the door to the ACIS. This moment was pregnant with memories. After graduating at the top of her class at Berkeley, she had her pick of graduate programs. In her mind, there was no question about where she would go. Stanford. For five long years she toiled, rarely seeing the light of day.

She half-smiled, shaking her head to free herself of the flood of memories and images. She pulled open the door and strode across the lobby toward the elevators. Rachel greeted her at the door to her cubicle-sized private office.

Despite its miniscule size, Kaitlin was impressed. Ph.D. candidates don't often merit a private office. Rachel must have landed in someone's good graces to score this trophy, regardless of its claustrophobically small size.

Kaitlin extended her hand to Rachel. "I'm very sorry about Darren," she said sincerely.

"Thanks. Me too," Rachel said as she shook Kaitlin's hand.

"I understand that he was your boyfriend," Kaitlin continued.

"Was," Rachel said flatly, without embellishment.

Kaitlin looked at Rachel. She was tall. Very skinny. With a mane of wavy red hair that landed in the middle of her back. She was dressed in the uniform of a graduate student. Blue jeans, oversized Gap sweatshirt and Birkenstocks. Her complexion was naturally pale and made more so by the indoor demands of studies in computer science. She wore no make-up; a scattering of freckles across her nose accentuated her attractiveness rather than diminishing it.

The only thing that betrayed the picture of the typical graduate student was the diamond pendant necklace that peeked out above the collar of her sweatshirt.

Kaitlin noted that, based on Darren Park's driver's license, he would have stood a good three to four inches shorter than Rachel. She knew a lot of guys would not have been comfortable in that situation. For women, it was a problem easily remedied by wearing flats. But guys usually worried about stuff like that. Then again, the power of attraction and what made couples successful was hardly Kaitlin's forte.

"Was?" Kaitlin said gently. Rachel had made a point of conveying the past-tense nature of her relationship with Darren. Kaitlin's tone was that of an inquiring classmate, not of a detective conducting an investigation.

"Yes," Rachel said. "We broke up about six months ago. Actually," she went on after a brief pause, "*he* broke up with me." Tears started to well up in her soft blue eyes. "I was still trying to make us work, you know. I thought we were good together..."

"What happened?" Kaitlin asked.

"I...I don't know." She raised her eyes and looked directly at Kaitlin. "I wish I did." She lowered her head. "It was probably his family. He would never admit it, but it probably was."

"His family? I don't understand..." Kaitlin prompted.

Rachel laughed a sad laugh. "Well, on the one hand you have his nice, traditional Korean family and on the other you have me... tall, redhead, Jewish me." She frowned. "I was hardly their leading candidate for their firstborn son." She sighed. "And there was Darren's brother, Bobby. He was very different than Darren. Very intense and not in a good way. I *know* he didn't like me."

Cultural differences were common in a diverse community like the Bay Area. It seemed every family had a "Romeo and Juliet" story to tell of star-crossed lovers. Kaitlin wasn't surprised to learn that Darren's family was resistant to his relationship with Rachel, but she was curious as to why Rachel was so emphatic about it.

"How do you know?" Kaitlin asked.

Rachel considered the question.

"I don't think it was ever personal with him. Bobby didn't like any of Darren's lifestyle choices – job, work ethic, or me. He was pretty vocal about his feelings. Bobby was involved in the family business, and he was always criticizing Darren because he didn't want to be part of it."

"So you think that because of the pressure he was getting from his brother and his parents, Darren decided to break up with you?"

"He never admitted that was the reason, but I think so," Rachel said as she nervously fingered her necklace.

"That's a lovely necklace, by the way," said Kaitlin. Probably a gift from wealthy parents, she thought. At Stanford that wouldn't be the exception but the rule.

"Thanks," Rachel said, looking down with a smile and clasping the pendant. "Darren was always surprising me with beautiful things." Tears welled up in her eyes again. "He bought me this for our one-year anniversary."

Rachel was not unattractive and obviously smart, but Christ, Kaitlin thought – she had guys giving her diamond necklaces. Kaitlin had gotten gifts from boyfriends before, but they were things like ugly sweaters, tickets to sporting events, and, on one occasion, a used bicycle. But diamonds? Never.

Kaitlin regained focus. So Rachel and Darren were past tense. But Kaitlin knew that "over" did not always mean "done." She'd need to dig deeper if she really wanted to know where things stood.

"So you guys were no longer a couple. I understand." Kaitlin waited a beat. "Did you see each other after you broke up… or talk?"

Rachel shrugged. "Once in a while…yeah, we talked on the phone. And we traded e-mails a few times a month."

"When was the last time you saw Darren?"

Rachel thought for a few seconds. "Probably last summer. August. He was traveling a lot for work. So even if he'd wanted to see me more, there wasn't a lot of time."

Rachel's comment surprised Kaitlin. "He did a lot of work-related traveling?"

"Sure. All the time."

"Did he go anyplace interesting?" Kaitlin asked, regaining her composure.

"Mostly he traveled to Asia," Rachel said, trying to remember the places Darren had visited. "Maybe New York once or twice. He didn't talk a lot about it. It was all just work to him."

Kaitlin moved away from any more discussion of Darren's travels. Maybe Darren had told Rachel he was traveling on business to hide new girlfriends. Nothing extraordinary about that. But, whatever the reason, there was a disconnect between what Kaitlin had learned from Gupta and what she was learning from Rachel.

"Rachel, did you ever know Darren to drink or use drugs?"

"No," Rachel replied with certainty. Kaitlin accepted the response at face value. But from painful, personal experience, she knew that Rachel, as close as she was to Darren, could be totally wrong.

"Did he owe anyone money?"

"I'd be surprised if he did. His family was well off and he had a very good job. I can't imagine that he ever needed to borrow any."

"Was he argumentative? Have enemies? Anything that would make someone angry with him?"

With Kaitlin's line of questioning, Rachel became alarmed. She had believed Darren's death was just an accident, but these questions were firing up her neocortex.

Rachel shook her head. "No. Nothing that I know of. Darren was a good, hardworking guy. He got along with everyone."

Kaitlin listened to Rachel and then asked her the question she had been holding until she was ready to leave. "Rachel, were you angry with Darren?"

Rachel's expression turned hard. She didn't need her 140 IQ to know where Kaitlin was going with that sort of question, and by now her brain had connected lots of dots. She'd been quite forthcoming in all her answers. However, as was the case for Synergy's Pradeep Gupta, that was a straw too many.

"*Why would you ask me that?*" she challenged Kaitlin. "What would my being angry with him have to do with a car accident?" She twisted her necklace nervously. "You don't think that *I* had anything to do with what happened to Darren, do you?"

Kaitlin was too good a detective to answer that question directly. Instead she held her gaze steady on Rachel. "Rachel, this is all routine follow-up to an accident that involved a fatality. We can't make assumptions. I'm sorry if any of my questions offended you. Now," she said, standing up, "I'm sorry I've taken up so much of your time. I have a good idea how difficult your schedule is…"

"Let's get one thing straight," Rachel said in a cold, direct voice. "I had absolutely *nothing* to do with what happened to Darren." Then she stood up so that she was eye to eye with Kaitlin. She held Kaitlin's gaze for a moment before turning to collect several books and papers on her desk. "I've got to get to class. Do you have any other questions?" Rachel asked, still ruffled.

Kaitlin shook her head. "Not right now, no. You've been really helpful. Thank you."

Rachel nodded, thinking that was the end of it.

"But," Kaitlin went on, "it would be helpful to have your e-mail address, just in case I do."

Rachel paused. She opened her mouth to speak, but then stopped short. Kaitlin was eager to hear what Rachel would say next, but Rachel didn't oblige.

"Sure, of course," Rachel said. She took out a pen and scribbled her e-mail address on a scrap of paper and handed it to Kaitlin.

"Thanks again," Kaitlin said. "And I really am sorry about Darren."

"Yeah, me too," Rachel said.

Kaitlin extended her hand to Rachel. "Good luck."

"Thank you," Rachel said, accepting Kaitlin's hand. "Now, I really do have to get to lecture." She turned and walked down the narrow hallway.

Kaitlin watched her until she turned the corner and disappeared. As she did, she had the strange sensation that she had been watching a red-haired version of herself, hurrying down the linoleum hallway for the hundredth lecture of the fifteen-hundredth seminar on advanced embedded computer systems design or similar topic.

Kaitlin couldn't shake the image of herself going through those motions again. Even the heft and feel of the heavy office door upon closing was a visceral experience. Her thoughts were so jumbled with the past as she walked out onto the sidewalk that she hardly noticed that the cloud cover had returned.

It would rain again. And soon.

# Chapter 8

Kaitlin shivered as she descended the cold, hard steps that led down to SJPD's computer crime lab. Its cool, dehumidified environment was hospitable only to circuits, chips, transistors, and resistors. As she came to recognize after spending the vast majority of her adulthood locked away in similar dungeon-like computer rooms, she was *not* any of the above.

Signs of life in such places were scarce. Fast-food wrappers. Pizza boxes. Coke cans. An occasional life form that appeared more vampire than human.

Despite her feelings about computer rooms and the physical discomfort she felt, Kaitlin moved down the steps with some degree of anticipation. Darren Park's cracked Palm awaited her. And her mind was racing at the prospect of piercing through the contradicting layers of his young life.

Her excitement came to an abrupt halt when she came to the lab's heavy, steel door. Through the reinforced window panel, she was stunned to observe FBI Special Agent Alex

Renfro standing across a lab table from the white-coated technician. And there in Renfro's grubby hand, the very same hand that had been on her ass, was Park's Palm V.

Shit.

Kaitlin pushed open the door. She ignored Renfro and marched directly to the lab technician. "Officer Palance phoned me last night indicating that a piece of evidence would be available for my review this morning. Why does he have it?" she demanded, glancing over her shoulder at Renfro.

"I'm sorry, Detective Hall," the technician apologized, looking more like a worried hamster than a man, "but this device has already been checked out of evidence by Special Agent Renfro. It's his for seven days…unless you have a subpoena," he added hopefully.

She caught the smile that flashed across Renfro's sensual lips.

"Damn," she said under her breath. She turned and watched Renfro studiously avoid looking at her while he played with the buttons on the PDA, trying to figure out how to get it functioning. Kaitlin leaned closer to the technician. "Look at this," she said, mockingly. "Special Agent Renfro of the *FBI* is liable to push the wrong button and erase all the information from the damned thing!"

That worked. Renfro immediately stopped what he was doing and looked up at Kaitlin.

She smiled. "Hello, Alex," she said.

"Hey, Kaitlin."

She narrowed her eyes. "Why is the FBI interested in Darren Park's traffic accident?" she demanded.

Now it was Renfro's turn to smile. "Nice to see you again too," he said in a lighthearted and infuriatingly sweet manner. "I guess we're going to dispense with the pleasantries, huh?"

She gave him an impatient look and crossed her arms over her chest.

"Thought so. Well, I really cannot confirm or deny whether the Bureau is interested in Darren Park's traffic accident." He cleared his throat. "The Bureau *is* interested to know why you're so interested in it, however."

The ball was in her court. If he wanted to play games, she would go along. The trouble was she was at a disadvantage. She had no idea what Captain Torres told Renfro after she'd left the other day.

When bluffing was a weak hand, the rule was to stall. She shrugged her shoulders. "As far as I can tell, it was a routine accident. However, it happens that the deceased's employer is a software company in San Jose. Captain Torres refers to my investigation as a "constituent service," if you know what I mean." Renfro skeptically raised an eyebrow, but she plowed on.

"I'll do a little legwork. After I file my report, he'll call the CEO and express his condolences and let him know that the SJPD gave the case its full attention. Blah, blah blah. That sort of thing..."

Renfro nodded. Kaitlin knew that the bullshit she'd just served up was reasonably credible. Anyone who knew Torres would appreciate his desire to look good to the CEO of a software company. The question was, would Renfro buy it?

Kaitlin didn't want to give him too much time to consider what she'd said. "All that being the case, I don't suppose you'd mind checking that device, that you clearly don't have a clue how to operate, back into evidence so I can have a look at it."

Renfro smiled briefly, catching a glimpse of the same woman who had rocked him that night in Vegas. She was no one to trifle with – that was for damned sure. And sexy. Even under the fluorescent lights of the computer lab.

Not for the first time, he realized that alcohol had played little role in the attraction he'd felt in Vegas.

"You know how hard it is for me to say no to you," he said flirtatiously. "However, I'm not quite ready to check this baby back in." He extended his arm and checked the time on his Casio wristwatch. "But I am way overdue for a cup of coffee."

Just as she was feeling that she'd lost the battle, he surprised her by handing her the Palm.

"Tell you what," he said. "You hold on to this little gizmo for about an hour while I go find a cup of joe." Then he winked at her. "You're right about one thing – I'm liable to erase every goddamned thing on it." With a grin, he turned and made his way out from the lab.

She clutched the PDA in her hand. She looked down at it and then at the grinning lab technician. "What are you looking at?" she demanded.

"Nothing, nothing," he stammered. He scurried away, leaving her alone. She slid onto a stool and rested the PDA on the table. She had sixty minutes.

⅄

Sixty-two minutes later, Renfro returned. "Well, Detective, find anything interesting?" he asked before he drained the last from his cardboard cup. He tossed it in a graceful arc and landed it directly in the wastepaper basket. "Well?"

She powered down the device and folded the leatherette case closed. "All yours," she said.

He looked at her curiously.

"What?" she asked, reading his expectant expression.

"Nothing," he said, shaking his head.

"The guy was a typical nerdy engineer," she said. "You know the type. Not much of a social life." She frowned, hoping that her frown suggested her disappointment. "But thanks for the chance to take a look at it. You didn't have to do that."

"I know," he said with the certainty of a guy who was holding all the cards.

Kaitlin hated that. She hated that self-assured macho thing that Renfro did so effortlessly. And charmingly.

He held her with his deep, perceptive eyes. "I figured you wouldn't find anything interesting." He shrugged. "I thought I'd do Torres the favor."

She nodded. "You know how he is about the political thing," she said, masking the frustration she felt dealing with him. "At least now he can call Park's employer and cover his bases."

Renfro smiled. "That's not really what I meant," he said.

"No?" she asked, suspecting she'd just been caught in a trap of her own making.

"No," he said. "When I last spoke with him, Torres mentioned that you get easily distracted by cases you aren't assigned to. Like Darren Park's," he added with obvious delight. "He mentioned that he really needed your attention on some burglary cases."

Kaitlin wished she could have said what she was thinking. But, drawing deep down into herself, she held back. "All in a day's work," she said obliquely, trying not to become furious by his boyish grin. She breathed slowly, controlling her emotions. "And you know how the Captain appreciates any assistance the FBI can offer," she said with smooth sarcasm. "I'll be sure to make a note of your cooperation in my report."

"That'd be swell," he said.

"Thanks again," Kaitlin said as she turned and headed for the door.

"Talk to you soon," he called after her.

"Not if I can help it," she seethed under her breath as she pulled open the steel doors and hurried into the hallway. The only thing that kept her from exploding was what she knew about Darren Park that Renfro didn't. The information she'd just culled from the PDA gave her a new direction. A direction that would take Renfro and the FBI time to figure out.

Most of the entries in the device were mundane. But there were a number of them that piqued her interest. Mr. Park had indeed become quite the world traveler in the previous six months. His calendar revealed an entry at least every other Friday that read simply, "SFO." There were a handful of other entries that she couldn't fully decipher – including a number of calendar items which were marked with single names like "Bob," "Elizabeth," and "Shane." They could have signified anything – lunch plans, racquetball games, or something else altogether.

The checkbook feature of the Pilot also troubled her. Up until a couple of days before his death, his spending habits were striking only in their utter regularity and moderation. He seemed to be a direct-deposit kind of guy. A good portion of his paycheck went to rent, groceries, gas, and some electronic toys from Fry's.

There was nothing to explain an expenditure of say, a diamond pendant necklace or chrome wheels for a Beemer. There was no entry for travel expenses. Not even a single airline ticket.

Someone wasn't telling the truth about Darren Park.

# Chapter 9

"Nice digs," Kaitlin said to herself, looking out her car window. Given Darren Park's PDA entries for monthly rent expense, Kaitlin wasn't expecting the Taj Mahal when she turned up Coddle Road in San Jose. After all, thirteen hundred dollars a month didn't get you much anymore in the Bay Area. Maybe a modest little shoe box.

So she was a little taken aback when she pulled up in front of a lavish, two-hundred-unit condo complex. With a doorman and a valet.

"A doorman?" she thought to herself. "Where the hell do these people think they are? New York?"

She quickly glanced down at the street address she had written in her notes. Then she looked up at the address on the condo complex. This was definitely the place. Kaitlin's mind was already trying to make sense of the apparent contradiction. Roommates? No one mentioned roommates, but it was a possibility.

She shook her head. "Where was Darren Park when I was looking for *my* apartment?" she thought, giving a cynical spin to the evidence presenting itself to her.

She held up her badge to the concierge at the marble-topped desk in the building's lobby. "San Jose Police Department," she said simply.

The nonplussed concierge peered at the badge over the rim of his glasses. Then he looked directly at Kaitlin. "Yes, I believe I spoke with you earlier," he noted with the insouciance of a Manhattan waiter.

Kaitlin was not in the mood for pretense.

"Darren Park's apartment?"

"Yes, of course," he said. "I'll have one of our people take you up." He spoke into an intercom system and then looked back at Kaitlin. "It'll be just a moment," he said as he gave her an artificial smile.

"Thanks," Kaitlin said, returning the false smile.

The concierge turned his attention back to the financial page of the *San Jose Mercury News.* However, seeing as Kaitlin didn't remember walking into the reading room of the library, she reached forward and gently lowered the newspaper. "Did you know Darren Park?" she asked.

He raised an eyebrow at her forwardness. Police officer or not, he felt she was showing remarkably bad manners. He drew a slow breath. "Not particularly. I knew who he was, of course. I know all the tenants. But I become friendly with very, very few."

"How long had Mr. Park lived here?"

The concierge brought his hands together and rested his chin on the tips of his fingers. Then he closed his eyes. "Let's see. I believe he moved in not long after the building opened last summer. I do remember that he drove a black BMW," he added, as if that might have been an important piece of information.

"Like who doesn't?" Kaitlin thought to herself. "Thanks," she told the concierge. She hadn't decided whether he was holding back information, or if he was seriously pathetic. Seeing a person every day for the better part of a year and knowing nothing more about him than the kind of car he drove?

In either case, it was pointless to continue questioning him. If there was more information to be gotten from him, it would happen at headquarters. She turned away from the concierge as he returned to the newspaper. She strolled around the lobby, pausing to pick up one of the brochures that advertised the many features of, what she thought was appropriately named, "Coddle Manor."

The back page of the brochure listed rentals beginning at "$3,500 per month." She raised her eyebrow. That was nearly three times the $1,300 Darren Park listed for his monthly rent.

When the security guard led her up to Park's apartment, she immediately realized that this apartment was not one of those that "began" at $3,500. Instead of the disheveled bachelor pad she was expecting, she walked into an elegantly furnished apartment. Leather couch. Overstuffed chair. Handsome wood and iron coffee table. Art Deco lamps. Coffee table books.

The walls were adorned with brightly-colored, signed lithographs. She was both impressed and disappointed. There was something more real about a bachelor's apartment that had stacks of beer cans, swimsuit and rock `n roll posters, and cinderblock and lumber bookshelves.

It was clear that Darren Park was not a run-of-the-mill bachelor techie. The entertainment center opened to reveal a state-of-the-art home theater system. Sixty-inch Pioneer theater format monitor, DVD, and just about every NAD, Harmon Kardon and Nakamichi audio and video components Kaitlin had ever seen advertised in an audiophile catalog.

"Man, this was one bachelor living large," she thought to herself.

The bedroom boasted a neatly made, queen-sized bed. If she hadn't met Park's girlfriend, Kaitlin would have wondered if Park had been gay. Nothing had prepared her for a bachelor apartment so tastefully and neatly arranged.

It gave her the creeps. In no small measure because it raised more questions than it answered.

It was not much of a surprise when Kaitlin found a walk-in closet filled with Armani, Calvin Klein and Hugo Boss. The fact that Park had worked for a Silicon Valley company with a "jeans and tee shirt" dress code seemed to have no effect on his sense of style.

She wasn't sure at what point in her exploration of Park's apartment that she began to make mental comparisons between his world and her own. From the size of the apartment to the quality of clothing to the tasteful furniture. His watch collection, housed neatly in a velvet-lined teak cabinet, included a TAG Heuer, a gold Rolex, a stylish Breitling chronograph, and an elegant Art Deco Hamilton in mint condition. Kaitlin let out an appreciative sigh. She'd had an uncle who collected fine watches and she knew he would've given up quite a lot for that Hamilton.

When she hit rock bottom in the side-by-side comparison between her life and Darren Park's, a single question emerged: *Where the hell did the money come from for all this?*

Kaitlin was now more familiar with Park's reported finances than she was with her own. After taxes, he reported bringing home just over forty-five thousand dollars a year. Hell, $45K could hardly pay for his rent. She shook her head. Forty-five thousand would barely cover his dry cleaning.

So, how did Darren Park, systems administrator for Synergy, manage to cover his rent, his car, his furniture, his home entertainment center, his clothes, his weekend jaunts to the Far East, his baubles for girlfriends… and his own ego?

Nothing on paper had given her any indication that he was living a life like this – not his payroll information, not his check register, not his personal notations in his Palm. There remained the possibility that Park could have received a fair amount of money from his family. They were, by all accounts, well off. She had gone to school with bright young Korean princes – first generation American-born and well-compensated by their parents for staying out of trouble and garnering straight As in school.

Kaitlin knew that only an interview with Park's family would address the financial incongruities of Darren Park's lifestyle. For a couple of reasons, though, Kaitlin hesitated to initiate that interview. Without direct evidence of a crime, she was reluctant to intrude upon the Park family's grief. And she was more than a little conscious of the fact that she hadn't actually been assigned to Darren Park's case. A family interview would clearly put her beyond the bounds of mere investigative curiosity and personal initiative.

As far as the SJPD was concerned, there was no case. Period.

Her visit to Darren's apartment left her more troubled than eased. She sensed something wasn't right. She just couldn't put her finger on it. Somehow, she was certain that his family's wealth would not be enough to explain the incongruities in his lifestyle. She had no choice. She had to have a chat with Mr. and Mrs. Park.

# Chapter 10

The Park family's address in Hillsborough was an honest indication of their financial status. Hillsborough was home to some of the area's wealthiest residents. Large houses situated on wooded tracts of land. The Park family home, an elegant Mediterranean, was not the largest estate in the neighborhood, nor the smallest. Many of the residents boasted at least two live-in servants. For the most part, this was Bay Area old money, sprinkled with some new money, dot-commers who had cashed in stock options early in order to snap up choice property.

She buzzed in at the bottom of the long driveway and was greeted by Mrs. Park at the front door. Despite their obvious wealth, Mrs. Park struck Kaitlin as a modest and traditional Korean woman. She wore a conservative silk print dress. At five foot one inch, she was several inches shorter than Kaitlin. Her expression was one of confusion and sadness – of grief borne with graciousness and silent pain.

As Mrs. Park led Kaitlin into the house, Kaitlin noted that the house was decorated with understated elegance. Massive Oriental rugs covered the bleached, hardwood floors, softening the sound of their footsteps as they walked toward the living room.

They were midway through the room when Mr. Park, seated at a large desk, looked up from the telephone. Seeing Kaitlin, he paused in his conversation. He spoke several hasty words to the caller and then hung up the phone. He composed himself and rose to greet Kaitlin.

"Mr. Park, thank you for taking the time to speak with me," she said. "I'm very, very sorry about your loss."

The briefest emotion passed across Mr. Park's face. Then he motioned for Kaitlin to have a seat in one of the high-backed chairs flanking his desk.

As she sat down, she nodded toward Mr. Park. "I know you've already spoken with several of my colleagues, so I'll try to be brief – "

"Detective Hall," Mr. Park said with some impatience, "whether you make this brief or not makes no difference. Our son cannot be brought back to us."

Kaitlin was taken aback by the sharpness in Mr. Park's tone. She glanced down at her hands then looked at Mrs. Park who averted her eyes. She proceeded with the standard investigative questions that were always asked, the very same ones that she had asked Darren's girlfriend, Rachel. It wasn't until their Filipina housekeeper brought in a tray bearing three porcelain cups and a porcelain teapot that she delved a little deeper.

"Had Darren traveled recently with the family, or perhaps on family business?" she asked.

Mr. Park stiffened slightly but said nothing.

"Mr. Park?" she asked, prompting him.

"No," he said. "There have been no family vacations. And no family business involving Darren in the past few years."

Kaitlin jotted down the remark. "Mr. and Mrs. Park, I have already spoken with Darren's employer and, according to him, Darren had not traveled on business either. Yet, he had been traveling to Asia quite a bit in the past few months," Kaitlin said. "I assumed his travel would have been personal."

"Detective Hall," Mr. Park said in a voice that combined pride, pain, and formality, "I am sorry to say that, while Darren has always been a...good son, he had not been close to the family for the past few years."

"Was there a falling out?" she asked, probing gently.

Mr. Park paused before answering. "He was a young man. More American than Korean in his attitude. He..." Mr. Park said, lowering his eyes. "We had some differences of opinion. Those differences caused Darren to keep much of his private life from us."

"Like his relationship with Rachel Weinstein?" Kaitlin asked.

Mrs. Park shifted uncomfortably. She folded her hands on her lap and studiously kept her eyes on them. Mr. Park looked up. His gaze remained fixed on Kaitlin. His expression was blank. After a moment, he nodded.

"Yes, like his relationship with Ms. Weinstein," he conceded.

"Mr. Park, I know this is difficult," Kaitlin said, softening her questions. "Was there anything else?"

Mr. Park looked downward again. "Darren was not interested in participating in the family business," he said.

"Please tell me a little about your business."

He raised his eyes and looked at her with genuine pride. "It is the Great Fortune Trading Company – an import company that I began when I was in Korea. Household products. Textiles. A variety of things. We import them into the United States."

"And your other son, how does he participate in the business?"

"Bobby? Bobby is in charge now. I have retired."

"And you wanted Darren and his brother to run the company together?"

"Of course," Mr. Park said. "What father could have asked for anything more? But Darren refused," he added, the hurt evident in his voice.

"Did he give you any reason for his refusal?"

"I'm afraid Darren never had a clear sense of family obligation. Even when he was not doing well financially, he put distance between us. He seemed to prefer… a more American orientation," he said with soft bitterness.

Mrs. Park looked disapprovingly at Mr. Park. Then, surprising Kaitlin, she spoke: "Detective, it is true that we would have preferred Darren to live his life in a different manner, but we had come to accept Darren for who he was. He was our son and this, after all, is America." She looked down again, overcome by her emotions.

"Of course, I understand," Kaitlin said. She felt her stomach knot up. This interview was painful for all involved. The emotions were raw, the hurt so evident. "I know this is very difficult for you. I'll only ask you a couple more questions."

Mr. Park waved his hand, inviting her to continue.

"Can I ask whether you gave Darren any financial assistance?"

"No," Mr. Park said sternly. "Absolutely not."

"Gifts, perhaps?"

"Detective Hall, both our sons were raised to respect hard work and to live within their means. We never spoiled Darren as a child and we certainly did not as an adult. He made his decisions. He supported himself. "He had a job. It was a good job. Not the best job, true. But a job that allowed him to live his life the way he chose."

"What about Bobby?"

A quick smile crossed Mr. Park's lips. "Bobby does very well. The business is more successful than ever."

"Might he have provided any financial support to Darren?"

"I doubt it," Mr. Park said. "You would have to ask him."

It was clear that Jong Ma Park was not in the habit of buying his son Beemers, Nakamichi audio components, or Hamilton watches. He was barely giving him the time of day.

Darren Park was certainly not a trust fund baby.

While the incongruities of Darren Park's life could yet prove to be the result of extreme generosity on the part of brother Bobby, Kaitlin was fairly sure they wouldn't be. She was a long way off from any clarity regarding Park's death, and the more she learned about his life, the less clear it became.

As she drove away from the Park family's Hillsborough home, Kaitlin punched the buttons on her car stereo. A Pearl Jam song ended as the news came on. Kaitlin half-listened to the reports of traffic jams, rain on the way, and another stall in the Arab-Israeli peace talks. However, the next story caught her immediate attention.

> *"In Santa Cruz this morning, a tragic discovery. The body of Michael Owens of Los Gatos was found on Cowell beach, bringing the extensive search that followed his disappearance to a halt. Early reports suggest that he drowned while surfing the area's rough waters.*
>
> *"Owens was reported missing two days ago when he failed to show up for work at Entrex Semiconductors in Palo Alto..."*

Kaitlin's heart was pounding and she wasn't exactly sure why. So a guy drowned in Santa Cruz. It was sad news but hardly uncommon. What was it that troubled her about this report?

The guy had been reported missing two days ago. Today was Friday. That meant he'd failed to show up for work on Wednesday. Okay, if he had failed to show up Wednesday, he must have shown up for work on Tuesday. Right?

"Now who the hell treks to Santa Cruz for a Tuesday evening or Wednesday morning frolic in the ocean?" she wondered. That water was way too cold for Kaitlin. But hardcore surfers, even in winter, would go whenever and wherever there was a decent swell.

"Okay, reel it in," Kaitlin cautioned herself. "Pause the surfing skepticism before you fall in love with it."

She soon realized the piece of this puzzle that had caught her attention. Michael Owens of Los Gatos had failed to report for work at *Entrex Semiconductors.* Entrex employed over a thousand people, so it was doubtful that anyone would have been concerned about a low-level employee failing to show up for work on a Wednesday morning. Or failing to show up at all.

But what if Owens was a key employee in cutting-edge silicon chip design that Entrex was world famous for? What if he was involved in designs that were the lifeblood of all semiconductor companies? Designs that were multi-billion-dollar trade secrets. Secrets like the encryption technology developed by Synergy. Secrets that, like encryption technology, were restricted from foreign export without U.S. government approval. Approval that was never granted.

Kaitlin wondered where her thoughts would be right now if she hadn't turned on the radio exactly when she had. She chuckled as she eased onto 280 South heading home. Thanks to that fortuitous radio selection, suddenly there was an awful lot to think about. Darren Park. Michael Owens. Silicon chips. Encryption technology. Traffic accidents in Half Moon Bay. Surfing accidents in Santa Cruz.

"You're letting your imagination get ahead of you, Kaitlin," she told herself.

What she needed to do was get home and get out of her clothes. She needed a decent meal and a long, hot bath. And then she needed sleep.

"Umm," she purred. She smiled as she looked forward to tomorrow, her day off.

"Sleep is good…"

# Chapter 11

Whatever fantasy Kaitlin might have had about sleeping through her day off went out the window when she opened her eyes at 6:15 a.m. and couldn't go back to sleep. "No, no," she said, pulling her pillow over her head. She tossed and turned. She pulled the blankets over her head. She threw them off.

"Damn it," she said to herself. "Why can't you just be a *girl* and sleep late just once in your life?"

When she was young, the girls she grew up with slept until noon on Saturday and Sunday mornings; she was up at the crack of dawn with the boys, playing ball or working on computers. Even in adulthood, she still could not master the art of sleeping in.

By 8 a.m., she was showered, dressed, and out the door. She viewed herself in the rearview mirror and narrowed her eyes. "Sometimes, I hate you," she swore at her reflection. She bristled with momentary self-loathing. What had she done to be cursed with a Type B personality trapped in a Type A body?

Then she started the car and rolled out. Her destination was the Port of Oakland and Bobby Park's office. "Oakland: the Bay Area's weekend relaxation destination," she muttered sarcastically. It was not the place where most people chose to spend their day off.

She glanced once more at herself in the mirror. "Promise me that at some point you will seriously consider getting a life," she said to her reflection. "Promise me," she added, more insistently.

⅄

An hour later, she arrived at a metal-clad guard booth outside a massive dockside warehouse, the perimeter surrounded by chain link fence topped with razor wire. Inside the booth, a very large Asian man was bobbing his head back and forth to the loud beat of gangsta rap pounding through his boom box. When she pulled up alongside the booth, the man turned down the boom box, but only slightly. He looked over at her, eyeing her up and down.

"Yeah?"

She held up her badge. "Detective Hall. I'm here to speak with Bobby Park," she said.

He shifted his weight uncomfortably in his chair. "He expecting you?"

"I don't think so. His father suggested I come and speak with him." Over the frame of the fat guard's Ray-Ban sunglasses, Kaitlin perceived a singular arched eyebrow.

She hadn't alerted Bobby to her arrival. She wanted him a little off balance. She felt it was only fair. After all, it was her day off.

"Just a minute," he said. He picked up the phone from the booth's console and closed the window. Noticing Kaitlin watch him intently from her car, he turned away before he spoke to the person on the other end of the line. She couldn't actually hear his conversation through the thick security glass, but perhaps he thought she could read lips. Or maybe he was just paranoid.

The guard was a behemoth of a man, not your typical rent-a-cop. He was most likely a buddy of Bobby Park's who was paid to hang out and keep the riff-raff from bothering the boss. Kaitlin waited to find out whether a SJPD detective was considered riff-raff.

A moment later, he opened the window. "Go on in," he said, jerking his head and motioning toward the warehouse across the parking lot. He stepped out of the booth. Kaitlin's eyes widened. She could now see he was a mountain of man. She was surprised that he fit in the small booth.

The man grabbed the gate and shoved it along its track, opening a narrow space for Kaitlin to drive through.

"Thank you," she said sweetly. She didn't mind pissing off men, she just didn't see the sense in having a mountain mad at her.

If the security personnel were any indication, this was going to be a very interesting meeting. She pulled up to the building's entrance nearest the wharf. She parked in a spot alongside a Mercedes 500 sedan, a fire-engine red Acura NSX, and a white Jaguar convertible.

As she closed the door to her Chevy Lumina, she was suffering from a very definite inferiority complex. Did everyone in the Bay Area but her drive a $70,000 car?

Other than the high-end cars, the sights and sounds of the pier were classic. The heavy sky. The faraway sound of a ship's diesel engine. The bellow of a fog horn. The cawing of seagulls and albatrosses.

She stepped up to the building's loading platform where she found two young men in their twenties. Both Asian. Both wearing identical black, leather jackets. Both smoking.

One of them flicked his cigarette to the ground. "Can I help you?"

"I'm here to see Bobby Park," she said.

He jerked his head. "Inside."

"Thanks," she said, wondering why the guy bothered.

Inside, the scene was no less strange. At the end of the room, an attractive young Asian woman with full make-up and two pounds of metal earrings and bracelets feverishly tapped the keys of a ten-key adding machine. *Clack-clack-clack, jingle-jingle, jingle.* Although her desk sported a state-of-the-art, one-inch thin flat screen computer monitor, it was dominated by ledger paper covered with ink notations. She glanced up at Kaitlin through her stylish eyeglasses and then, just as quickly, glanced down again.

Another large black and gold-trimmed lacquered desk occupied the opposite side of the room. It was bereft of anything other than a laptop computer, telephone, and a holder for neatly stacked business cards that read, "Bobby Park, President."

In the dead center of the room, a man stood with his back to her. He was stooped over slightly, gripping a golf putter. His shoulders swung back slowly. The wrists cocked just a bit. And the golf ball, tapped gently, rolled straight and true down the center of the eight-foot-long Astroturf putting green.

As the ball rolled along, the room grew silent. The *clack-clack-clack* of the adding machine and the jingle-jingle-jingle of the jewelry stopped. Then the ball dropped into the cup with a thud and the noise of addition and adornment resumed.

The man walked over to the cup and retrieved the golf ball. He rested the putter over his shoulder and turned around. Dressed more like the golfer he was practicing to be than an import-export executive, Bobby Park looked Kaitlin up and down, clearly impressed with what he saw.

"You're the cop?" he asked, incredulously.

She nodded. She took out her badge and displayed it to him. "Bobby Park? Detective Hall. San Jose Police Department. I'm sorry for your loss."

He nodded. He stepped toward Kaitlin and extended his hand toward her. After shaking her hand, he offered her the putter. "Care to take a swing?"

She shook her head. "Maybe later," she said.

"My father mentioned you might be calling," Bobby said.

Too bad, Kaitlin thought. He *was* prepared.

"Have a seat," he said, gesturing to a high-backed leather chair in front of the desk. He moved behind it and sat down.

He opened the top drawer and took out a pack of Winston Lights. He waved the red and white box in front of Kaitlin. "Smoke?"

She shook her head. "No thanks."

"You don't look like a smoker," he said, lighting a cigarette and inhaling deeply. "So," he said, exhaling a cloud of smoke, "how can I help you?"

"About your brother…"

"Shoot," he said, disturbingly nonchalant.

"Darren was driving a tricked-out BMW when he crashed. A black M3. Do you know the car?"

He nodded. "Sure. Darren got it about three months ago." He smiled and exhaled again. "Big man got himself a fancy car. He showed up here to impress me."

"Really?"

"He'd never had a nice car before. He was a Honda Accord sort of guy."

Kaitlin noted his cocky tone and even cockier attitude. A man with a Mercedes outside the office could be dismissive about his brother's Honda. Having grown up in California, she was very familiar with guys trying to impress her with their cars. During her freshman year in college, one of her dorm mates suggested that boys think that every extra ten thousand dollars they spend on a car adds another inch to their manhood.

Kaitlin had blushed then. But the years had taught her that her dorm mate wasn't so far off.

"If he was such a Honda Accord guy, why'd he spring for a Beemer?"

Bobby shrugged. “Hard to say. He made a bunch of money on his stock options or something.” He took a quick drag on the cigarette. “Maybe he thought it was time to make a statement.”

“A statement?” asked Kaitlin. “To whom?”

“You know, to his girlfriend. What’s her name?”

“Rachel,” the attractive secretary chimed in.

“Mind your business!” Bobby shouted at her in English. Then he shouted something louder in Korean. The secretary lowered her eyes, hunched her shoulders and went back to work.

Bobby turned to Kaitlin. “To Rachel. To my parents. To me. Who knows?”

Kaitlin didn’t have any trouble with what Bobby was saying. Except for his line about where Darren’s money had come from – it didn’t ring true. Synergy was privately owned. There was no way he could have made money cashing in stock options. The shares were restricted and there were no buyers.

“Any idea what Darren might have been doing out on the road to Half Moon Bay on a weeknight?”

He shook his head. “I don’t know if you’ve gotten the story yet, but me and my brother weren’t all that close,” Bobby said.

Kaitlin nodded. “I’m getting that.”

She waited, giving Bobby a chance to start thinking and, with any luck, talking.

Finally, he obliged. “He was alone in the car, right?” Bobby asked casually, blowing out another stream of smoke.

Kaitlin nodded. “Alone, yes. Why do you ask?”

He shrugged. “Curiosity.”

Kaitlin didn't buy that for a second.

She pressed on. "Was Darren in any sort of trouble? Enemies? Drug problems?"

Bobby laughed. "I doubt it. Darren was the good boy. I was the troublemaker. I can't tell you how many times I tried to get him to loosen up and have a good time. But not my big brother Darren."

Kaitlin watched Bobby closely. "You and Darren had any arguments recently? Everything all right between you two?"

Bobby narrowed his eyes. "What the hell are you getting at? I told you we weren't that close…"

"Just a routine question," she assured him.

"Doesn't sound like a routine, goddamned question," he said as he mashed his cigarette into the ashtray and then lit up another one.

"It really is," she said.

"Well, anyway, things were cool between us. He did his thing. I did mine. Period."

"Your father wanted Darren in the family business."

"My father has an old world vision of the new world," Bobby said dismissively.

"How would you have felt about Darren working with you?"

"I wouldn't have given a shit," he said. "It would have made my parents happy. Hey, he set up the computer system. But he didn't have the head for business. He was a computer geek."

Before she could continue her questioning, the phone rang. Bobby picked it up. "Yeoboseyo?" he answered gruffly, continuing in Korean.

He held his hand over the mouthpiece and looked up at Kaitlin. "I have to take this call," he said. "Are we finished?"

She nodded. She got up from the chair and headed for the door. Kaitlin knew that Bobby hadn't been entirely straight with her. But, as she well knew, even lies tell a story. She just had to figure out what story Bobby's lies told.

Before driving away, Kaitlin scribbled down the license plate numbers of the cars outside. As she backed out of the spot, she was determined to remember everything about the Great Fortune Trading Company.

She did a three-point turn and began to head toward the gate when the large, multi-colored stack of cargo containers on Great Fortune's dock caught her eye. Each container bore a seven-digit tracking number on its side.

On a whim, she wrote down the numbers. On Monday, she'd call the Asian Criminal Enterprise task force and ask a few questions. She wasn't sure what those questions might be, but by Monday she'd figure it out.

# Chapter 12

The weekend passed by in a blur. By her standards, Kaitlin had slept in Sunday – until 8 a.m. Yet Kaitlin remained mystified. Why couldn't she lounge around like other human beings?

The morning was spent cleaning the kitchen, bathroom, and bedroom. After that, grocery shopping, getting the oil changed, picking up a few things – the kinds of errands that drove home the fact she didn't have much of a life. The sad reality that she had no dates, or even prospects for one, only added a cherry on top of the whipped cream of her pitiful existence.

She was well-known by first name to everyone who worked at *Blockbuster Video,* where she rented a second-rate action flick that she'd missed seeing in the theatres earlier in the season. She would watch it that night and know why it had quickly gone to video. She bought a coffee at Starbucks and picked up a copy of the *New York Times* on the way home. Perhaps she'd spend the next three hours luxuriating in the *Times,* and after that, a long bath, a video, and bed.

Although she spent a good portion of the weekend reflecting on her lack of a life, those introspections were as much a consequence of her investigation into Darren Park's death as they were with any deep dissatisfaction with her life. Whatever else she suspected about the case, it troubled her that a young man with so much potential had lost his life before he'd had the chance to really enjoy it.

"Get out of that thought process," she told herself. Although she felt a 'stop and smell the roses' self-lecture coming on, she was very conscious of the vast differences between her and Darren. She had lots of friends in the area and a multitude of interests that engaged her enthusiasm. But this weekend she couldn't get up the energy to be social or to do more than the bare minimum – and dwell on Darren Park.

This weekend, while she cleaned, ran errands, and watched a mediocre video, her thoughts returned to work. Not, of course, to any of the messages that kept cropping up on her answering machine. Instead, her thoughts remained on Darren Park. And on Michael Owens, the formerly missing might-be surfer. By 6 p.m. Sunday afternoon, a mild case of the blues had set in. She couldn't shake them even with another bath before bed. Kaitlin got into bed and read for a while. She turned off the light just before midnight and spent the next five hours tossing and turning.

⅄

"There really is no justice," she decided groggily when turned off the alarm at five o'clock Monday morning.

"Thank God for coffee," Kaitlin thought as the aroma from her timed coffee maker wafted into her room. Even so, she groaned a protest at the thought of having to pull herself from under the all-too-comfortable flannel sheets and out into the cold dark room. Not sleeping was bad enough. But that first jolt of cold air in the morning was painful to contemplate. She could hardly think of a worse punishment.

"Come on, Kaitlin," she urged herself. "Let's get a move on."

She pushed aside the window curtains and looked out at a Bay Area downpour. "Yuck," she said, looking desperately upward for any hint of blue sky. As dreary as that sight was, she knew if she didn't get herself out of the house and on the road, most of her morning would be spent in traffic. That was more than enough motivation to get her into action. She quickly showered and dressed. She stopped in front of her automatic coffee maker and poured the French Roast into her stainless steel commuter mug. She raised the mug in a silent toast to herself and the task ahead, heading for the front door.

Her hand was already on the doorknob when she realized that a rain jacket was in order. She grabbed it off the hook in the closet, said a silent prayer in praise of Gore-Tex, then dashed out the door toward her car.

She turned on the radio, set the wipers on high, and pulled out onto the road. As she sped along, with only light traffic around her, she smiled to herself. "Early bird catches the worm and misses the traffic," she chuckled. Five o'clock in the morning might be a cruel time to climb out of bed, but she'd take that pain anytime rather than sit in morning commuter traffic.

Even better than beating the morning traffic was arriving at work and finding the station house deserted. She was the only person there. "Ah, blessed peace," she said to herself as she settled down at her desk. She had a lot of work to do and she didn't need any distractions. Her weekend thinking had given her some ideas, and she wanted to get some things down before Captain Torres returned from his morning pow-wow in Woodside.

She shook her head as her computer was booting up. Torres' ambition and strategy made him as predictable as clockwork. Two or three times a week – and always on a Monday morning – Torres met some company CEO for breakfast at Buck's, home of Silicon Valley's power breakfast, to talk politics, golf, and business. Not necessarily in that order. She knew it didn't matter what the topic was, the objective was always the same – Torres making sure his power base was happy.

When he had those power breakfasts, Torres didn't arrive at the squad room until 11 a.m. Kaitlin knew that she had a good couple of hours to work before she had to worry about Torres.

By seven o'clock, Kaitlin was working her computer and the telephone at the same time. The halogen desk lamp on Kaitlin's desk provided the sole illumination and cast Kaitlin aglow in the otherwise dimly lit room. The staccato of the keyboard echoed in the stillness of the squad room. With each passing minute, she felt a greater urgency to get more done.

She knew that she was stretching the limits of her official responsibilities. So before anyone showed up to snoop over her shoulder, she tried to collect as much information as possible, as quickly as possible, regarding the death of Michael Owens. At the same time, she followed up on some loose ends dangling from the Darren Park death.

Friday morning's meeting with Bobby Park had opened an entirely new area of inquiry that she was anxious to pursue. She still didn't know much about the Great Fortune Trading Company. But what little she did know convinced her that all was not on the up and up.

She looked up at the clock on the wall. Funny. Despite a perfectly accurate clock in the lower right corner of her monitor, she always opted for the slightly inaccurate analog clock with the sweeping second hand that hung on the wall. In any case, the constant sweep of the red second hand and the constant ticking away of the minute hand indicated how little time she had left to put together an argument to get officially assigned to the Park "case."

In only three hours Torres would arrive. There was no way of knowing what kind of mood he'd be in. That always depended on how the breakfast went. So she knew she'd have to put together an airtight argument to convince him that her "case" was indeed a case. And that *she* should be assigned to it.

As she continued her research, Kaitlin knew how limited her ability to gather information was without a subpoena. She had made progress, no doubt. Using Darren's passport, she'd been able to assemble a rough chronology of his entries into various foreign countries. She was awaiting a report from the U.S. Customs Service that would be dispositive as to the dates and times of his re-entries to the U.S. Unless he'd declared that he was taking out over ten thousand dollars in cash, the Customs Service wouldn't have a record of his departures. But the various airline computer systems would.

As she worked her computer, the information she continued to gather suggested nothing more than the obvious: Darren was pocketing substantially more income than reflected in his financial records and as revealed from discussions with his employer, friends, and family. His pattern of weekend travel was regular, extreme in its scheduling and, so far, inexplicable.

Even as she worked the various information sources at her disposal, Kaitlin was developing a strategy for gaining more information. She knew that a ripe source of information would be Darren's e-mail accounts. Access to his e-mail accounts would allow her to track his various communications over the past six months.

She knew there was the likelihood that he maintained a number of personal e-mail accounts in addition to his account at Synergy. She would need help to begin rooting out those accounts. Pradeep Gupta was an obvious choice for help, but she was reluctant to call him just yet. Given Gupta's business jitters, it would be tough getting him or anyone else at Synergy to cooperate willingly.

But there was Rachel.

Kaitlin leaned back in her chair. She closed her eyes and thought about her conversation with Rachel. "What weren't you telling me, Rachel?" Kaitlin whispered. Tension had quickly filled Rachel's small office when Kaitlin questioned her about the circumstances surrounding Darren's death.

Had Rachel felt defensive? What was she hiding? Or was Kaitlin reading too much into a young woman's natural response to Darren's untimely death?

Regardless of the reason for the tension, Kaitlin felt that Rachel was her best hope for any real assistance she might get. At the very least, she felt that Rachel's agreement, or refusal, to cooperate would give her some insight into any complicity on her part with respect to Darren's activities before his death – or perhaps even his death itself.

With all that in mind, Kaitlin drafted an informal e-mail to Rachel:

> *Rachel,*
>
> *Thanks for taking the time to meet with me the other day. I hope you're doing well. I am continuing my investigation of Darren's death. I've made considerable progress since our meeting, but I could use your help. Can you tell me any e-mail aliases Darren used during the last year? Was Synergy his only account, or did he have a personal account? Thanks in advance for your help.*
>
> *Kaitlin Hall, SJPD*

So as not to place all her eggs in one basket, Kaitlin drafted another e-mail, this one to Slim Yamazaki. Slim had yet to return her last phone call, but she could count on him for assistance. She knew that Slim was more likely to respond to e-mail than a phone call. Without providing much in the way of detail, she solicited Slim's help.

Hackers like Slim had an uncanny ability to gather information – both on the Internet and in private computer networks – as the need arose. She paused before hitting the "send" button on the e-mail to Slim. She drew a deep breath, the kind she would take before diving off a cliff. Which was exactly what she was doing. Asking for Slim's cooperation on an investigation was definitely a breach of protocol. And, officially, there wasn't even an investigation yet. Her finger hovered above the left button on her mouse. She knew the risk she was taking. But she also knew that she was taking an even greater risk by *not* sending the e-mail. What would take her days to accomplish, even with her computer expertise, Slim could accomplish in hours. Kaitlin didn't have that kind of time. She either got Slim's help or she packed any hope for continuing the investigation.

She clicked the "send" button.

She looked again at the clock. Ten o'clock. Time flies when you're having fun. Kaitlin hit the phones again. Until now, she hadn't been successful in her attempts to reach Ken Barnes, Director of Human Resources at Entrex. He hadn't shared her sense of urgency in returning the various voice mail messages she'd left him.

"Doesn't anyone get to their desk before noon on Monday?" she lamented.

"What's that?" Rob Newmeyer asked as he walked by her desk.

"When did you come in?" Kaitlin asked, startled to discover that there were a number of other people in the squad room.

Rob laughed. "Oh, about an hour ago," he said. "You've just been too busy to notice. What're you so involved with?"

She made a face, indicating that he should keep his voice down. "I'm still trying to figure out what happened with that car accident," she told him sheepishly.

He furrowed his brow, making it clear that he thought she'd taken leave of her senses. Even so, he wished her good luck. "You'd better finish up. Torres is sure to be here soon."

Kaitlin looked up at the clock. "I know, I know," she said impatiently.

By 10:30, she had managed to get Detective Frank Ward of the Santa Cruz P.D. on the phone. He had responsibility for the Michael Owens case.

Kaitlin held the receiver away from her ear as the detective coughed repeatedly before speaking. There was something about the cough that made her worry about contagion even over the phone lines.

"Now, how *exactly* can I help you?" Ward asked gruffly, clearing his throat at the same time.

Kaitlin thought he had a lot of nerve sounding annoyed with her. She'd paged him twice in the past hour and he hadn't responded. This call was her third effort to contact him. Maybe if he called people back promptly, he wouldn't hear from them three and four times in an hour…

"I'm interested in Michael Owens," she told him.

"Yeah, why's that?"

She frowned. There was a limit to what she wanted to say. "Following up on some loose ends from another case," she said vaguely. "What can you tell me about the victim?" she asked.

Ward paused, as if considering whether to bust her chops some more. But then he was wracked by a violent coughing fit. "We have a positive I.D. One of his co-workers came down and identified his body. Family lives back East."

"How long had he been in the water?"

"The body was in pretty good shape. Probably no more than a couple hours."

"Do you have a cause of death?"

"Haven't gotten the word from the examiner. So, nothing definitive."

Kaitlin focused on Ward's every word, pulling meaning from not only what he was saying but how he was saying it. "The news reports describe his death as a surfing accident. What exactly does that mean?" she asked.

"It means a drowning or a broken neck. Or both." He hacked up a large cough, abruptly punctuating his sentence. His annoyance was still very evident in his tone. "What's the San Jose Police Department's interest in this again?" he asked, his throat raspy and half-clogged with phlegm.

"Not entirely sure yet," Kaitlin said, determined not to show her hand. "Maybe none. Did he have any personal effects on him?"

Her vagueness was not lost on Ward, who was getting even more annoyed and terse. His next response was a single word: "Nothing."

"Not even car keys?" Kaitlin asked, her own voice getting edgy in response to Ward's. "How do you think he got to the beach in the first place?"

"Listen Detective, we know damn well how he got to the beach. We didn't find a car key, but we did find his car. A couple of miles south, near the boardwalk. Now, you want to tell me what the hell this is about?"

Kaitlin ignored his question. Her thoughts were elsewhere. She'd lived her entire life in California and had spent the better part of her childhood on the Pacific Ocean's sandy beaches. Something about what Detective Ward was telling her didn't seem right.

"Detective, which way do the currents run along the beach there?" she asked.

She could hear the hesitancy in his voice as he answered, "It depends on the season and the weather, but generally north – south."

"Meaning that, out on the water, a surfer on his board would drift towards the south."

"I'm no surfer but, yeah, that's right."

"Don't you find it curious that you found the car to the *south* of the body? And with a couple of miles between them? You did say that the body looked like it hadn't been in the water for more than a couple of hours, right?"

Detective Ward was silent.

"Detective Ward?"

Then he coughed and cleared his throat again. "Well ... I guess that's right. Possible he could have walked a ways to the north before he started surfing."

Kaitlin didn't need to be a surfer – or a detective – to figure out that it wouldn't make sense to park your car, take your surfboard off the roof rack, and then walk a couple of miles to get into the water. The direction of travel aside, Kaitlin was also puzzled by the distance. "Detective, could a body drift that far in that short period of time?"

He paused before answering. "It's been pretty windy down here ... but well ... no . . . that does seem like a long way."

Kaitlin interrupted Ward's thoughts with what must have seemed a non sequitur to him. "What sort of car was Owens driving?"

"Umm ... let's see . . . a BMW. Five Series. Looks brand new; still has the dealer tags on it. Damn shame ..."

Bingo. It wasn't much, and it wasn't scientific, but Kaitlin was sure that the Beemer was a link between Michael Owens and Darren Park. However, she would keep that little bit of intuitive inspiration to herself for the time being.

"I'll come over to Santa Cruz this afternoon. Can I plan on meeting you at the station?" Kaitlin asked.

"Well ... let me see ... " Ward said tentatively, flipping the pages of his pocket calendar, completely uninterested in meeting a meddling detective from another jurisdiction.

It was while Ward searched for some excuse to put off being bothered by Kaitlin, that Captain Torres made his grand entrance. He paused at the doorway to survey the squad room. He nodded his head silently in acknowledgment of those in the room as they looked up from their desks to note his arrival.

"How's four o'clock?" Ward offered reluctantly.

"I'll see you then," Kaitlin said, anxious to get off the phone. "Thank you, Detective Ward." As she placed the phone in the cradle, she watched Torres as he completed his promenade through the squad room and settled himself in his office.

After what seemed like five minutes, she took her first breath since Torres appeared in the doorway. She pressed her hand flat against her stomach, settling the butterflies that had suddenly made their presence known. Breathing slowly, she began to gather her thoughts. At the same time, she also gathered the stack of documents that she'd assembled relating to Darren Park, along with the much smaller stack relating to Michael Owens. She reviewed her line of thinking, then mentally rehearsed how she'd present it. She knew she'd have to have her story straight and her wits about her before pitching her hypotheses – or, rather, her collection of hunches – to Torres.

She raised her eyes upward and wished herself luck, hoping he'd had a really successful breakfast that morning.

"Okay, here goes everything," she said to herself as she slid from her chair, gathered her piles of paper, and began to walk slowly over to his office. Despite Kaitlin's self-consciousness, none of the other detectives in the office so much as looked up from their desks. Kaitlin was grateful no one seemed to pay any attention to her approach to the lion's den.

She knocked on the outside of the open door. Torres looked up, smiled quickly, and gestured for her to come in and have a seat.

Kaitlin breathed a sigh of relief. He seemed to be in a good mood. The morning breakfast must have gone well.

"Good morning, Detective Hall," he said as he watched her sit down and rest her paperwork on her knees.

"Good morning, Captain," she answered, bringing to bear her "cheerleader" smile, as her mother called it,. She pushed a wave of brown hair behind her ear, revealing the outline of her face. A face blessed with a beautiful complexion and featuring cute little dimples.

Since Kaitlin was fifteen years old, Kaitlin's mother knew that her daughter's smile, and other powers of attraction, held considerable force over the opposite sex. She believed that her daughter should exercise those powers to her full advantage. And she often told her so as she got older.

"Mother!" Kaitlin argued. "That's despicable!"

But her mother eyed her knowingly. "Nothing's despicable if it works," she said.

Kaitlin knew that she was too smart – and too much the feminist – to rely on her womanly charms to achieve her aims. But at certain times, and with certain men, she did find herself paying homage to her mother's practical wisdom. A quick smile, a short skirt, or a slightly tight blouse on occasion helped tremendously when her superior intellect was not fully appreciated.

Nothing's despicable if it works.

This morning, Kaitlin was willing to use every angle she could. There was no way to know if her cheerleader smile benefited her pending case, but it was clear that it wouldn't hurt. Torres smiled back with a particularly bright smile.

"Let me get the door," he said, getting up.

"I'll get it," Kaitlin said, reaching back to push the door closed and almost knocking over her paperwork.

He smiled quickly and then glanced at his monitor. He'd been checking his e-mail when she came in. He tightened his lips and then hit a key on his keyboard. The screen saver came on. He waved a hand toward the files perched on her lap. "Looks like you have your hands full."

Kaitlin glanced down at the documentation she was balancing. "Yes. I wanted to discuss some of this with you – " Kaitlin began. But Torres cut her off.

"I've just come from having breakfast with Art Berg of Comtak." Torres watched her closely, gauging her recognition of the name. "He was wondering how we've been doing in our efforts to recover that stolen semi-trailer of his.

"You remember the one, don't you, Detective? The one filled with three hundred thousand dollars in Comtak computer monitors? Not the big ugly ones. The nice flat panel monitors, like the one my kid keeps asking me to buy for him."

She nodded. "I remember."

He nodded at the paperwork on her knees. "Looking at all those files, my sixth sense tells me that you've got good news for Art," he added, picking up his Montblanc writing pen off the desk and rolling it between his fingers.

Kaitlin lowered her eyes and studied the manila folders she was holding. She knew Torres was busting her chops. And she knew he had a right to. Nonetheless, it was essential that she mask her emotional reaction. Amongst his many talents, Torres was the master of the mind game.

He tapped the fat black pen gently on the desk in a steady rhythm, like a game show clock timer. He patiently awaited her reply. He had all the time in the world.

Kaitlin looked up and focused her eyes directly at Torres. "I'm sure you told Mr. Berg that the San Jose Police Department is making every reasonable effort to get to the bottom of that horrible crime," Kaitlin said with a quick smile. She lifted the files and rested them on the edge of Torres' desk. "And that in our spare time, we're also trying to get to the bottom of an apparent double-murder linked to controlled technology, industrial espionage, and other illicit activity."

Torres stopped tapping his pen and held it in mid-air. He liked playing mind games as much as anyone, but Kaitlin was clearly not playing a game.

"Care to run that by me again?" Torres asked, calmly. He looked at her incredulously, his brown eyes gazing above the frame of his glasses.

"Darren Park and Michael Owens," she answered, matter-of-factly.

"Detective Hall," Torres said, "this better be good. I've heard of Darren Park. Who the hell is Michael Owens? And what exactly do you mean? 'Industrial espionage ... controlled tech ... illicit activity'…?"

"Michael Owens *was* a silicon chip designer at Entrex," Kaitlin answered. "His body was found last Thursday in Santa Cruz. On the beach."

Torres took off his glasses and rubbed his eyes. He had the horrible feeling that this was going to turn into one giant headache. "And what does that have to do with Darren Park?"

Kaitlin shrugged. She knew she had his attention now.

"At first blush, nothing. The news reports suggest that Owens died in a surfing accident. A drowning," she said. Then she opened a manila folder and lifted the top sheet of paper from it. "But, like Darren Park's apparent car accident, a lot of things don't add up. I've done some digging ..."

Torres stopped rubbing his eyes and glared at Kaitlin. "You've done *what*?" he demanded, his temperature rising.

Kaitlin let the piece of paper, a summary of the evidence she'd gathered, drop back to the opened manila folder. "I've done some digging," she repeated, her voice a little softer now.

"Okay, now let's get clear on this…That is all right with you, isn't it, Detective? That I, as Captain, get clear on something?"

"Of course," she said.

He frowned. He didn't appreciate his rhetorical questions being answered. "Detective Hall, you have not been assigned to an investigation regarding Darren Park. Is that correct?"

"Yes, it is ..." Kaitlin replied.

"*And*, you have not been assigned to an investigation regarding this Michael Owens. Is that correct, Detective?"

"Yes, Captain, that is correct," Kaitlin replied evenly, and without a hint of guilt. "But …"

Captain Torres looked at her as if she'd lost her mind. "But?"

"Captain, I believe that after you hear what I'm going to tell you you'll agree to formalize those assignments before I leave your office."

Torres put his glasses back on. "Okay," he said, quickly regaining complete control. "Let's hear what you've got."

He had taken a no-nonsense attitude. He saw what Kaitlin was up to. He didn't like it. He was not someone who appreciated being manipulated. But he admired her skills and her intellect. He knew perfectly well the reasons she'd made Detective as soon as she was eligible under department policy.

She wondered if she had overplayed her "special" status this time?

Kaitlin remained silent for a moment, trying to read the situation.

"Come on," Torres said, pointing to the documentation on his desk. "Tell me about Darren Park and Michael Owens. Tell me about illegal and illicit activity." As she leaned forward to take the folder from the top of the pile, he reached for his pen, rolled it in his fingers, and began tapping softly on his desk pad.

Kaitlin knew Torres better than Torres imagined. She could read his body language and the subtleties of his behavior. The pen signaled that he wasn't playing with her. He was giving her a real opportunity to make her case. But he was only giving her this one shot.

"Thanks, Captain," she said. Kaitlin knew she had to pitch her case to him intelligently, succinctly, and convincingly. She began with a portrait of Darren Park. "Young, low-paid sys admin with full network permission. He's got unfettered access to some of the world's most powerful encryption software and his brother operates a lucrative import-export company."

Torres shifted slightly in his chair, but said nothing.

"He's living high on the hog – brand new Beemer, plush apartment, all the clothes, electronics, and other goodies a guy could want. He buys diamonds for the girlfriend. But if you look at his W-2 income from Synergy and his Quicken entries, the guy is living way beyond his means.

"And then there's frequent weekend travel to Asia. But not with family – or for his employer – contrary to what he tells his ex-girlfriend."

Kaitlin paused for emphasis.

"Someone is giving Darren money – lots of it – and I've ruled out all the usual legal sources. If you ask me, he's on the take…"

She could have gone on talking about Darren Park for an hour, but wisely she stopped short.

At some point in the presentation, Torres had stopped tapping his pen. He continued to listen but, even before she had finished laying out her theory, Kaitlin knew what his response would be. She felt her stomach tighten. It seemed pointless, but she would not give up.

Before Torres could stop her, she shifted her presentation to Michael Owens. Here, her explanation was a good deal sketchier. She hadn't yet done the background. She was direct in pointing out the weakness of the connections. She hoped to bolster her lack of knowledge with the strength of her conviction.

"The connection between the two deaths is real," she posited. She emphasized the similarities between Darren Park's life and death and Michael Owen's. Both were young employees of Silicon Valley firms with access to highly sensitive technology, both were dead within days of one another, the result of apparent mishaps, and both had been driving brand new Beemers.

"I appreciate that what I've presented is not exactly rock-solid at this point. But I hope you can see that the information I've put together is the beginning of a very compelling case, Captain," Kaitlin concluded, trying to end on a strong note.

The silence that filled the room when she stopped talking took on a physical reality. She felt it pressing against her, making it difficult for her to breathe. It only lasted mere seconds but seemed much longer. Torres checked his Montblanc to make sure it was closed. Then he slid it gracefully into his shirt pocket.

"Not rock-solid?" he asked, his voice colored with sarcasm. "*Are you kidding?* You couldn't sell a television movie on the premise that you've just outlined, let alone justify a criminal investigation," he said. "So they were young and worked for high-tech firms – and they both drove BMWs. You've just described a third of the Silicon Valley population!"

"And both dead," Kaitlin said. "That hardly describes a third of the Silicon Valley population."

Torres frowned and then continued. "And as for 'illegal and illicit' activity, you don't have any evidence which remotely suggests anything's actually happened!" Torres expression turned quickly. "This case is as close to rock-solid as San Francisco Bay mud!" he said excitedly, laughing lightly at his own metaphor.

Kaitlin was silent.

Torres chuckled. "Look," he said, trying to sound sympathetic. "I can understand how you might find this kind of mental exercise more interesting than your current caseload ..."

She stiffened. *So*, the fact that she was assigned to the worst cases in the office was undisputed. She felt a jolt of anger and resentment that focused her thinking. She'd been feeling defeated and unappreciated. However, now she viewed what was happening a bit more critically and objectively. The fact that Torres was laughing at her was a good sign.

He wasn't going to boot her from the detail over her presentation. A revelation occurred to her – she had absolutely nothing to lose.

Kaitlin decided to press her case. "Captain, I know that I haven't done the homework on Michael Owens. And I know that in Park's case, what I do have is purely circumstantial. But assign me these cases and give me some time to track down a few leads. I promise you I'll come back with a case you can bank on."

"Detective, if you are right about what's going on – homicide connected with illegal technology exports or espionage - then this is an FBI matter, not ours. The FBI and the Commerce Department," Torres countered.

"Probably," Kaitlin agreed, nodding her head. "And after I've completed my initial investigation, we may have to turn it over to both those agencies. However, right now, I'd like to investigate it as a possible homicide – and *that* is well within our jurisdiction."

Torres was thinking about what she was saying.

Kaitlin knew she had to handle this delicately. No one, least of all Torres, was going to risk stepping on the FBI's toes without good air cover.

"Captain, I promise as soon as I have something concrete that ties the deaths to any federal offense, we can call your friend Renfro."

She paused for dramatic effect.

"He's already showing more than a little interest in the Darren Park case, isn't that right?"

Torres sat silently, propping his elbows on the desk. Renfro's visit with him *had* immediately followed Darren Park's death. And Kaitlin knew that Renfro had asked Torres a few casual questions regarding the preliminary findings on the case. *Why else would he have shown up in the morgue, looking for the Palm Pilot?*

Torres didn't answer.

Kaitlin watched his thoughts reflected in his expression. She ascertained that he was torn between wanting to move forward aggressively – and garner potential rewards – and wanting to move cautiously – so as not to risk anything. She did not share any of his hesitance.

"Captain," she said, forging on, "until we have a solid reason to consult the Feds, I suggest that we continue to treat this as a local matter. At least until I can tie up some loose ends."

Torres looked into Kaitlin's eyes. Kaitlin wasn't the only one in the room with some expertise at sizing up another person. He knew she had the potential to be an excellent detective. In what might have been a surprise to Kaitlin, most of Torres' considerations at this point had to do less with his own lofty aspirations as with his feelings about her as a professional. He knew that a positive decision would motivate her, while a negative one might break her spirit. In that context, Torres evaluated the upside and the downside; something he was particularly good at doing.

The corporate guys he golfed with were always asking for his advice and counsel on issues that affected them personally and professionally. Some instances stood out vividly in his mind: *"Henry, I've got a great sales guy – but I think he's got a problem with the nose candy. What would you do about it?"* Or, *"Torres, even though it's over, I want to tell my wife that I had an affair with my assistant. Do you think that's the right way to go?"*

It was easy playing armchair quarterback, and Torres enjoyed it. But when it came to his department he didn't have the luxury of psychological distance. This department was *his* company, his baby.

Finally, he sided with his intuition that Kaitlin would grow as a professional by moving forward – and she'd be unnecessarily minimized if he sent her back to the garbage cases on her desk.

He pulled his elbows back and onto the leather chair's worn armrests. "All right," he said softly. "I'll add the Park case to your roster. Provided that you continue to work up your other cases on a timely basis. I want to see every single status report."

A smile lit up Kaitlin's face. She started to say something but he held up his hand to stop her. "Go track down your loose ends," Torres said gruffly.

"Thank you, Captain," she said. "You won't regret this. I promise you that."

"I hope not," he said with a shake of his head. "And, you're welcome." He watched Kaitlin gather her folders.

"Oh ... since we're assigning you cases today, here's another one." He leaned back in his chair and pulled a thin manila folder out of the credenza. He slid it across the desk. Kaitlin rotated it, so that she could read the fresh white folder label: *Eugenia Hammond, Case No. SJ-2001-484824.* Kaitlin flipped open the cover and started to look at the case intake summary.

"Mrs. Hammond is an unfortunate older woman in Los Gatos," Torres told her as she was reading. "Four hundred and eighty two of her hard-earned social security dollars were taken from her after she responded to an Internet ad. Some sort of a get-rich-quick scheme. It appears Mrs. Hammond was going to make a fortune buying and selling real estate with no money down. She sent in her check, but they didn't send her the promised real estate secrets. Two weeks later, the web site is gone and the phone's been disconnected.

"Surprise, huh?"

Kaitlin looked up from the folder and stared at him in mild disbelief.

"Please pay Mrs. Hammond a visit. *Today*," Torres said, trying hard to sound serious.

Ordinarily, Kaitlin would've been fuming. Yet another idiotic "case" dropped into her lap. But today was different. Torres had also assigned her the Darren Park case. She flashed Torres a grin as she scooped the new file off his desk and plopped it on top of the stack of papers that she'd brought in. "No problem, Captain."

"Good."

"You said that old Mrs. Hammond lives in Los Gatos?"

"That's right," Torres answered.

"That works out great. I'll stop by her place on the way back from Santa Cruz. I'm meeting the coroner there in an hour."

Before Torres could reply, Kaitlin hefted the stack of files and papers off his desk. She stood tall and smiled her best smile. "Thank you, Captain. You won't regret this," she said, turning for the door.

"I damn well better not," Torres whispered to Kaitlin's back after she had left his office.

# Chapter 13

Kaitlin had no sooner pulled out from the department's parking lot and onto the street, when her cell phone rang. She reached for her jacket pocket. But it wasn't there. "What the…?" Mercilessly, the phone rang again. Then again and again. She knew that if it rang once more, the call would automatically forward to her voicemail. And she was waiting on too many important calls to miss any of them.

"Where's that cursed phone?" Kaitlin wondered as she searched her jacket and purse while desperately trying to keep her eyes on the road. "This is how people get killed," she noted to herself as she swerved back into her lane. Cellular technology will be our salvation or our damnation, Kaitlin thought as she shuffled through papers and notebooks covering the passenger seat. "Yes!" she proclaimed, finding the cell before it could ring again. She quickly flipped it open.

"Hello?"

"Yes, Detective Hall?"

"Speaking," Kaitlin replied, trying not to pant audibly.

"This is Ken Barnes of Entrex ..."

"Mr. Barnes! Hello. Thank you for calling me back," Kaitlin said. Then, remembering the context of her phone call, she showed her concern by asking how everyone at Entrex was doing.

"I've got to tell you, not real well," Barnes admitted. "A lot of us – and I include myself – are taking this very hard. Mike was a good guy and he had a lot of friends."

Kaitlin searched for the appropriate words. Condolences were not her strong suit. As a young detective, she was not adept at disregarding her emotions about death before offering routine sympathies to the grieving.

"Sure, I can understand that...you have my condolences," she said sincerely into the low crackle of the cell phone,

A brief silence followed. Kaitlin pulled onto Guadalupe Parkway.

"Thanks," Barnes said. Then he added something under his breath that made Kaitlin clench the steering wheel: "And people were just starting to get over what happened to Dale Cho."

"I'm sorry?" she said, struggling to control her car with just one hand on the wheel. "Who's Dale Cho?" Kaitlin gripped the steering wheel more tightly with her left hand as she merged into the traffic flow.

"Dale was on the same project team as Michael. He was killed in a traffic accident in San Diego a couple of months ago."

There was a brief silence. "He'd been down there on vacation," Barnes added, not quite sure what to say next.

Kaitlin struggled to process what she'd just heard over the phone while avoiding a collision. "Can you tell me, in general terms, the nature of Michael and Dale's work at Entrex?"

"Sure, I don't see why not. Michael was a project manager and Dale was a senior engineer in the ASDG."

"The ASDG?" she asked. Technology companies were almost as bad as the military in being acronym crazy. She wasn't going to try to decipher this one on her own.

"I'm sorry – that's our Advanced Silicon Design Group," Barnes said.

Focusing on her conversation with Barnes, Kaitlin had avoided a collision but almost missed her stop. She swung the car quickly into the Noah's Bagels parking lot and pulled to a stop.

Another dead techie. Another untimely accident. Two at the same company in a span of two months. Kaitlin calculated the probabilities.

"Mr. Barnes, can I ask you to pull both Michael Owens' and Dale Cho's personnel files? I'd like to stop by this afternoon and take a look at them."

"Sure," he replied.

"Also, can you make sure no one goes into Michael Owens' office or alters anything in his computer directory?"

"No problem ..." Barnes said reluctantly upon reflection, "but ... one question for you."

"Yes?"

"Will you be wearing a uniform?"

"Excuse me?" Kaitlin hadn't gotten that question before, and wasn't sure where Barnes was headed.

"People might get freaked out having a police detective rummaging through Michael's office. You won't be wearing a uniform, will you?"

Kaitlin smiled. "No, no uniform. I'm a plain clothes detective."

She could hear his sigh of relief. "I'll see you this afternoon – sans uniform," Kaitlin said.

She walked into Noah's and ordered her usual – a toasted onion bagel and large coffee to go, her thoughts swirling from the conversation with Mr. Barnes. While she waited for her order, she placed a call on her cell phone to the San Diego Police Department; she had to know more about Dale Cho's fatal traffic accident.

She was still on the phone when she returned to her car with breakfast. With a flimsy plastic utensil, she smeared cream cheese on the bagel with one hand as she held the cell phone with the other. Kaitlin took a bite of her bagel and washed it down with coffee as she waited to be connected to a person who could assist her. This was the modern age of dining. One couldn't just eat a meal: you had to eat while doing something highly productive.

Mid-bite, Kaitlin was finally put through to a police liaison who called up Dale Cho's case summary on the computer.

"Here we go," the liaison said.

"Excellent," she murmured to herself. She quickly washed down more bagel with coffee.

Kaitlin feverishly jotted down notes as the liaison officer read from the summary. Well before he'd finished reading its entirety, which described in detail how Dale Cho, age 27, had driven off a steep mountain road near the small town of Julian, Kaitlin knew that his death was no coincidence.

Three young engineers. Two closely connected to each other. All working directly with, or having access to, very sensitive high technology. All three dead as a result of unusual accidents within a matter of months.

Trying to maintain objectivity, Kaitlin told herself that statistically, such a mortality rate was insignificant. "Shit happens," she reminded herself. But she didn't think weird coincidence was what was going on here.

And learning the make, model, and year of Dale Cho's car did nothing to ease her growing suspicion. Kaitlin thanked the liaison officer for his help. Then she finished her bagel. Mission accomplished. After several gulps of the rich black brew, she secured the cardboard cup of French Roast in the Lumina's cup holder.

"Another day, another dead BMW driver," she told herself turning the key in the ignition for her drive to Santa Cruz. "I never thought I'd be so happy to drive a Chevy."

# Chapter 14

The soft glow of computer monitors illuminated the windowless room. Cables twisting in their rainbow hues snaked along the floor in multiple diameters like unruly, clumpy mats of spaghetti before bellying up the walls like some psychedelic imitation of a Salvador Dali painting. The low hum of the CPUs provided a gentle white background noise to which the room's sole occupant remained oblivious. He perched on a rolling chair, typing on one of the various keyboards arrayed on the countertop. Oversized Sennheiser headphones pressed against his ears. His head rocked steadily as he listened to Led Zeppelin's *Black Dog* at a solid 110 decibels. His typing kept time with the beat of the music. His bare feet tapped evenly on the hardwood floor.

Slim Yamazaki was at the center of a supply of computer processing power that easily surpassed the entire computing power of the known world as it existed until 1973. That bit of trivia didn't concern Slim. He had more pressing things on his mind.

At the moment, he was in the process of hacking into an online banking center. Six hours previously, he had unleashed an attack on the computer nerve center of Bank of America – one of America's largest banks. He smiled and rubbed his hands together in silent glee.

He was well on the way to realizing his best-case scenario, which was to gain access, manipulate account information and then transfer a large sum of money from a BofA account holder to a German bank account held in the name of Hans Gerrmann – a long-deceased German SS officer.

Once the money was in Hans' account, Slim would transfer it, via the Swiss Interbank Clearing System, to a numbered bank account he'd established at Credit Suisse.

That was the best-case scenario. The worst-case scenario would allow Slim to surreptitiously gain access to the bank's webservers and disable their public web page. Mess with them a bit.

In either case, Slim was fully mindful of the fact that BofA would pay him a hefty sum of money for the effort. Since the previous year, Slim had been in the employ of BofA – and a number of other large financial institutions – with the sole purpose of hacking into their computer systems and disrupting their business services.

His entrepreneurial metamorphosis from renegade hacker to hacker consultant had been the result of necessity rather than a change of heart. "By any means necessary," admonished a rifle-toting Malcolm X from the oversized poster that hung on the Dungeon's wall. The quote, however radical its origin, led Slim down a more conventional path when personal need intruded.

Slim's younger brother, Kenji, was diagnosed with leukemia. A catastrophic event made worse when he discovered his health insurance had lapsed two months prior. The insurance company would no longer have anything to do with him. Preexisting condition and all that. Forget that Kenji had held the same policy for ten years. Once out, he might as well have never been in. Without health insurance, the family needed a substantial amount of money in order to fund chemotherapy.

"By any means necessary," Slim cursed as he'd distanced himself from his friends and acquaintances in the Cult of the Dead Cow, the Legions of the Underground, 2600, and other hacker collectives.

Converting his skills and his favorite pastime into a lucrative source of income required nothing more than a single e-mail to BofA's security czar. In that e-mail, Slim identified at least three defects in the bank's electronic security system and provided the fixes for free.

He offered to identify the remaining defects in return for a consulting gig. Only the most cynical amongst us would have suspected anything remotely like blackmail in the offer.

BofA was thrilled by the offer. And, the less anyone else knew of the arrangement the better. The last thing the institution wanted was for the public to learn how vulnerable their system had been.

That first $20,000 assignment saw Slim's reputation as a world-class hacker threat become a reputation as a world-class hacker ally. And with that trust came job after job working for many Fortune 100 companies. As a result of Slim's intervention, and the diligent efforts of U.C. San Francisco's oncology staff, Kenji Yamazaki survived his bout with cancer. By virtue of the experience, Slim changed his stripes. He now hacked for cash.

Situated in the Cimmerian nerve center of his Oakland Hills house, Slim was confident that he'd achieve some measure of success against Bank of America's network. Even as he worked with them to improve security, they continued adding new online services – and, in the process, vulnerabilities to the system. Each of the new services inevitably had holes; holes that improperly motivated individuals were determined to find. While the CPUs churned with the glorious hum of a celestial chorus, currently programmed by Slim to hack their way into the bank's secure logon algorithms, Slim turned his attention to Kaitlin Hall's project. He re-read the e-mail that she had sent him several days earlier, feeling a twinge of guilt that he hadn't returned her phone call.

Kaitlin had essentially asked him to develop a rather scattered pattern of information into a concrete model of events and facts. Although he knew next to nothing of the underlying case that Kaitlin was working on, he could already see curious patterns of information emerging from the research he had completed over the past 48 hours. He just didn't fully understand what those patterns meant. Yet.

He was a patient man. After all, he was and always would be, at heart, a hacker.

The first data point Kaitlin provided was one Darren Park, deceased. And then, just this morning, Kaitlin had provided him with two other data points: Michael Owens and Dale Cho. Both deceased.

Kaitlin's instructions that accompanied the names were broad: "Find out everything you can about these people. Concentrate on any connection that exists between and amongst them."

Slim eagerly put the Sun workstations to the task of sweeping the Internet for any information regarding these people. The computers, his babies, were enabled with a proprietary search agent technology that Slim had developed. That search agent, dutifully nicknamed "Spock," could parse millions of pages on the Internet in seconds. Spock would also launch automated searches in thousands of financial, business, real estate, and genealogical databases and survey the multitude of Usenet and discussion groups where those names appeared.

Spock was no ordinary search engine. Spock had smarts.

Slim's initial concern was not that Spock would have difficulty finding information about these three people. His worry was that it would retrieve too much, making any meaningful review of the collected information lengthy and tedious. Fortunately, Spock returned with less than one gigabyte of fascinating information.

"A juicy morsel, little more," Slim concluded.

Slim downloaded the fruits of Spock's search onto a laptop computer. He'd been in the perpetual glow of the computer room for the past six hours and he'd had enough. He needed to come up for air. With his laptop in tow, he pushed open the door and came up the steps to retreat to his favorite place – his deck.

The redwood deck in his home's backyard granted Slim a majestic vista of the entire San Francisco Bay. "Jesus," he groaned as he placed his hand over his eyes, blocking out the bright sunlight. Moving forward gingerly, he squinted as his eyes slowly adjusted to daylight.

The Oakland Bay Bridge gleamed like a silver ribbon across the glittering Bay; its colossal steel spans arching over Treasure Island into the city. As usual, despite the East Bay sunshine, the Golden Gate Bridge was shrouded in dense fog; its two orange towers standing rigidly at attention, like sentinels.

His eyes finally comfortable with daylight, Slim enjoyed several meditative minutes gazing at the wide expanse beneath him, admiring from bridge to bridge the only city he could ever love.

"Ah, lovely, lovely," he sighed.

Having soaked up his fill of the awe-inspiring beauty of his surroundings, Slim was ready to tackle the analysis of Kaitlin Hall's strange data request. He engaged the challenge with special enthusiasm – as he always did when Kaitlin asked for his assistance. Although the task was, on the surface, not much different than the tasks he performed most of the time, he approached it much differently than he did hacking for work. This was for Kaitlin.

Just thinking about her made him smile. They'd never dated, and he had no doubt that that was for the best. But she was, quite simply, unlike any other girl he had met. Truly unique. He was in awe of this fantastically beautiful creature who could hold her own in any debate – from `70s exploitation films, Avogadro's number, or UNIX system architecture. In all the years Slim had known her, she'd never once said no to an all-night session of Dungeons & Dragons or an all-day session of mountain biking on Mt. Tam. Moreover, she was someone that Slim always felt perfectly comfortable talking to. Over the past ten years he'd been waiting to find some flaw in her, but so far no luck.

Kaitlin was the perfect system – no vulnerabilities. And coming from a hacker, that was no small compliment.

"Okay then, Kaitlin, what have we got here?" Slim asked himself as he began to assemble the information he'd retrieved. First, there was the cross-dimensional relationship mapping between the different data points: three personal names and two companies. Darren Park, Michael Owens, and Dale Cho; Synergy and Entrex.

As he studied the data, Slim could find no connection between the personal names. The review of dense biographical information suggested no material links between them. They were from different towns, had different college affiliations, and had no known common business interests, other than the fact that Dale Cho and Michael Owens were co-workers at Entrex.

"Hmm," Slim sighed, fighting the vague feeling that he was somehow letting Kaitlin down by not finding anything. "Okay then, let's move on to the professional." He moved on to a comparison of Synergy and Entrex.

Slim was quite familiar with both companies. Synergy was an encryption house, and all hackers took a personal interest in anyone who would taunt them with the challenge of cracking sophisticated security algorithms. Oddly, encryption companies and hackers shared a common, vocal dislike: the intervention of the U.S. government in personal affairs.

Two sides of the same coin, was how Slim characterized the dynamic.

Slim was equally familiar with Entrex but for a different reason. It was fast becoming a household name. Not nearly as large as Intel, Entrex was an upstart in the chip business. Still, they had quickly developed a reputation for very low-cost, extremely high-power microprocessors.

Entrex's latest design project, code-named MEGA-Soft, was the best-kept secret in Silicon Valley. The industry was waiting with bated breath to learn the details of what it had only been given hints about. In one of the few public statements made about MEGA-Soft, Entrex's CEO had touted it as an innovation that would "change the world." The industry was used to that sort of hype. Silicon Valley was built, and sometimes burned, on such claims. Nevertheless, while made with remarkable frequency, those claims were being realized with almost equal frequency.

Even people outside Silicon Valley had ceased to remember a world that had been unchanged by the miracle workers of the Valley. How many people remembered using a slide rule? Or a world that had not been dominated by the PC and the Internet?

As he studied the information Spock had retrieved, Slim noticed several superficial connections between the companies. They were both less than ten years old. Both were in the same industry and both were headquartered in Silicon Valley.

Of the two, Entrex was a publicly-traded company. That meant there was voluminous publicly available information on file with the Securities & Exchange Commission, not to mention the commentary of various industry analysts that followed companies in the semiconductor field. Slim skimmed page after page of information, hoping a light bulb would illuminate. There was not nearly as much information on Synergy, and not much that Slim did not already know.

Slim pensively rubbed his goatee between his thumb and forefinger. “Nothing easy here,” Slim said to himself as he gazed up from the laptop after half an hour of focused attention. The bright daylight was giving way to the creeping fog. The sun, muted orange as it dipped into the moist shroud over the Bay, was now a mere five or six degrees above the top span of the Golden Gate Bridge. The bridge’s orange towers now appeared black due to the sun’s dramatic backlighting. Slim rubbed his eyes and looked back at the computer’s LCD screen.

With the preliminary company comparisons not drawing any obvious results, Slim descended upon the review of the broader statistical sampling that Kaitlin had requested: fatalities among people employed by Silicon Valley high-tech employers within the past twenty-four months. To limit the results of that search, Kaitlin had asked that he exclude reported fatalities of persons over sixty, deaths of persons not having some technical training or background, and deaths in hospitals following protracted illness. Spock had run a rigorous composite search, accumulating information from newspaper obituary columns, church newsletters, hospital listings, and numerous other sources. It had also assembled various census and actuarial data, giving him birth, death, and accident statistics of the relevant population, by age, race, industry, geography, and other criteria. He scrutinized the search results that now appeared on screen.

A good half-hour had passed. Suddenly, Slim thought out loud: "Weird. Very weird ..."

Where statistically he should have found no more than four or five deaths within the relevant group, fourteen deaths were listed – including the deaths of Dale Cho, Michael Owens, and Darren Park.

He might have started this process for Kaitlin, but now Slim was engaged. He was into it. Slim typed furiously. "Right on!" he shouted as he drummed his fingers on the top of his teak patio table. Of the fourteen deaths, eleven *appeared* accidental in nature. Given the population in question, he should have found only two or three accidental deaths. But here they were: car crashes, drowning, snowboarding wipeouts, and accidental O.D.s. Given the information he evaluated, Slim took pride in the search results. The fact that the deaths of Dale Cho, Michael Owens, and Darren Park were included in Spock's output list validated, in a somewhat unscientific way, that Spock's search algorithm had been properly written.

"Okay, Kaitlin," Slim said as he grabbed the cordless phone off the patio table. "Bet you'll want to hear about a whole bunch of dead guys."

# Chapter 15

Kaitlin walked in as the machine clicked on. *"Hello, sorry I missed you. Please leave your name, number, and the time you called, and I'll get back to you as soon as I can."*

"Kaitlin, it's Slim…"

Hearing Slim's voice, Kaitlin practically dove at the phone. "Slim! Slim, I'm here, don't hang up." She waited until the second beep on the answering machine before speaking again. "Slim, okay. What's up?"

"Well, you aren't going to believe it," he said, not quite sure how to go about telling her what he'd found out.

"Try me," she said. "You'd be amazed at how I've become a believer in the unbelievable."

"Kaitlin," Slim began, "I gave him your parameters. And Spock gave me a 'death list' - the names of *fourteen* males between ages 23 and 35 working for high-tech companies in the Valley." Slim waited a moment. "All deceased. All *accidental*." Slim waited quietly, filled with pride at Spock's achievement.

Kaitlin kicked off her shoes and put down her day pack. On the way home, she'd been thinking about what to make herself for dinner. But she wasn't thinking about dinner now.

"That's incredible, Slim – *fourteen deaths*? That a lot of young men. What do the statistics suggest?"

Slim smiled. "Ah, I knew you'd ask that very question."

Kaitlin chuckled. "And I knew you'd know the answer," she replied, plopping on the sofa and curling up against the soft pillows.

"I do," he said proudly. "According to my calculation, this death rate represents about a *five hundred percent* higher rate of accidental death than you'd statistically expect to find within that population.

"Statistically, we should see one ... maybe two ... fatalities. At first, I thought I may have miscalculated, or that something about Silicon Valley techies makes them more accident-prone than their counterparts outside the Valley. So I re-ran Spock just on the individuals other than Darren Park, Michael Owens, and Dale Cho, cross-referencing the companies that employed them at the time of death."

"And…?" Kaitlin asked anxiously, drawing up her knees to her chest.

"My dear, of those eleven fatalities, we can remove four. For the remaining seven I found definite connections."

Now Kaitlin was on edge. What had simply been intuitive suspicion on her part was on the verge of being validated. Although Torres had gone along with her desire to pursue the investigation, she knew he was just humoring her. And, over the past few days, she wondered if maybe she'd let her imagination get the better of her.

She silently chided herself to maintain her objectivity. "What sort of connections?" she asked, her voice more critical than she'd intended.

Slim heard the criticism and doubt in her voice and, for an instant, thought it was directed at him and his research.

Kaitlin sensed in his pause the hurt she'd caused. "Slim, I'm sorry for the tone. It's just…this is a very weird case."

Slim immediately felt sympathy for her, as he always did.

"You can bet your life on that," he said. "It's downright bizarre. I mean, check this out. First, although the deceased were employed by seven different companies, each of the companies is involved with developing cutting-edge or sensitive technology. All technology covered by the F.A.R. and D.F.A.R. export controls. Second, *all* of the deceased had positions where they were involved in developing, or otherwise had access to, internal computer systems. And get this – *four* of the seven were sys admins."

Kaitlin knew that Slim's results were compelling. But she also knew that they were all circumstantial. In other words, it gave her a great argument for continuing her investigation, but nothing to show Torres.

"Anything else, Slim?" she asked.

"Yeah," he said. "Last thing, and I think this is the weirdest thing of all, all seven companies, nine if you include Synergy and Entrex, had private venture capital investments from a firm named Harriman & Co."

"*Harriman*?" Kaitlin exclaimed as she swung her feet off the coach and planted them firmly on the hardwood floor. "Are you sure?"

"Positive," he said.

Kaitlin stood up and paced. She'd heard that name recently. But where?

Slim waited patiently in silence on the other end of the phone. He could hear Kaitlin pacing and muttering to herself, pondering the information that he'd just downloaded to her.

"That's it!" Kaitlin yelled suddenly, snapping her fingers.

"What?"

"Harriman," she said. "Now I remember where I heard that name."

Slim nodded to himself and said in a barely audible whisper, "You go, girl."

Kaitlin recalled the guest book on the security desk at Synergy. And she remembered Gupta's assistant calling him into the conference room for his meeting with "Harriman & Co." Pradeep Gupta's much needed financing source. The cash infusion.

"Slim? Slim, you still there?" Kaitlin nearly shouted into the phone.

"Yes, I'm here. I was worried for a second that you'd fried a synapse or something," Slim joked.

"Close, but I think I'm okay," she laughed. "Listen, I know he's been working overtime, but I need Spock to pull together all he can on Harriman & Co. – as soon as possible."

Slim hesitated. He hated saying no to anything Kaitlin wanted. But this time he had to.

"Kaitlin, I'll be happy to start the work, but I've got a deadline for this BofA project. It'll take some time for me to free up the bandwidth. I'm really sorry,"

Kaitlin felt the letdown in Slim's voice. She understood. "Hey, no problem," she said. "No need to apologize. You've already gone beyond the call – like you always do for me. And I can't believe what you've managed to pull together so quickly. If you get a chance, do what you can, when you can."

"You know I will," Slim said earnestly.

"Meanwhile, if you can just do a core dump and e-mail the information on the guys on the death list, I can start parsing through that," Kaitlin said. "That should give me plenty to chew on for the next 48 hours."

"Excellent," Slim said. "And that'll give me more than enough time to finish the other project and pay the rent." He was silent for a moment. When he spoke again, his tone had shifted and was filled with concern. "Kaitlin?"

"Yeah, Slim?" she answered.

"I hope you're being careful out there. If the connections go deeper, then there's someone out there who has no problem getting his hands dirty."

Kaitlin hadn't considered that her investigation might pose a real danger to her. But Slim was right. If her suspicions were more than intellectual imaginings, then she was dealing with someone who played for keeps.

As much as that realization shook her, she was moved by Slim's concern for her safety. Not for the first time and definitely not for the last, she realized just how fortunate she'd been to have him as a mentor and as her friend.

"I'll be careful," she said.

"Promise?"

She smiled to herself. "Yes, I promise," she said. Then her smile disappeared as she considered the difficulty in actually keeping her promise.

# Chapter 16

Any potential danger involved in her investigation quickly became background noise. Like every other cop, she knew her job was dangerous. But to fixate on the danger would paralyze you. Get you or your partner killed. Instead, Kaitlin learned quickly to push danger to a far corner of her mind, a distant sector of read-only memory, accessible only while off duty.

In this moment, Kaitlin felt excitement. Not danger. She felt the thrill that comes with pieces of a puzzle coming together. That it was her intuition that formed the initial picture... well, that just made it even better.

"Torres will flip when I show him this," she thought to herself.

Not that she was showing Torres anything yet. The last thing Kaitlin wanted was her investigation handed over to the Feds. To avoid that, a little more groundwork on this case needed to be done.

Her excitement took over all thoughts of dinner. Sitting down to eat was no longer on the agenda. She started pacing again. Her energy was electric. Kaitlin felt ready to explode. Her body was too energized for her to think in a clear, linear fashion. So she decided to do what she'd always done when she needed to catch up her body to her brain. Go for a run.

First, she grabbed a bottle of water from her small refrigerator. She took a long drink and strode toward her closet.

"Oh, my God!" she exclaimed as she stood in front of the chaos that was the interior of her closet. "They're here someplace," she muttered to herself as she got down on her knees and began digging through the pile of clothes, towels, jackets, sports gear, and other assorted things that, for want of another home in her small house, ended up in her bedroom closet.

"Eureka!" she cried as she unearthed first her left and then her right running shoe from the mess. Before getting up, she pulled out a blouse she'd been searching for the week before. "So, that's where you were, huh?" she said, tossing it onto the bed so she wouldn't lose it again.

She hadn't gone to the gym since she began investigating Darren Park's accident. She was beginning to feel a little sluggish. Rigorous physical activity was her one outlet, as it had been since her years in the Academy. She needed to work up a sweat in order to maintain mental focus. Being in good physical shape was an added benefit and a professional requirement.

After getting out of her work clothes, she paused to study herself in the full-length mirror attached to the interior of the closet door. Her sober appraisal was not too damaging. Like any woman, she could always find fault. A little cellulite. *Where the hell did that come from?* A need to take a pound or two off the thighs and bottom. Still, she knew that an objective view had her looking pretty damned good. A few days off hadn't done too much damage to her slender body. She turned her back to the mirror and looked at her reflection over her shoulder. Then she shrugged. "You'll do," she said with a laugh.

She changed into running shorts and a top and headed out the front door. After a brief stretch on the front steps, she slipped on her headphones and turned on the radio. Discreetly, she deposited her house key in the terra cotta planter filled with pale purple hydrangeas and ran onto the black asphalt street.

"Shut up and play some music," she whispered to the DJ's voice coming over the headphones. As if he heard her, an old *Police* tune came on. She smiled. Sting's voice always made her feel good. With his amazingly smooth and high, nearly falsetto, voice he was unequalled.

Sting wailed, *"Because it's murder by numbers, 1-2-3. It's as easy to learn as your A-B-C..."*

Kaitlin recognized the song and tried to remember which *Police* album it was on. "You're getting old," she told herself as it took her time to remember. The song continued, bringing to mind the conversation she and Slim just had.

> *"Now if you have a taste for this experience, and you're flushed with your very first success, then you must try a twosome or a threesome, and you'll find your conscience bothers you much less..."*

The song was tongue-in-cheek. Kaitlin had once read an interview with Sting in which he explained that it was intended as a statement on politicians more than anything. Even so, in her mind, it certainly applied to someone who could deliberately lure a host of young, successful men to their deaths.

As her feet pounded the pavement in a steady jog, Kaitlin stopped her imagination from running wild.

"Sting's good but he's not my muse when it comes to police work," she told herself. Reluctantly, she acknowledged the coincidence of hearing that song so soon after her conversation with Slim, and right in the middle of her investigation into Darren Park's death.

She'd hoped the run through her Menlo Park neighborhood would clear her mind, and that the music would alleviate her boredom, not cloud her thinking. As she ran a steady warm-up pace the length of her flat block, she envisioned running along the shore or a mountain path. Anywhere but here in middle-class suburbia, where every house and every street looked similar. Like so many suburbs, there was almost no one on the streets. In fact, the only people she saw were those getting in or out of their cars, going in or out of their houses. At times it was a veritable ghost town. On some streets, hours could pass before a single car drove by.

Kaitlin's headphones blared music from the KFOG radio station. She reached the end of the block and Sting sang on, *"Because murder is like anything you take to. It's a habit-forming need for more and more. You can bump off every member of your family, and anybody else you find a bore..."*

"*Synchronicity*, that's it!" she said out loud, finally remembering the name of the *Police* album. She also remembered the first time she'd listened to it and how that particular song made an impression on her, because of the story it told.

Under the current circumstances, it gave her the chills. The cynical lyrics left a bad taste in her mouth. Kaitlin listened for another few seconds and then she'd had enough. She reached up to the headphone radio and pushed a preset button, tuning it to the classical music station that was playing a piece of chamber music.

She couldn't determine the piece or the composer. Schumann or Schubert. She always mixed up those guys. Not that it mattered. It was soothing. Kaitlin liked it. She settled into an easy rhythm as she picked up her pace.

Although Menlo Park's sleepiness generally bothered her, it was good for running for exactly that reason – few cars and even fewer people. The orchestration was lovely. The pace was challenging. Fifteen minutes later, she was fully warmed up and running at stride. She could hear herself breathing under the classical music.

She wasn't sure when she became aware of the car cruising slowly behind her. But her gut told her it wasn't one of her neighbors heading home from Safeway. She ran a bit faster, and the car sped up. When she slowed, it slowed. She was being followed. She didn't look back. She was better than that.

Recognizing the street names at the next intersection, she calculated that she was two-and-a-half miles from her house. She ran one more block to Bryant Street and turned the corner to head home. As she did, she caught a quick sideways glance at the black Mercedes slowly following her. It remained about two hundred yards back, traveling at four to five miles an hour. Keeping pace with her.

She felt a momentary panic rising within her. She could sprint into a backyard. Cut through some houses. Head toward the commercial strip. Any of these would be a smart thing to do. As a police officer, it's what she would have counseled a woman running alone on a suburban street in the early evening to do.

But, as soon as she got ahead of her panic, she became intrigued. Why was someone following her? A black Mercedes was not a vehicle she'd suspect for a random crime against a woman.

No, if this car was following her – and she was certain it was even before it made the turn at Bryant – then running from it would only postpone a confrontation.

Intrigued or not, the reality of the situation was finally making its impression on her. No matter what, she had to remain in front of the car. She prayed that she might see a cruising police car but, in this particular corner of Menlo Park where crime was essentially non-existent, the chances were slim to none.

About five miles into her run, she neared its end. She rounded the corner onto her street. She counted to twenty and then turned her head.

"Damn!" she whispered.

Not only was the car still following her, it had closed the distance. No longer two hundred yards away, it was now only a couple of hundred feet away. Kaitlin summoned all her strength and sprinted.

The Mercedes easily matched her pace.

"Don't go home… keep running!" Kaitlin thought to herself, panting hard. Home would be the absolute worst place to go. When she reached the property line of her house, she kept going. Her heart pounded in her chest. She groaned audibly, pushing herself much harder than usual. She didn't have the wind to run much further. She'd seek refuge at a nearby neighbor.

About ten houses down from hers, Vernon Taylor stood in the driveway hosing down his prized, fire-engine red 1965 Mustang convertible. At sixty-five, Vernon had a full head of silver hair, a deep tan, and a very active lifestyle. He was the very picture of a California "active senior" in his shiny blue Nike track suit.

More importantly, he was one of the few neighbors Kaitlin actually knew.

Still sprinting, Kaitlin cut sharply up the steep brick driveway, running right past Vernon, and into his garage.

"Hey Kaitlin!" Vernon sputtered as she ran past him. He turned to see where she was going, jerking the garden hose and accidentally spraying his wife's Oldsmobile, which he'd just finished washing and drying. "Aw, man!" he shouted, redirecting the hose downward.

"Kaitlin, where the hell did you get to?"

Meanwhile, the Mercedes rolled to a complete stop in the middle of the narrow street at a slight angle to Vernon's driveway. Vernon, still mystified by Kaitlin's behavior and not quite sure where she'd gone, turned to look at the sedan. Being a man who appreciated a nicely detailed car, Vernon took notice of the beautifully polished S500 sedan. He also noted the darkly tinted windows, illegal in California, which prevented him from seeing the driver or any passengers inside the vehicle. The car remained stationary in front of the house. The windows remained closed tight, and no one got out.

After idling for a few moments, the car suddenly accelerated into a U-turn and vanished down the otherwise deserted street. Vernon just stood there, hose in hand. "That's odd," he murmured to himself. Then he shook his head and turned off the hose. He quickly coiled the hose and walked into the dark garage, stepping gingerly until his eyes adjusted to the darkness.

"Kaitlin? Are you in here? Kaitlin? What the hell's going on?" Vernon asked, bewildered as he navigated around the vintage 1950 Studebaker pickup truck parked semi-permanently in the garage.

A sweaty Kaitlin emerged from underneath the pickup. She rolled out on her back, lying on a mechanic's dolly. Her face was bright red and she was still breathing hard.

"Hey, Vernon. What's up?"

"Why don't you tell me?" Vernon said, looking down worriedly.

"Is that Mercedes gone?" she asked.

He looked out the garage door to confirm that it hadn't returned. "Yes, it's gone." Vernon offered her his hand and helped pull her up to her feet.

"You didn't happen to get the license plate number, did you?" Kaitlin asked hopefully, wiping her hands on her shorts.

"I didn't know I was supposed to. Who was that?" Vernon asked, with a helping of fatherly concern.

Kaitlin wiped the sweat from her forehead with her sleeve. "I wish I knew," she said with sincerity.

Kaitlin walked to the garage's threshold and peered up and down the street cautiously.

"I told you it was gone," Vernon said.

"I know," Kaitlin said as she exited the garage, still looking up and down the street for any activity. The car was gone. She let out a sigh of relief.

"Kaitlin, what's going on here? Should I call the police?" Vernon asked.

"Vernon," Kaitlin said, placing her hands on her hips and smiling, "I *am* the police."

"Yeah, yeah, I remember. But sometimes cops need help too," he replied.

"Everything's fine now. Don't worry about it," Kaitlin said. She knew that she didn't sound wholly convincing. There was a reason for that. She wasn't totally convinced herself.

She glanced at the beautiful Mustang in the driveway. "You'll want to start drying that Mustang before you get water spots," she said lightly.

Vernon smiled. "I almost forgot about that..."

"You must have been pretty worried to forget about the Mustang," Kaitlin said with a laugh.

He chuckled too. "Well ... I guess you're right." Before he went back to his task, he looked at her directly. "Are you sure you're alright?"

She nodded, "I'm sure."

"Okay, if you say so," he said, reaching into a large plastic bucket for several dry towels. He started to gently dry off the Mustang's hood.

Before heading back to her house, Kaitlin stood there and watched Vernon. She had a vivid recollection of her father from her childhood. Her dad was washing his old green Pontiac LeMans in the driveway. He sprayed her and her friends with the hose as they rode their bikes back and forth on the sidewalk. She remembered laughing and giggling endlessly. She smiled at the memory.

Kaitlin's dad had died of a heart attack during her freshman year in college. He would've been about Vernon's age now, Kaitlin thought. She shook her head, trying to remember the last time she'd thought of him. It had been a long time. When he died, she thought she would never stop thinking about him.

As she watched Vernon, she realized how much she missed her father – even if she didn't think of him every day.

Her breathing slowed to normal. There was still no sign of the Mercedes, or any other car, on the street.

"Thanks for the use of your garage," Kaitlin said, politely patting the fender of the Mustang as she walked down the driveway and proceeded up the block to her house.

She was eager to take a long hot shower and think through what had just happened. On her porch, she maneuvered her arm behind the potted hydrangeas and felt around for the key. She tapped about blindly but came up empty handed. She jostled the plant at its base, thinking the roots were obstructing her reach. She still couldn't feel it. An odd feeling crept over her; she grabbed the big round planter with both hands, spinning it around. Her house key was gone.

The squad cars arrived at Kaitlin's house within minutes. They entered the house with guns drawn and proceeded to check every inch. Later, three specialists from the burglary division arrived, including Mike Torvino, one of Kaitlin's classmates at the academy. Kaitlin sat pensively at the kitchen table as the detectives did their work.

Finally, Torvino came back into the room. "Kaitlin, we've dusted for prints on everything, including the front door and the planter." He looked away from her.

"Nothing, huh?" she said, not surprised.

He shook his head. "No, it doesn't look like it."

Nothing had been taken and there was no sign that anyone had even entered the house. But the key *was* gone.

"So, what now?" Kaitlin asked aloud, but mostly to herself. She knew the answer. She'd been on the other side of that question too many times.

"Get your locks re-keyed – maybe consider getting a burglar alarm," said Torvino, trying to sound as if doing either was no big deal.

"I've got an alarm," Kaitlin said, pointing at the keypad by the front door. "I just don't use it."

"You might want to start," Torvino said with a smile as he drank the last of his coffee. "Thanks for the coffee," he said, putting the cup down in the sink.

With that, the herd of cops took their cue, finishing their coffee and filing out of her house. It was midnight.

So much for a cop's bravado. Whoever was in that Mercedes and whoever took her key – she had no doubt the two were connected – had her attention. She was gutsy. She wasn't stupid. While she had been reluctant to succumb to fear, Kaitlin gave attention to Slim's suggestion: She'd spend the night at a friend's place. She showered, changed, packed a small overnight bag, and drove to the Los Altos Hills home of the formerly Cathy Goodwin, now Cathy Epstein, one of her best friends from high school.

As she pulled out of her driveway, Kaitlin's feeling of concern shifted to one of anger and suspicion. She didn't like being chased out of her own home.

"Screw you," she said to her new, faceless enemy. "You can kiss my ass."

She proceeded up Page Mill Road, past Hewlett-Packard headquarters, countless law firms, and biotech companies nestled in low-rise campuses, and headed into the mansion-dotted hills. When she pulled into Cathy's driveway, she fought the momentary desire to turn around and head home. Reason prevailed, ego surrendered, and Kaitlin got out and slept at Cathy's.

Tomorrow would be another day to get to the bottom of what was becoming an increasingly complex, and possibly dangerous, investigation.

# Chapter 17

"Hey, you awake?"

Kaitlin rolled over and opened her eyes drowsily to the sound of Cathy's gentle tapping on the bedroom door.

"Kaitlin?"

"Yeah…umm….what?" Kaitlin groaned. *What time is it? Two in the morning?* It felt as if she had just fallen asleep.

"Come on, sleepyhead. Pancakes and coffee downstairs in five," Cathy said cheerfully, her head peeking in between the door and the jamb.

"What time is it?" Kaitlin asked with a yawn; it was still dark outside.

"Just after five. Alex goes to work early. So I get up early. There's a robe on the back of the door for you."

Kaitlin was no late riser but *just after five?* "Thanks," Kaitlin grumbled. She was half-tempted to roll over and drift back to sleep. But she reasoned that wouldn't be hospitable. She pulled herself up and landed her feet on the carpeted floor. She shuffled downstairs in the robe, taking the stairs cautiously as she poked the sleep from her eyes. In the kitchen, she hazarded a smile as she squinted into the bright light.

"Good morning, Alex," she said, walking to the table and giving Cathy's husband a hug.

"Good morning to you," he said, embracing her warmly. She could hear the concern in his voice. He'd been asleep when she'd called Cathy the night before. She knew by now he'd heard the whole story – at least as much as she'd told Cathy.

Alex's concern and the warmth of his embrace was genuine. He had gotten to know Kaitlin well during all the years he'd been with Cathy. Although Kaitlin and Cathy didn't speak all that often, their relationship had the integrity and resilience grown from years of long-term friendship. They were like sisters, but more respectful of each other. To Alex, Kaitlin was like a sister-in-law.

"How's life on the Internet?" Kaitlin asked him, jokingly referring to his job.

"It's still paying the bills," he responded good-heartedly, "and keeping the rain off of our heads." They pulled up chairs to the table. Cathy poured three cups of coffee for them. Alex poured orange juice. To Kaitlin, they were the model couple. The perfection of their life together made her own single life seem all the more bleak.

Alex was on his third Internet venture. The first had made him a millionaire many times over when, after only a couple of years, a much larger company bought out his company in a merger. His second business venture skyrocketed … and then promptly crashed and burned. With his knowledge of the industry and his tremendous professional drive, Alex didn't miss a beat getting into another project. Of course, it would be the next big thing. In less than six months, and in a down market, Alex's new company raised twenty-five million dollars in venture capital. Even still, Alex was smart enough to know that he'd be either out of a job or vastly richer within a couple of years.

Anything was possible. Kaitlin wished Alex and Cathy only the best. "Good for them," Kaitlin thought with genuine sincerity. In Silicon Valley, success was wasted on enough jerks; it should occasionally bless people deserving of it.

Alex poked at a pancake with his fork. He glanced quickly at Cathy and then spoke. "Kaitlin, we're looking to hire a Chief Technical Officer. We could really use someone like you."

Kaitlin looked over at Cathy, who offered an apologetic smile and then lowered her eyes. Her parents weren't the only ones who thought Kaitlin shouldn't be in police work. Kaitlin smiled and took a sip of coffee. "That's sweet Alex, but you know I already have a job."

"I know, I know ..." Alex said, "I thought I'd ask, just in case. We've stopped giving new hires a signing bonus – remember those BMW Z3s we gave out last year? But I think there's still one of them that we've already paid for. I'm pretty sure I could get that added to your comp package." He smiled wryly.

Kaitlin raised an eyebrow. Alex didn't know what to make of it, so he pressed on. "And, if you work with me, you won't have to come here at midnight because people are following you and breaking into your home," he said seriously.

"Alex!" Cathy said, kicking him under the table. "Leave her alone, would you?"

"All right ... all right," he said sheepishly. "Sorry to hound you." He took a bite of his pancakes and then looked up at Kaitlin. "You know it's just because we're worried about you."

"I know, Alex. You have nothing to worry about. I'm a big girl," Kaitlin said, drowning her pancakes in maple syrup.

"Besides, with what's left of my technical skills, I'm sure I would single-handedly derail your entire business plan. But, as long as you guys are offering, I *will* take one of those cute little Beemers." She smiled and fluttered her eyelashes in exaggerated cuteness.

They all laughed and resumed eating their pancakes. Cathy and Alex had made their point. Kaitlin had acknowledged it. No hard feelings all around.

Alex downed his coffee and was out the door by five-thirty. Kaitlin was happy to hang out with Cathy until eight, when she left for work at the local junior high school. She taught seventh graders. Now *that* was a job Kaitlin was happy not to call her own.

After a hot shower, Kaitlin lined up her priorities. Research Harriman & Co. and its founder, Warren Harriman. And change the locks on her house.

She got the number for Harriman from 411, called their office in the City and introduced herself to the receptionist.

"Fortunately, Detective Hall, Mr. Harriman is presently in the country," the receptionist crisply informed Kaitlin, "Please hold a moment."

As Kaitlin waited, she drew a mental picture of the woman on the other end of the phone. She envisioned a too-thin, not-too-intelligent blonde-haired waif perched behind a large marble reception desk. The receptionist quickly came back on the line.

"Detective Hall, I informed Mr. Harriman that you were calling on official police business. While his schedule is quite busy, he is available to meet with you between two and two-thirty this afternoon."

"Thank you, that'll be fine," Kaitlin said. She wasn't sure whether to be excited or anxious about the meeting with Harriman.

Kaitlin would spend the better part of the morning online, reading every scrap of information she could find about Harriman & Co. and its business activities.

She would not walk into this meeting unprepared.

# Chapter 18

As she approached the large, white letters adorning the mountainside just west of the freeway – SOUTH SAN FRANCISCO – THE INDUSTRIAL CITY – Kaitlin's thoughts turned to baseball and her childhood memories of going to the Giants games at Candlestick Park. The park, which she now drove past, was officially named 3Com Park and would later be branded Monster Park. Naming rights tied to corporate sponsorships were laying claim to every major sports venue in the nation, but San Franciscans would never truly adopt any renaming of their familiar Candlestick.

Despite the seriousness of her upcoming meeting with Harriman, Kaitlin smiled. She felt privileged to live in this beautiful piece of the world. The proximity to the ballpark, the day's sunshine, the impressionistic palette of the Bay Area… it all added up to an amazing morning. Kaitlin found the puffs of white cumulus clouds dotting a deep blue sky, the rich earthy hues cloaking the hills, and the wind-whipped aquamarine water of the bay inspiring.

The old ballpark stood somewhat awkwardly on the edge of the water. There was a greater chance of it sliding into the Bay after the next earthquake than there was of a ballplayer hitting a homer into the water. And after years of bickering and politicking, the people of San Francisco had voted to build a new mega-stadium right in the heart of downtown.

She'd grown up going to Giants games, but now she couldn't remember the last time she'd been to one. And she certainly hadn't been to the new AT&T Park. *Maybe after this case wraps up, I'll track down a couple of Giants tickets ... I might even bring a date ...*

The unlikelihood of that happening bothered her.

A few moments later, the old and the new stadiums were behind her. She turned up the radio, rolled down the window, and concentrated on the coming meeting. Sooner than she anticipated, she was pulling up to the Embarcadero Center. The office, hotel, and business center development that had put San Francisco's modern real estate market into high gear, occupied several blocks on the City's easternmost waterfront. "Could they have made this sucker any bigger?" Kaitlin thought as she drove around for several minutes hunting for the visitor's parking entrance. After making her way down the right entrance ramp, Kaitlin stretched through the car window to reach the parking ticket. She descended, spiraling down level after level into the bowels of the massive concrete and steel office complex in search of a parking spot.

At last, she found a spot. She took the nearest elevator up to the lobby and then another elevator up fifty-two floors to the Harriman & Co. reception area.

As Kaitlin exited the elevator, she walked into a space very much like the one she imagined when she'd spoken to the receptionist over the phone. She took in the breathtaking view of the City and the Bay from the windows that faced Alcatraz and Marin. Kaitlin was not surprised to discover that the receptionist was very much as she'd pictured her.

But Kaitlin admitted to being wrong about a couple of details. The desk was dense gray-black granite, not marble. And the receptionist who greeted Kaitlin was an incredibly beautiful brunette wearing a smart black suit; she was on the thin side, but rather than the vacuous woman she'd anticipated, this receptionist had an intelligent look.

Kaitlin shrugged and thought to herself, "Can't win them all.

As Kaitlin approached the desk, the receptionist, Miss Perfect in her smart black suit, looked up.

"You must be Detective Hall," the receptionist said, smiling over her remarkably efficient job at sizing up Kaitlin.

Clearly Kaitlin was not the only one with preconceptions. Kaitlin wondered how well the receptionist had done in anticipating her.

"That's correct. Thanks for scheduling me in."

The receptionist hit a button and spoke into her elegant headset. Then she gestured to the plush seats in the reception area.

"Please have a seat. Mr. Harriman will be with you in a moment."

Kaitlin walked over to a black leather sofa, which afforded her the most advantageous view of the office. She settled on the one opposite the reception desk, despite the fact that it was closer to the receptionist than she preferred to be. She rested her bag on the floor and soaked in the surroundings.

A few phone calls came in and the receptionist smoothly routed them to unseen persons within the office. The room fell silent between calls.

"If you don't mind my saying so, Detective Hall, you don't look at all like what I expected.

"Oh, really," Kaitlin said, secretly pleased that the receptionist had missed the mark. "What were you expecting?" Kaitlin asked.

"In truth," the receptionist said with a slightly guilty smile, "I expected someone a lot more...*butch*."

Kaitlin was surprised by the directness of the response. Either the receptionist was foolish or more intelligent than Kaitlin gave her credit for. For a second, she wondered if she was being played.

Unsure, she simply smiled. "I'll take that as a compliment," Kaitlin said.

While ever the feminist, "butch" was a description that Kaitlin hoped never to be applied to her.

The receptionist returned the smile and went back to her paperwork. After an awkward pause, the room fell back into a comfortable silence.

The quiet was broken a few minutes later by the steady and assertive sound of high-heeled shoes approaching down the tiled corridor.

A beautiful blond version of the receptionist emerged into the reception area and approached Kaitlin with an outstretched hand.

"Detective Hall, my name is Paloma. I'm Mr. Harriman's assistant."

"Good afternoon," Kaitlin responded pleasantly, shaking Paloma's diminutive hand. Her thin fingers were bejeweled with large diamond rings. Kaitlin couldn't miss them. Either being Harriman's assistant was a lucrative position or someone was keeping this pretty blonde very happy.

"Mr. Harriman will see you now. Please come with me," Paloma said, as she guided Kaitlin toward the hallway.

As Kaitlin followed behind Paloma, she begrudgingly noticed Paloma's knock-out figure. She silently calculated how many miles she'd have to run to get that kind of body. She stopped when the number grew too large.

As they turned the corner, Kaitlin had a clear understanding of the criteria by which Harriman & Co. staffed its office. As offensive as it first appeared, Kaitlin realized that staffing an office with beauties like Paloma and the receptionist was more strategic than chauvinistic.

Having beautiful, intelligent women around could help recruit young male venture capitalists. Like the ones she noticed as she walked past several open office doors. These guys routinely worked sixteen-hour days under constant and incredible stress.

They made indecent sums of money for their hard work. But Kaitlin was sure that, in addition to the paycheck, it must be nice for these guys to have an ultra-vixen office staff to fantasize about – assuming that their relationships with the office staff were limited to fantasizing.

At the end of the hall, Paloma pushed open a large paneled door, depositing Kaitlin in Warren Harriman's massive corner office. There was a significant expanse of square footage between her and the large mahogany desk behind which Mr. Harriman sat.

This was an office descended from the robber barons of the past century, Kaitlin realized. It was a dramatic departure from the modern minimalist décor of the common areas. She found Harriman's office to be warm and inviting, and oozing with the message 'money spoken here.'

Turkish rugs adorned the floors, African tribal masks clung to the damask fabric covered walls, and Asian ceramics stood on elegant, carved pedestals. A large computer monitor at the corner of the desk was the office's sole compromise to modernity.

Although Kaitlin had seen Warren Harriman's picture on the Harriman & Co. web site, in person he looked quite different. As he rose from his desk to greet her, she was taken by his impressive stature. He stood about 6'4" and was solidly built. He wore a well-tailored, dark blue suit with a bright white dress shirt and maroon silk necktie. A full head of gray hair framed his handsome, tanned face. His eyes were a piercing steel blue. They were unblinkingly focused on Kaitlin's face.

"Hello, Detective Hall," he said as he offered his hand and gave a firm handshake.

"Please, have a seat," he said with a thick accent, waving her to sit in the overstuffed leather guest chair.

While Kaitlin couldn't place his accent exactly, the formal staccato sounded Germanic.

"It was very kind of you to make time for me," she said as she rested her bag against her chair.

"Please," he said, raising his hand in protest. "I am happy to cooperate in whatever way I can." His face remained expressionless. "However, I admit that I am a little in the dark about the nature of the visit."

She did not address the implicit question. Instead, she settled into the chair and removed a notepad from her bag.

"Can I offer you something to drink? Coffee, perhaps?"

"No, thank you," Kaitlin answered politely as she noticed his steely eyes still fixed on her.

He waited until she was settled before speaking. "Now, what can I help you with, Detective Hall?"

"Mr. Harriman, as your receptionist may have explained to you, I'm a detective with the San Jose Police Department's High Tech Detail. In that capacity, I investigate possible criminal activity that affects or involves high-tech concerns in Silicon Valley. I understand that many of Harriman & Co.'s portfolio companies fall into that category."

"That's correct," he nodded. "We are heavily invested in the technology sector. And we have a number of investments in Silicon Valley," Harriman answered softly and continued without breaking eye contact. "Although, I am unaware of any criminal activity that might have caused you to visit today."

She smiled quickly. "If you could just – " she began, but Harriman was not yet ready to allow her to speak.

"I understand you graduated from Berkeley with a bachelor's degree, *summa cum laude*, in electrical engineering and computer science and a master's degree in computer science and were awarded your Ph.D. in computer science by Stanford. You never accepted the teaching post that was offered to you at Stanford. Instead, you chose to enter the law enforcement field. You applied to the FBI for a position as Special Agent, but you were not accepted. You joined the San Jose Police Department. You graduated near the top of your class in the police academy and were the first in your class to make detective. Your mother lives in the Bay Area and your father is deceased. You're unmarried and live in…where is it? Yes, Menlo Park."

The hair on Kaitlin's forearms stood on end. She raised her eyebrows and let out a soft whistle, at once showing a degree of admiration and false comfort with the situation.

"That's not a bad little snapshot. Nice homework," Kaitlin said, neutrally.

She noticed his eyes twinkled slightly and his lips flashed a barely perceptible smirk.

"Success in this business depends upon doing the proper homework, Detective," Harriman said, in a slightly patronizing tone.

"After all, knowledge is power," he added smugly.

Kaitlin shifted in her seat. She knew that he had taken charge of the interview, and she was trying to determine how to change the dynamic.

"As you can imagine, I've also done my homework," she said, not elaborating.

This time, Harriman smiled. "So, now that we know a little bit more about each other, what was it that you wished to discuss?" he asked in his thick, cultured accent that Kaitlin suspected was Austrian in origin.

"I'm interested first in some general knowledge. Could you tell me a little about Harriman & Co.'s investment approach?" Kaitlin asked calmly, managing her composure. The fact that he'd unearthed a mountain of information about her, some of which was extremely personal in nature, had unnerved her. She was sure he knew even more than the morsels he'd shared with her. Her concern was how he could have compiled so much information so quickly, and why.

"We currently manage a fund of over $500 million invested by wealthy individuals and institutions throughout the country. Our investment strategy is quite simple. We focus on high-quality, early-stage U.S. companies with innovative technology products and explosive growth potential."

Harriman had just offered her the polished, SEC-approved response. He'd probably made the same statement hundreds of times to investors, analysts, and the press. It was now Kaitlin's job to squeeze him a little.

"I see ... well then, please tell me about companies like Synergy Secure Computing and Entrex Semiconductors."

Kaitlin paused, then added the names of the seven other portfolio company names that Slim had identified as having lost employees in the past year. "Or … Taditron, Omega Electronics, and Advanced Circuit Systems …"

If Kaitlin's listing the names of those specific companies had any effect on Harriman, he didn't let it show.

"Our investments in the companies you have mentioned is completely consistent with our investment approach," Harriman answered offhandedly. "As I am sure you know from your homework."

Indeed, he was right when it came to her doing her homework. Although these nine companies fit into the Harriman investment strategy, there were some inconsistencies. "But you must find those nine companies to have been disappointing choices?" Kaitlin persisted.

"How do you mean?" he asked, unfazed.

"Well, from what I've read, and I'm not much of a financial wizard, the companies I just mentioned have been among Harriman & Co.'s poorest performers. Half have yet to turn a profit and the others have shown very weak profits at best. Overall, they've fared even worse than your Internet investments."

Harriman was silent.

"Did I read those financial statements correctly?" Kaitlin asked coyly.

Now it was Harriman's turn to shift in his seat. She knew he was wondering how she'd seen the financial statements of several privately held companies. Those financial statements were strictly confidential. Even as a detective, she would not have been privy to that information without a warrant.

Kaitlin had done what she intended to do – she had leveled the playing field with Harriman.

"Yes, Detective Hall, your interpretation of the financial information regarding those companies is essentially correct... On paper most of those companies have not delivered the performance we like to see. However, as I am sure you know, they have excellent prospects due to their technology holdings." He smiled, although a tension hung in the room. "Remember, the stock market is awash with multi-billion-dollar technology companies that have not yet turned a profit ..."

"That's true," Kaitlin conceded, "but there's something different about these nine portfolio companies."

"What would that be?" Harriman said, showing interest.

Although he viewed Kaitlin as an adversary in this conversation, Harriman had gained some respect for her. He was enjoying the banter – for now.

"The nature of their products," she stated simply. "I'm no expert, but it seems their multi-billion dollar potential is severely limited when they aren't free to export their technology outside the U.S."

Harriman paused ever so slightly before responding.

"I would agree with you that the government of this country has been quite impractical when it comes to export policy regarding technology. We will all be better off when the government recognizes the importance of technology and the narrow-mindedness of restricting U.S. exports."

Kaitlin wasn't a big fan of the government's position, but she wasn't about to get into a political discussion with Harriman. She just smiled, and Harriman kept talking.

"Silicon Valley is spending a considerable amount of time and money lobbying Washington to bring about a change in policy. Because I am confident that this view will – must – ultimately prevail, we do not feel that current export controls will hamper the long-term success of our investments. Meanwhile, we find value elsewhere in those companies, and we are in them for the long run. The same cannot be said for many of the remaining Internet companies out there."

Kaitlin nodded her head and made quick notes on her pad. She still wasn't saying anything. Not yet. She had accomplished what she wanted with her opening gambit. She got Harriman talking. And she wanted him to keep talking, to anticipate her next question. To her satisfaction, he tired of waiting and resumed speaking.

"Can I assume then that your visit today has something to do with technology exports?"

Kaitlin stopped writing and rested her pen gently on the writing pad. "To some extent," she said, ambiguously. "I won't argue with you on the rationale behind the export controls. But the law enforcement community is concerned about companies subject to export controls. You know, theft of their trade secrets, industrial espionage. That sort of thing…"

"Of course," Harriman said. "That makes perfect sense. We are all grateful for the fine job your police department is doing."

That gratuitous bit of fawning was out of character for Harriman.

Kaitlin thought it was an interesting slip, but she didn't know where to go with it. She needed to move the conversation along and proceeded boldly.

"The reason I contacted you was that each of the nine Harriman portfolio companies mentioned had at least one employee die in the past twenty-four months. The individuals were young and their deaths untimely," Kaitlin concluded.

Harriman paused, measuring Kaitlin carefully.

"Ms. Hall, if you're suggesting workplace safety issues, I'm not aware of any deaths, or injuries beyond the ordinary, having occurred at any of our portfolio companies. You'd have to talk to the management at each company for that sort of information – "

"I'm not investigating workplace safety issues," she said firmly, cutting him off. "Each of the employee deaths that I referred to happened *outside* the workplace."

Harriman had a puzzled expression. He spread his hands out in a gesture of surrender. "Well then, I'm not sure how I would even know about those deaths. Collectively, our portfolio companies employ thousands, tens of thousands, of people. I'm not even surprised that each experienced the loss of one or more employees – as unfortunate as that might be. The chief value of these companies is the intellectual strength of its workforce. So it is regrettable to lose even one," he concluded.

Kaitlin couldn't tell whether Harriman cared about the loss of life, or just the loss of "intellectual strength" and its impact on the bottom line.

Kaitlin countered, "Statistically speaking, Mr. Harriman, the number of accidental deaths represents a mortality rate *five times higher* than normal, given the total number of portfolio company employees." She paused. "Does that surprise you?"

Harriman folded his hands. "I don't know if I would say it surprises me. It seems troubling. But this entire discussion is troubling me, quite honestly. Certainly, the statistical anomaly you mention is interesting. However, statistical theory is a delicate art."

He reached swiftly into his suit jacket and pulled out a quarter.

"Detective, as this coin rests here in my hand, I can tell you that if I throw it in the air, the probability of it landing on one side as opposed to the other is exactly fifty-fifty. But I can assure you, if I were to flip this coin in the air one hundred times, it most definitely would not land on heads fifty times and on tails fifty times."

He put the quarter away, as if he had proven his point.

"Well, Mr. Harriman, I can certainly appreciate your assessment of statistics. But let's just say that I have a more confident opinion of statistical analysis ... when properly applied."

"Don't get me wrong, Detective. I respect statistical analysis. As an investor, I must. But I am very careful not to draw conclusions based solely on statistical patterns, and inference."

"So, you can't think of anything that those employees – the deceased – might have in common?"

"Detective, I don't even know who the employees are," he said, a tone of mild exasperation and offense in his voice. "I couldn't even guess at anything those employees might have had in common."

He clasped his chin with his hand and looked at Kaitlin earnestly.

Kaitlin knew that she'd gotten all she was going to get from Harriman at this meeting.

She'd succeeded in getting an impression of him. Now, she wanted to leave before he drew any firmer conclusions about her.

"You're right," Kaitlin said. "If there was a commonality, some direct connection between them, it would be unusual. And I certainly haven't found one. But because of your familiarity with these companies, I was hoping you might think of something that I've overlooked. I guess I'll have to go back to the books on this one," Kaitlin sighed, feigning disappointment.

She deposited her notepad into her bag and clicked her pen closed.

Harriman slowly pushed his chair back on its rollers and stood up. He straightened his tie and flattened it gently against his crisp white shirt.

"Detective Hall," he said, looking down at her and adopting a fatherly tone. "I understand that you are a trained officer of the law and a scientist at heart. But you are also very young," he said, the smallest hint of condescension in his tone.

"People often look for reasons to justify the loss of life. My years of experience, here in the U.S. and in my native Austria, have shown me that such justifications are usually not found.

If I were you, I would not overlook the obvious before seeking unwarranted justifications for these tragedies."

Kaitlin listened intently, but she wasn't buying it. She was confident enough not to be swayed by the unctuous tone of a handsomely dressed man.

Harriman sat on the edge of the desk opposite Kaitlin. He was nothing but casual.

"I'm sorry for philosophizing to you, Detective Hall. That is surely no help to you. I am sorry I cannot offer any insight on this subject."

"No, that was very helpful," Kaitlin said, thinking it best to maintain a good rapport with him.

Kaitlin surmised she'd be back here soon, asking him much more pointed questions. She scooped up her bag and rose.

"I appreciate the benefit of your experience. Thanks for taking the time out of your schedule to meet with me," she said, shaking his large hand.

"My pleasure. Please feel free to contact me again if I can be of any assistance to you, Detective Hall."

As if on cue, Paloma opened the door and escorted her out of the office and into the lobby. The receptionist gave her a fake smile, which Kaitlin reciprocated, and placed several validation stickers on her parking ticket.

Kaitlin couldn't wait to get the hell out of Harriman & Co.

As soon as the chrome doors to the elevator closed, Kaitlin took several deep breaths and let the adrenaline dissipate through her body. She didn't let herself relax too much, as she was sure there was a camera in the elevator.

Harriman had been pure ice. Lecturing her about the randomness of death! *Please*, she thought.

Still, his had been a practiced and solid performance. He'd laid Occam's razor flat on the table: Where there are multiple explanations for a specific event or phenomenon, the simplest one is most likely to be correct. The scientist in her was predisposed to agree with the theory. But the cop in her told her that these nine deaths, Darren Park, Michael Owens, and Dale Cho included, were not simple, unconnected accidents. The statistics indicated otherwise. *But what was that connection? What, if anything, did Harriman, or Bobby Park for that matter, have to do with them?*

Her visit to Harriman had strengthened her determination to find out.

The elevator deposited Kaitlin in the Embarcadero's cavernous lobby.

From the lobby elevator, Kaitlin walked for what seemed like a quarter mile to the elevator bank servicing the parking structure. She didn't remember the area being so vast on her way in.

"Damn it," she said quietly as she studied the numerals on the interior wall of the elevator car. Mystified, she looked down at the parking ticket in her hand. It held no clues. Despite her usual attention to detail and superior memory, she couldn't remember which floor she'd parked on. She'd been so focused on her meeting with Harriman that she hadn't given the least thought to finding her car after the meeting. It could have been the fourth level as easily as the seventh. "Good thing there are only eight friggin' levels to choose from," Kaitlin thought sarcastically.

She pushed the button for the fourth floor, thinking it was as good as any other place to start. At least if the car wasn't there, she could walk down the ramps to the lower levels, rather than having to walk up them.

She'd checked two levels without success. After experiencing the breathtaking 52nd floor view of Harriman & Co., the parking structure's decidedly low ceiling made her claustrophobic. She was getting antsy. Kaitlin disregarded the large posted signs that cautioned "NOT A WALKWAY – VEHICLES ONLY" and proceeded down to the sixth level, where she felt confident she'd find her car. Kaitlin shivered in the cold and damp garage. She was looking forward to getting into her car and cranking up the heater.

As soon as she'd reached the bottom of the ramp leading to the sixth level, Kaitlin saw him.

In search of her Lumina, she'd quickly scanned the cars lined along the eastern wall of the structure. There she spotted the large black Mercedes sedan with heavily tinted windows that had followed her during her jog. However, the car's windshield was untinted, and she could see the driver inside. The driver had Asian features. His head was cocked all the way to the left.

Kaitlin stepped back behind the concrete pillar that supported the ramp. She carefully angled her head around the pillar, following the driver's line of sight. In the southernmost portion of the lot, about two hundred feet down and ten cars from the elevator doors, was her car and the focus of the driver's gaze.

From her bag, she drew her service weapon.

A closet pacifist, she soon came to appreciate that her pacifism was for a war thousands of miles away. Here, in a cavernous parking structure where she was alone, the 9mm Glock semi-automatic pistol in her hand was reassuring. She'd been one of the best shots in her class at the academy and had kept her aim sharp by frequent visits to the range.

The truth was that she found target practice exceedingly therapeutic.

"No wonder guys are scared of you," a girlfriend had once said to her, commenting on her more than professional interest in guns and target practice.

She made herself "thin" behind the concrete pillar and brought the weapon up to her chest. With her other hand, she pulled her cell phone out of her pocket. The LCD screen read "NO SERVICE." Deep in a concrete parking structure she wasn't surprised, but she was disappointed.

She drew a breath. She was on her own. She pushed the useless phone back in her pocket. She inhaled deeply, steadying herself. Gracefully, she swung her body around the concrete pillar. She leveled the gun chest-high with both hands and aimed directly at the driver. With arms outstretched, she walked determinedly through the center of the dimly lit structure head-on towards the Mercedes. At about thirty paces, the driver, who had been attentively watching Kaitlin's car to the left, jerked his head around.

Kaitlin froze in her tracks as they locked eyes.

"Out of the car!" she yelled forcefully. "Out of the goddamn car!"

The driver was completely surprised. He'd obviously been waiting for her to exit the elevator doors and head to her car. And if she had, she never would have seen him waiting in the darkened sedan.

He sat motionless. His left hand was clutching the steering wheel, but his right hand was out of view. Kaitlin had given him enough time to comply.

"Out of the car, *now*!" she yelled again, training the Glock on the driver's head.

In an instant, and without breaking eye contact, the driver fired up the engine. He slammed on the accelerator, and the Mercedes hurtled out of its parking space with its tires screeching loudly.

With incredible precision, the massive sedan veered sharply to Kaitlin's right, taking the driver out of her line of fire. Reflexively, Kaitlin dodged to her left and assumed a crouched shooting position on the cold concrete floor. But by the time she brought the barrel up, the car's red taillights had disappeared up the ramp to the next parking level.

She could hear the screech of the car's tires on the upper levels as it rounded the structure's corners. The car's high-pitched sound grew faint as the car rose through the structure, exiting at street level several floors above. A cloud of white smoke and the acrid smell of burnt rubber hung heavily in the air. Kaitlin raised herself from the floor. She gently cursed herself.

She smacked her forehead with the palm of her hand. She'd missed getting the car's license plate numbers. *Damn it.*

Still, she had learned a few things. One, she was definitely being followed. Two, the person following her was a professional. Three, the person following her didn't want her dead.

Although Kaitlin had surprised him, the driver had a clear opportunity to gun the car left and easily take her out. But he'd elected to swerve the other way, avoiding her. Kaitlin was perplexed.

# Chapter 19

"What about that?" Kaitlin asked hopefully, pointing up at the camera.

She had cruised through the parking lot slowly and quizzed the parking lot attendant thoroughly before leaving the Embarcadero Center. It was almost comical, but not surprising, that no one seemed to remember seeing the Mercedes or its driver. Looking up above the parking attendant's booth, Kaitlin noticed a security camera. It would have recorded the license plate numbers and perhaps captured an image of the driver.

The attendant looked at her sheepishly. "*No funciona*," he said.

Kaitlin didn't speak Spanish but she knew that it meant she had nothing – except the fact that she was unharmed.

Smiling apologetically, the parking attendant went on to explain in broken English that the camera was designed to scare the parking attendants from pocketing cash out of the register. But they all knew it was just for show and didn't really work.

As soon as she was on 101 South, Kaitlin picked up the cell phone. She thought about calling in the incident that had just occurred, but she decided against it.

Instead, she made the mistake of checking her voicemail at the station.

Kaitlin navigated into the fast lane as the first message queued up: "Hello, Detective Hall, this is Eugenia Hammond. I am calling to find out whether you've managed to crack the case!"

It was the old lady from Los Gatos who'd been scammed on the Internet.

"On *Murder She Wrote*, Angela Lansbury *always* solves the crime within a matter of days – sometimes sooner! It's been three weeks, and I haven't heard a peep from you or any of the other detectives working on this case," Mrs. Hammond continued heatedly.

Kaitlin smiled. There were *no* other detectives working on Mrs. Hammond's case. In fact, she herself hadn't spent more than ten minutes reviewing the file since she'd received it two days ago. Nor had she visited Mrs. Hammond in Los Gatos, as she'd agreed and as Torres had instructed her to do. Kaitlin appreciated Ms. Hammond's annoyance, but she wasn't thrilled with being compared to an octogenarian television detective. She'd made a mental commitment to put in a couple hours later this afternoon researching the swindlers that had walked away with Mrs. Hammond's money.

Kaitlin hit the pound key and the next voicemail message played. It was from Darren Park's father, Jong Ma Park. He spoke in the dignified voice and perfect English that Kaitlin remembered. As he spoke, she gently bit her lower lip.

"Detective Hall, I was notified today by the building management at 2115 Coddle Road that our son Darren's apartment was broken into. The movers had been scheduled to pack up Darren's belongings and take everything out next week. The building manager said it was a burglary. Apparently, not much was taken. But because you have been investigating Darren's death, I assume you should be aware of this ..."

Kaitlin's pulse started racing again. This was no random burglary. With all that there was to steal in Darren Park's residence - designer clothes, collectible watches, top-of-the-line electronics, original art - not much was taken?" Kaitlin would have to get another look in the apartment to draw any sort of conclusion.

Mr. Park's final words on the voicemail caught Kaitlin's attention.

"Detective Hall, if you learn anything regarding this, please let me know as soon as possible."

His last comment struck Kaitlin as rather out of character. In her past discussion, Darren's father, while upset, had been stoic to the extreme. He'd seemed almost disinterested in the circumstances regarding his son's death. Now, he wanted to know right away if Kaitlin learned anything about the burglary.

"Curiouser and curiouser," she sighed, recalling a favorite line from *Alice in Wonderland*. Kaitlin wasn't sure what to make of Mr. Park's message. Why was he interested now? Did he have new information? Or had he simply been cautious with his knowledge and suspicions when he'd met Kaitlin?

It was plain to Kaitlin that something in Darren's family life was not as it appeared. The dynamic was strange – between Darren and his parents, and between Darren and his brother Bobby.

She also felt strongly that Harriman was somehow connected to Darren.

But she had absolutely nothing to back that up. Not even a theory. Which made her angry with herself: conviction without proof was the hallmark of undisciplined thinking.

She shut off the cell phone, dropped it on the passenger seat and gunned the Lumina to eighty.

Kaitlin raced toward Darren's apartment.

# Chapter 20

She'd flashed the badge at the building's unfriendly concierge. If he had remembered her, he didn't show it. She proceeded without fanfare up to the 2nd floor and then down the long corridor, her feet barely making a sound against the plush burgundy carpet.

"Ah, gift wrapped," Kaitlin said as she approached the apartment's front door, cordoned off with bright yellow plastic tape, marking the site as an active crime scene. Kaitlin reached under the tape and found that the door was closed but unsecured – the door had been pried open with a crow bar. The jamb was splintered and the yellow tape dangled to the carpeted floor.

At first glance, the apartment seemed unfamiliar. When she'd last set foot in it, it had been cloaked in darkness. Now, with the blinds having been drawn all the way up, it was drenched in harsh sunlight. Kaitlin paused to wonder who might have pulled up the blinds, but continued her entrance into the apartment.

As she peeked in the kitchen and the other rooms, she gave an involuntary shudder. Darren had been dead only a week and the place had already lost its human feel.

"How quickly places forget us," she thought, "though we remember places all our lives."

While the apartment hadn't been trashed, it certainly had experienced a very thorough and professional going over. The sofa cushions stood on the sofa at odd angles. Most of the cabinet doors were ajar, the interior contents visibly shuffled about. Dresser drawers were opened and clothes lapped over their edges.

Kaitlin looked over at the large wooden entertainment center; all the high-end electronics were still there. Kaitlin wasn't terribly surprised. Removing them would have been a challenge. And challenges were not high on the list of local burglars. Their M.O. was different. The smart ones stuck to small, expensive stuff that they could easily pawn or fence in East Palo Alto or West Oakland.

Fast turnaround was the name of the game.

But then again, Kaitlin wondered why she was even considering burglary. Smart burglars usually hit cars and single homes, not apartments with doormen and concierges. She shrugged. Stranger things have happened.

In a moment of social consciousness, she considered the people who overlooked the pockets of need in the Bay Area. Drenched in their prosperity and nestled in their SUVs, people easily ignored the blighted communities of the Bay Area that had not shared in the region's off-the-charts economic boom. In fact, the downward spiral continued in those areas, with urban degradation worsening. The rise in the number of Silicon Valley millionaires had no correlation to the number of Bay Area mothers on welfare. Crime inspired by poverty would get worse, Kaitlin thought, before it would get better. As she considered the popped bubble of the market, she concluded those pockets of need would grow, and grow quickly.

Kaitlin moved along the hall and walked into the bedroom. The scenario was much the same. Someone had been here, and it was clear that whomever it was had been anxious to find something specific.

Making her way to the bedroom window, she looked out into the bright sunlight. She rested her hands on the small writing desk below the window. "Not a bad set up," she thought, gazing at the large sycamore trees lining the street.

The desktop was essentially barren. A writing pad, a few pieces of mail, and a couple of magazines lay scattered. Even the magazine choices were predictable to Kaitlin now that she had gotten to know a bit about Darren Park: *Stereo Review*, *Dr. Dobb's Journal*, and *Sys Admin*.

The white sheets had been stripped off the bed, and the mattress and box spring were askew. The single small drawer had been pulled out of each matching bedside table.

Their contents were visible – assorted pens, paperclips, Post-It notes, and the like.

There was nothing in the room that didn't belong.

And then her heart skipped a beat.

The one thing that should have been there was not. She almost smacked herself, it was so obvious. *Where the hell's Darren's computer?*

Someone unfamiliar with the tech world might suggest that a person who lives, breathes, and sleeps with computers at work would be happy to be free of them at home. Such a person would be wrong. There were many in the Valley – system administrators in particular – who couldn't tolerate being more than a few feet away from a computer at any given time. Sure, they had other interests: movies, hiking, Ultimate Frisbee and the like. But when in a fixed place for any length of time, they weren't quite whole unless tinkering away on a PC or UNIX workstation.

"So," she asked herself again, "where the hell's Darren's computer?"

She couldn't believe that she'd overlooked an absent computer the first time she'd scanned the apartment. If she'd seen one, she would have definitely removed it and taken it to the computer crime lab for a work over. A Palm Pilot is an evidence treasure chest; a computer is a gold mine.

"Maybe he left a laptop in his office the night he died?" It was a possibility she'd have to check out with Synergy.

But she knew a laptop would also have been of interest to a burglar – easy to remove, just stick it in a backpack, and it would bring a quick five hundred bucks.

If this was a burglary, what else would have been taken? She paced around the room.

The closet door was slightly ajar. Its brass knob was still covered with fine gray-white fingerprint powder from the burglary detail's check for prints. Opening the door by its edge, Kaitlin pulled it wide open.

Inside the closet, several suits dangled from their hangers. The previously neat rows of shoes were scattered about. The dresser at the back of the closet, however, looked as she'd recalled during her first visit. Only one of its drawers was open a few inches.

"What the…?" she whispered out loud. On top of the dresser sat the handsome wooden box that housed Darren's watch collection.

If the box still contained Darren's impressive assortment of fine watches, then there would be no doubt that this had not been a burglary.

If the watches were gone, she'd have to concede that there had been a burglary. Occam's razor required it.

As she carefully lifted the antiqued brass clasp and gave it a half-turn, she didn't know what she hoped to find - watches or no watches. With both hands, she raised the wooden lid, revealing the plush burgundy velvet liner. And a dozen brilliant timepieces. Even the Hamilton. Undisturbed. All keeping perfect time.

Kaitlin's heart beat more quickly as she lowered the lid to the box, the thumping sound replacing the delicate ticking of the watches. Something was going on. She knew it now with total certainty.

# Chapter 21

It was late afternoon by the time Kaitlin returned to the office and settled behind her desk. With a sigh, she reached down and booted up her computer. After a few seconds, the ubiquitous Microsoft Windows logo popped onscreen. The familiar Microsoft jingle sounded on the speaker, and, in a jarring departure from the normal boot up sequence, Captain Torres stuck his head out from behind his office door and yelled out into the squad room, "Detective Hall! May I kindly speak with you in my office?"

Consistent with the irritated and urgent tone of his voice, his expression was more than a bit agitated. But, otherwise, he was looking quite dapper in a light gray suit and navy blue tie.

Kaitlin looked at her computer screen and rolled her eyes. Then she pushed her chair out and walked to Torres' office. With four of her fellow squad members seated at their desks, she felt the back of her neck burning as she passed each one.

They shared her discomfort and did their best to keep their heads down and their eyes on their computers, log books, or whatever they happened to be working on.

Kaitlin's lips pressed together in a tight frown. If Torres had wanted to, he could just as easily buzzed her privately on the phone system's intercom rather than shouting out into the squad room.

But she knew why he'd done what he'd done.

He wasn't interested in talking to her so much as he was in making it known to the entire department that she was being called on the carpet.

It was part of being a cop. They all knew it and understood it. But that didn't make the experience any more pleasant.

To Kaitlin, it smacked of bullshit power.

She'd experienced the same thing in grad school. How many times had professors, or even fellow students, publicly humiliated, chastised, or unnerved a student that they felt particularly threatened by? Too often.

She'd never liked being called on the carpet, but she had gained a great deal of composure being a cop. She strode toward Torres' office with an air of confidence and a certain degree of annoyance.

Kaitlin stood in the office doorway. Torres didn't say a word; he mutely waved her forward. Kaitlin took a seat in the office's leather guest chair.

Only when she was settled and looking at him did Torres match her gaze.

"You've managed to do it to me again, Detective Hall," Torres said.

He had remained standing, pacing behind his chair. The shuffle of his footsteps was the only sound that broke the room's silence. Perhaps he hoped that she'd figure out her latest transgression and speak up.

Kaitlin remained silent. She wasn't sure what Torres was upset about, but she wasn't interested in guessing the wrong offense and possibly giving him more ammunition.

Torres looked at her expectantly.

"Captain, what exactly have I managed to do to you?" she asked innocently.

"Once again – and this is the second time in as many weeks – I've learned of your activities on behalf of this department from someone *other than you.*"

"Captain, you know exactly which cases I'm working on. You have my roster – "

"Detective Hall!" he snapped, cutting her off as the color of his face grew crimson.

"Did you, by using any of the various known forms of communication that our technologically advanced society possesses – telephone, cell phone, e-mail, *you name it* – let me know that you were planning to shake down Warren Harriman?"

"But I ..."

"But nothing!" he cut her off abruptly. "Do you have any idea who Warren Harriman *is*?

Taking his question to be a rhetorical one, she sank back into the soft leather of the chair and kept her mouth shut.

"Well, let me tell you who he is," Torres continued, his tone drifting into condescension.

"He's one of the most influential venture capitalists in the country. People in the financial community will tell you that he practically *made* Silicon Valley," said Torres. "Even now, with the Valley teetering, he holds incredible sway." Of course, with an abiding faith that your abilities as a detective are better than your judgment, I believe you knew that *before* you went knocking on his door." Torres pulled out his chair, and dropped into it with a thud.

Kaitlin said nothing.

He looked directly at her. His scowl slowly softened.

"*Please* tell me that you knew, Detective Hall," he pleaded.

"Yes, I did know that," she answered in an unwavering voice.

"Good. Very good," he smiled and nodded his head slightly with mock approval. "Did you also know that Harriman & Co. is one of the major corporate supporters of both the San Francisco P.D. and *this* police department? And that Warren Harriman was one of the leading proponents of establishing a high-tech crimes division here? This very division – the one that pays your salary?"

No, Kaitlin had not known any of that.

Sitting in Torres' office, watching him fuming behind his desk – and rightfully so – she wished she had. Not that the knowledge would've diminished her suspicions regarding Harriman one iota. But at least she would've had an opportunity to position herself with Torres before paying Harriman a visit.

She'd been heavy-handed. A rookie move in the truest sense of the phrase. She was not happy about that. She'd been unnecessarily clumsy at Torres' personal and political expense.

"I'm sorry," she said, looking at the Captain with absolute sincerity, "I wasn't aware of any relationship between Mr. Harriman and this department."

Torres grabbed the edge of his desk with both hands and leaned toward her. "I play *golf* with Warren Harriman for Chrissake!

"Shit," Kaitlin thought.

She'd really stepped on Torres' toes this time. Questioning one of his golf buddies, and an extremely powerful one at that, in connection with a rash of homicides.

"I'm sorry, Captain. I didn't know that either."

"I'm sorry too, Detective Hall. I am very sorry indeed. Enough for the both of us. In fact, that is *exactly* what I told Warren when he called me this afternoon."

He shook his head in a gesture that was hard for Kaitlin to read. Was he sympathetic? Angry? Pushed to his limit?

"Now," he went on, "perhaps you let me know exactly what's going on. While you're at it, maybe you could explain exactly why you thought it wise to question Harriman about the deaths of employees working at his portfolio companies."

Torres leaned back in his chair.

Kaitlin relaxed a bit, thankful that Torres had created a bit of space between them, physically and emotionally. The tension in the room eased.

Drawing a deep breath before beginning, Kaitlin spent the better part of the next hour filling in Torres on the investigative efforts, and the evidence that she'd gathered over the past few days. He listened patiently, interrupting her only occasionally with a smart question, asked with surgical precision.

The outcome of the conversation was no surprise: Torres remained skeptical.

"So, if I understand you correctly, you're telling me that you have at least three rival theories?"

Kaitlin shrugged. "Three. Two. Four. It depends on how you count them ..."

Torres was speechless, but kept his focus and held on to whatever patience he had left.

"Well, let's see. You've got Bobby Park. He's up to no good, but we don't know what that no good might be. Maybe his father, the respectable retired businessman, is also involved. Or, maybe not. We've got Darren Park's jilted nerd ex-girlfriend. And then we've got Warren Harriman. And, of course, there's the possibility that they're all working together," Torres said sarcastically. "I'm waiting for the theory that involves Elvis. Or aliens who secretly walk amongst us in human form."

Kaitlin flinched but she didn't say anything. She knew it was best not to respond. Not to react. Torres was venting. She would just have to weather the storm. She would reason with him later. She had powerful faith in information. She knew he needed more information to be convinced. And she was going to get it. But that would take time.

She also knew that Torres was a traditionalist. He was a backroom power broker. He moved forward based on relationships and intuition. The statistical significance of the deaths neither intrigued him nor had any real impact on him. Or, if it did, he was keeping it to himself.

Torres believed in the holy trinity of law enforcement: motive, opportunity, and means. When it came to Warren Harriman, he could certainly see means but not much in the way of motive. Torres knew Harriman as a powerful multimillionaire with a fondness for the law enforcement community – not a ruthless murderer.

Kaitlin viewed things differently. She believed that men with great power were capable of great harm. They were never satisfied. Their ambitions, at the very least, required them to achieve greater power.

Both could agree that Warren Harriman was a man of extraordinary power.

⅄

All things considered, Kaitlin had a great deal to be thankful for when she finally left Torres' office. Despite her egregious rookie blunder, she'd managed to get out of his office relatively unscathed; a brief tongue-lashing and a virtual rap on the knuckles. That was about it. More important than what Torres had done was what he had not done. He had not pulled her off the Darren Park case.

But Torres was very clear about how she was to proceed with Warren Harriman.

"Unless you've got something more than woman's intuition to go on, you stay far, far away from him. Do we understand each other?"

She nodded her head and held her tongue, despite the blatant sexism of his remark. Besides, she had no intention of disturbing Warren Harriman again. Per explicit instructions, she wouldn't contact him. But she sure as hell was going to keep investigating him.

As she made her way back her desk, Newmeyer was the only one to look up at her. He raised his eyebrows and looked her over, checking to see if she was still intact.

She gave him a slight smile and silently mouthed, "Cake."

He returned the smile, genuinely relieved. He took a deep breath, ran his hand through his curly brown hair and resumed working on his computer. As she passed his desk, Kaitlin gave him a gentle pat on the back. Even though he'd said nothing, his care and sympathy were apparent. He knew that the last thing Kaitlin needed right now was Torres calling her on the carpet.

She appreciated his empathy and hoped not to have to return Newmeyer's favor any time soon. Although he had a few more years of experience, he didn't have a particularly thick skin. The last time Torres had called him on the carpet, it had been ugly.

As she approached her desk, Kaitlin saw the red light blinking and heard the ring of an incoming call. Reaching for the handset from the aisle, she caught the call before it went into voicemail.

"Detective Hall," she answered abruptly.

"Detective, this is Victor Chan of the Asian Criminal Enterprise Task Force. I'm following up on some vehicle license numbers that you faxed over."

"Right," Kaitlin said, swinging herself around the desk and into her chair. She pulled out a writing pad.

"Find anything interesting?" she asked.

"Oh, yeah – you could say that," he said, with a chuckle. "Can I ask where you got those plates?"

Kaitlin wasn't sure how to read the ACE detective's response, so she decided to be honest – but not completely.

"A few were from some cars in the parking lot of an import-export company. The others were found … elsewhere."

She wasn't ready to give more information about the three plate numbers she cared most about, those on the cars belonging to Darren Park, Michael Owens, and Dale Cho. She wanted to know what ACE had put together.

The detective paused. He wanted more but he realized that he wasn't going to get it.

"Well," he said. "I've got a very definite idea about three of those numbers. The ones belonging to the Mercedes, the Jaguar, and the Acura NSX." Those were the ones that Kaitlin had gotten from Great Fortune Trading Company's parking lot, outside Bobby's office.

"Okay, tell me about those first."

"If you look at the current registration – everything is legit. The cars are owned by several different individuals: Albert Cho, age 59, Peggy Kwan, age 63, and a Jong Ma Park, age 60."

"Jong Ma Park is the owner of the import-export company," Kaitlin said.

"Hmmm ..." Chan said. "I'm interested to hear more about the current owners afterward, if you have anything on them. But in searching back through the chain of title on those cars, I found something of great interest ..."

"And that would be?" Kaitlin said earnestly.

"Each car went through a series of transfers between private individuals within the last year, but if you trace the title, they all originate from a place called Pacific Exotic Motors, in East San Jose."

"Got anything on that place?"

"Of course," Chan answered tersely.

Kaitlin briefly considered an apology, but Chan moved on.

"It's a used car dealership that specializes in high-end vehicles. Mercedes, BMW, Porsche. Actually, we've been keeping an eye on them for a while. We suspect it's a money laundering operation for the Triad. Haven't been able to pin anything on them, though," he concluded with obvious disappointment.

Kaitlin didn't like where this path was leading. Although it wasn't her area of law enforcement, she was familiar with the Triad. It was a well-known and very violent Asian mob organization. Narcotics, human trafficking, extortion. A whole list of nefarious deeds. In recent years, they'd moved into high-tech theft. In the famous West Chips case, they'd made headlines: "Southeast Asian Gang Steals Millions in Computer Chips." After a significant effort, over 140 suspects were arrested. Kaitlin knew that both the FBI and San Jose Police investigators had already seen signs that organized criminal factions from the Far East, like the Japanese Yakuza and the Hong Kong Tongs, were making inroads in the Bay Area.

These things were running through Kaitlin's mind as she formulated the one question that had direct bearing on her case: "So, do you think there is a connection between Jong Ma Park and an Asian gang?"

Although she hoped that Chan would elaborate on whatever connection might exist, he was circumspect in his reply.

"I wouldn't rule it out. But on the other hand, it could be that he's one of many innocent purchasers. Many restaurants and bars are used to launder money, but that doesn't mean their patrons are involved in wrongdoing."

Kaitlin was unimpressed by Chan's attempt at fairness.

"The odds don't support your uncertainty," she said. "I gave you the plates from six cars. And three were bought from the same dealership," Kaitlin said.

"Four," Chan corrected.

"Four? You mean one of the other cars was bought there?"

"Yeah. California plate 183KM6H. A 2000 BMW coupe. Registered in the name of Darren Park. That one was bought at Pacific Exotic Motors about three months ago."

"And the other two?" Kaitlin asked, referring to Michael Owens' and Dale Cho's vehicles.

"Those ones ... let me see," he said, rifling through his case file. "California vanity plate 'CHIPPER' and California plate

94IBJ59. I show current registrations in the name of Michael Owens and a Dale Cho. Those cars were bought at two different BMW dealerships. One in downtown San Jose and the other in the City. I called both dealerships. Interestingly, both cars were bought and paid for *in cash*."

Kaitlin mulled everything over. Darren's car had been purchased at the same place as Bobby's. As she recalled, Bobby had said that Darren's car purchase had been a surprise to him. That Darren had shown up one day to show it off.

Maybe Darren had asked his brother for some advice about where to buy a car, and his brother sent him to his dealer. But why would Bobby have lied about that? And what about the other two cars? Dale Cho's and Michael Owens?

"Detective Chan, why is the fact that the other two cars were purchased in cash of particular interest to you?"

"It's not to you?" he asked, chiding her. "Look, even when the economy was humming along like it would never stop, we still didn't see a lot of expensive cars being purchased in cash – except among a certain set of customers. Interest rates are low, Detective. Most people who buy cars are getting loans. Actually, most are just leasing these days."

"So, who are these cash customers?"

"Senior citizens who don't buy on credit. And people who have more cash than they should," he said directly. "I'm generalizing but this group is made up of your basic drug dealers, child-support deadbeats pleading poverty in the family courts, guys who're serial tax dodgers, and real estate developers. To those guys, cash is king. Everyone else pretty much uses plastic ..."

Kaitlin could empathize with the people who used credit, thinking about her own student loans. "Silicon Valley techies wouldn't fit the cash profile, would they?"

Victor Chan laughed. "No ... not at all. Sure, lots of guys in the Valley still have enough money to buy any car or house they want. But they rarely, if ever, use cash. Their accountants won't let them. They do like the rest of us; they use plastic. They just have ridiculously big credit lines."

Kaitlin respected the common sense position Chan was describing. It didn't make sense that two mid-level engineers like Dale Cho and Michael Owens – both working on the same design project – would independently go and buy BMWs *in cash* at separate car dealers, and then die in suspicious accidents within a few months of one another.

"Did you find out whether Darren Park paid for his car in cash?" Kaitlin asked.

"No. No, I didn't. I'd need to call Pacific Exotic Motors to do that. Frankly, I don't think they'll be too receptive to a call from their local police. In truth, I didn't think it important enough to risk compromising our surveillance of them." There was a pause. "Is it important enough to risk?"

"No, no. You were right. It's not worth it," Kaitlin said, knowing she'd find out for herself.

And she knew exactly how to do it. Not with a phone call to Pacific Exotic Motors, but with a call to Bobby Park. She had a feeling he'd be more cooperative this time.

"Thank you, Detective Chan. I'm going to digest this information, compare with my notes. You've been a big help."

"No problem. But before you hang up, I have some questions."

"Yes?" she replied, mildly surprised.

"About that import-export company ... what was the name of it again?" Chan asked.

Kaitlin's defenses were up and she wanted to get off the phone. Now. However, there was no diplomatic way to accomplish her goal.

"Detective Chan, I'm going to have to call you back," she said hurriedly. "My Captain's calling me, sorry, goodbye!" She hung up abruptly.

Okay, it wasn't subtle. And it wasn't true. But she wasn't going to compromise any details she'd managed to discover about the Great Fortune Trading Company. In much the same way that Chan didn't want to ring the doorbell at Pacific Exotic Motors, she didn't want him, or any other ACE detectives, sniffing around Great Fortune.

She didn't want Bobby Park getting spooked, unless she was the one doing the spooking.

It was now close to five p.m. She stared at the stack of case files lying on her desk. Once again, she didn't have the energy or the motivation to follow up on them. All her other tasks were black and white. There was only one investigation that was in full color.

She didn't want to be bothered with her other cases. The information she'd just received from Detective Chan completely occupied her mind.

She needed time to think. Her stomach grumbled, and she realized she also needed food. Even though it was on the early side, she decided to go home, grab a bite to eat, then spend the rest of the evening reflecting on the Darren Park case.

Just as she reached for her bag, her computer chimed, heralding the arrival of a new e-mail message. A sound that she'd come to loathe.

She struggled against her instincts to read the message, willing herself to push the sleep key on the keyboard and shut down the system. The e-mail message would wait until tomorrow, she argued silently.

But that plan never stood a chance. No self-respecting Type A personality would put the machine to sleep knowing there was an e-mail message to be read.

"Just a quick look," she promised herself in a futile attempt at pacifying her deep desire to go home and rest. "A scan. Nothing more."

As soon as she read the message, any hope of going home for a quiet, relaxing evening was shot. The message was from Darren Park's ex-girlfriend, Rachel. It was short, case insensitive, and to the point:

> *D. Hall,*
>
> *did a little research on Darren's email accounts. found one that I wasn't aware existed. led me to a few emails that hadn't been erased. pretty cryptic stuff -- financial information mostly – wire transfers details etc. Lots of $$$ references. Maybe related to brother bobby?? I think you might want to see these. let me know.*
>
> *Rachel*

*Kaitlin read the e-mail three times and each time its significance became more apparent. Hoping that Rachel was still online, Kaitlin fired back an e-mail as quickly as she could:*

*Rachel,*

*Thank you so much for the message. I am very interested in hearing about what you've found and how you found it. Can you meet me tonight at 7 at Café Sole in the Stanford Shopping Center? It's important that I meet with you asap.*

*Regards, Kaitlin*

She sat back and waited. She considered the significance of the e-mail. Rachel had done quite a bit of homework on Darren. All things considered, Kaitlin wasn't that surprised. She could tell from having spoken with Rachel that she hadn't gotten any closure on her relationship with Darren. How could she have? Things were going great, then she gets dumped with no explanation, and then he dies. If Kaitlin had been in her position, she would've done the same thing. Look for answers. You hope to find something, but if you don't, at least you feel like you did what you could. Then, hopefully, you move on.

But Rachel *had* found something. Perhaps Rachel didn't fully appreciate the significance of it now, but it was something. And Kaitlin suspected that it was something important.

Kaitlin drummed her fingers on the desk, hoping that Rachel was there to receive the e-mail message that she'd just sent. She hit the "Get New Messages" button and waited. "No New Messages" was the reply.

"Come on, come on," Kaitlin urged under her breath. She tapped her feet anxiously on the floor.

Kaitlin hit the "Get New Messages" button again. This time she was rewarded with the "Retrieving One New Message" pop-up onscreen.

"Yes!" Kaitlin softly exclaimed.

It was from Rachel. Her e-mail message read simply, "*see you there.*"

# Chapter 22

Kaitlin sat in the large booth and tapped her foot and looked at her watch – again. She was way beyond being annoyed now. She was worried. Big time.

When Rachel hadn't shown up by seven o'clock, Kaitlin was impatient. After all, what could have kept Rachel? Her office on campus was a five-minute drive, or ten-minute bike ride, to the Stanford Shopping Center. Maybe she had a last-minute appointment with a student or faculty colleague?

By eight o'clock, Kaitlin was perturbed. She began trying to track Rachel down using her cell phone. No luck. There was no answer to the unending ringing in her teaching assistant's office. And when she called her apartment, Rachel's roommates said that they hadn't seen or heard from her since that morning.

By nine-fifteen, Kaitlin was far beyond annoyed, impatient, pissed off. She was seriously concerned. The six glasses of ice tea didn't help her heightened stress level.

"This is ridiculous," she snapped at herself, "here I am sitting at the one place in the Silicon Valley that I know Rachel isn't at." Kaitlin got up, paid the meager bill, pushed in her chair, and walked from the restaurant into the shopping center's foyer. As she approached the glass exit doors, she could see that something was amiss in the parking lot.

"What the…?" she began, walking more quickly.

Flashing red and blue lights cascaded into the foyer. A half-dozen police cars and ambulances were jammed together near the doors to the mall.

"Shit," she said as she sprinted toward the doors. With each stride the sinking feeling in her stomach got deeper.

Fifty yards from the shopping center doors, a paramedic truck and two Palo Alto police cars were parked. Another several police and fire department vehicles were stationed elsewhere in the parking lot. Yellow tape crisscrossed the area and one of the cops was busy shooting pictures of the parking lot. The camera's electronic flash illuminated the parking lot intermittently.

Running to the scene, Kaitlin shouted to the nearest cop, "What happened? What the hell happened here?!"

The bored-looking cop looked up from the chalk-marked asphalt to eye the frantic woman coming right at him.

"Get back, lady," he said.

Kaitlin reached into her bag and pulled out her badge. "What's going on here?"

The cop shrugged. "Hit and run," he answered. "A bad one."

Breathless from her sprint and from a deep inner fear, she came to a stop directly in front of the cop.

"Who was it? *Who was hit?*"

"Female Stanford student," the cop answered. Then he glanced down at his clipboard. "ID'd as Rachel Weinstein."

"No!" Kaitlin cried out.

"You know her?"

"Is she all right?" she demanded. "Where did they take her?"

The cop's expression told Kaitlin everything she needed to know. Still, she wanted to hear the words.

"They took her to the University Medical Center. Not that it would have mattered where they took her. DOA." He paused. "Sorry," he said, as an afterthought.

Kaitlin's shoulders sagged. The color drained from her face. She was too stunned to react.

"Hey, you okay?" he asked, realizing now that he'd been overly detached in his tone.

Kaitlin's emotions were raw. But the cop in her gained control. She focused her thoughts. "Anyone get a look at the car? A license plate?"

"No plates, not even a partial," the cop said, shaking his head. "We have two witnesses that describe a big sport utility vehicle of some sort – Yukon or Suburban – dark in color. That's it," he said.

Kaitlin started to shake, not from grief but from anger. "Goddamn sons of bitches! Those bastards!" she yelled, on the verge of tears.

"Hey, take it easy," the cop said calmly as he gripped her elbow, trying to console her.

Kaitlin shook her arm free. "*You* take it easy!" she snapped, glaring at him. "Those bastards killed her. They killed her because of *me*."

The cop stared at Kaitlin, surprised by her assertion.

"What?"

She'd explain everything later. Right now, she needed to pull herself together and put the pieces together of what had just happened.

She did not believe that Rachel was killed in an "accident." Yes, hit-and-runs were a sad reality of life, but this was no ordinary hit-and-run. Kaitlin knew it. She couldn't calculate the odds of such an accident. The variables were too loaded. Intelligent Stanford grad student getting run down by errant SUV in the local shopping center parking lot on her way to meeting cop investigating ex-boyfriend's death?

"No goddamned way," she sighed.

Kaitlin knew in her gut that whoever killed Darren Park, Dale Cho, Michael Owens and perhaps seven others had now killed Rachel. The difference was that Rachel's death was personal.

It was Kaitlin who had asked Rachel to help with finding more information on Darren. It was Kaitlin who had arranged the meeting to discuss Rachel's findings in detail. Either or both actions likely prompted the killers to murder Rachel.

The other fatalities had only been names on paper, victims she'd had to construct abstractly in her mind based on third party accounts and investigative research. But Rachel was real. She had met Rachel. She'd shaken her hand and seen her tears. She'd taken her measure as a student, as a woman, as someone with feelings, intelligence, and emotions.

Kaitlin identified with Rachel. She too had trudged through Stanford's engineering buildings as a grad student. Kaitlin knew how those halls looked at three in the morning. She knew the dynamic between professor and student.

She *knew* Rachel. Rachel was a human being. And they'd killed her ruthlessly, in cold blood.

A chilling thought struck her. The same people who had killed Darren, who had killed Dale and Michael, who had killed Rachel, were watching and following her. At her home. In the City. And now, here.

# Chapter 23

Kaitlin remained at the scene until the on-site investigation concluded three hours later. The detectives examined hundreds of square yards of the parking lot. The Palo Alto police scoured the area. Searching for personal belongings, collecting hair and fiber samples, examining tire tracks, interviewing anyone who had heard or seen anything out of the ordinary. Anything that could possibly lead them to the vehicle that had taken Rachel Weinstein's life.

They were thorough and professional. They conducted a first-rate on-site investigation. And Kaitlin knew that it wouldn't do any good.

She threw her tired body into the driver's seat and slammed the door. She felt hopeless, helpless and exhausted. Objectively, she couldn't be optimistic about the little evidence that had been found.

"Hardly any physical evidence. No percipient witnesses. Weak vehicle description." She shook her head in disbelief as she headed up El Camino Real.

A professional, she'd concede that much. The killer was an expert at discreet and deliberate homicide. "Now there's something to put on your resumé," she said with bitter irony.

Kaitlin noticed the time on the dashboard clock. It was past midnight, ridiculously late. But there was someone Kaitlin felt compelled to call regardless of the hour.

With one hand on the wheel and quick glances at the roadway, she dug through her backpack's outside pocket, hunting for Bobby Park's business card. A part of her knew that calling this late wasn't professional. A professional call could wait until the morning. After all, nothing was going to change between now and the morning.

But Kaitlin's anger and suspicion got the best of her. She punched in his mobile phone number and brought her cell phone to her ear as it began to ring.

"What the hell am I doing?" she thought as she started to come to her senses. But the ringing stopped and Bobby Park picked up.

"Yeah, this is Bobby ...'"

No going back now. "Mr. Park, this is Detective Hall."

There was a brief pause. "Yes?" he said, sounding surprised.

"I'd like to ask you a couple of questions?"

"This really isn't a good time," he replied.

Kaitlin could hear loud music and conversation in the background.

Emboldened by having made the call, she wasn't about to be dissuaded by Bobby's mild protest.

"It'll only take a minute. Where are you, and where have you been all night?"

Bobby chuckled. "Aren't you supposed to read me my rights or something?"

Kaitlin was not amused. "Is there a need for that?" she asked, wanting to put him on notice.

"Not that I know of."

"Good. See, right now we're just having a conversation on a cell phone, and you're free to answer or not answer. After our conversation, I'll decide whether we need to have you come down to the police station tomorrow morning. And whether I'll have to read you your rights. Got it, Bobby? It *is* okay if I call you Bobby, right?"

"Yeah."

"So, where are you?"

He paused before answering.

Based on the background noise, the music, loud voices, and clinking glass, Kaitlin figured that he was in a crowded bar or restaurant.

"Luxy. It's a Korean nightclub in the City."

"When did you get there?"

"Around eight, I guess."

Kaitlin did some quick calculations. Rachel had been killed a little after seven p.m. It was possible for a person to drive from Palo Alto to the City within an hour. But it would've been a rush.

"Where were you before you went to Luxy?"

"The office. I came here from there."

She waited. She wanted her silence to lure him into thinking that she was going to ask him another question in the same vein but surprise him with a non sequitur. "Why'd you lie to me about Darren's BMW?" she said, throwing a curve ball.

"Huh?"

"You lied to me about Darren's BMW," she stated plainly.

"How do you mean?"

"You told me that he just showed up with it one day. To show it off. You said you didn't know anything about the car."

"Yeah ... that's right," Bobby said. His voice was flat and empty of emotion.

"Damn it, Bobby, I know that Darren bought that car from your car guy at Pacific Exotic Motors in East San Jose. So cut the crap. If you think that you can make the case that he just happened to go to your dealer without your recommendation, it's not going to happen."

There was another lengthy pause before Bobby spoke.

"I don't remember telling him to go there. Maybe he'd heard me mention that place before."

Then he added, somewhat defensively, "And even if he did buy his car there, what's the big deal?"

"Bobby, the big deal is that he was driving that car when he was killed. I think you know what I suspect ..."

"What?"

"I suspect that Darren's death *wasn't* an accident. And I think you know more about it than you're telling me."

"I don't know what you're talking about," Bobby snapped, obviously agitated. "If what happened to Darren wasn't an accident, what was it then?"

"I was hoping you could help answer that," she said.

"If you ask me, maybe he just got sick of his stupid life – and decided to pull the plug!"

That was a reply that Kaitlin wasn't expecting. She thought she'd been thorough in pursuing her suspicions about Darren's death. But now she was thrown for a loop. She'd never even considered that Darren had taken his own life.

It took her a moment to regain her bearings. When she did, her voice was not as forceful. "What makes you say that, Bobby?"

"How the hell should I know? You're the one with the conspiracy theories! From what I can tell, it was a car accident. If it wasn't an accident, then it was suicide. No one else was involved."

Bobby's final statement was delivered with absolute certainty. As if it were fact.

"So you've been asking your own questions about what happened to Darren?" Kaitlin asked.

"Listen, I've got to go. I've answered enough of your questions. I don't know why you're hassling me," he said, really annoyed. "You want anything else from me, arrest me."

"All right, Bobby," she said, easing off, "That's it for now." She felt a bit defeated but wanted to maintain her position of authority. "I'll call you back if I have anything else."

"Take your time," he said sarcastically, hanging up on her.

Kaitlin could tell that Bobby Park didn't like being squeezed by anyone; he had a particular aversion to being squeezed by authority figures. Especially if they were female. Standard machismo bullshit. By this point, Kaitlin had pretty much typecast Bobby as a smug bastard. During the call, she pictured him on the other end of the phone. Sipping Johnny Walker Red in the neon glow of nightclub lights, chain-smoking cigarettes. A pack of well-dressed male friends, all out to meet eligible young women of questionable morals.

Kaitlin had her suspicions but, as always, she tried not to jump to conclusions. She wasn't having an easy time of it. Her instincts told her that Bobby was involved in something crooked. But that could be any number of things. What was Bobby hiding about his brother's death?

"Kaitlin, think!" she implored herself. She was beyond tired; she was exhausted. And her emotional involvement in this case was compromising her critical thinking skills. Add to that her certainty that whoever had killed Rachel was watching her, and it made sense that she was thinking with her heart more than her head. She was only human.

But Kaitlin had never held herself to the low standard of being a mere human. A detective – a *good* detective – had to be better than that. Better mentally. Better physically. And absolutely better emotionally. But at present, Kaitlin wasn't living up to her extremely high standards.

Kaitlin settled her mind and returned her focus to the facts at hand. She carefully parsed what she knew from what she believed. She didn't believe that Bobby was responsible for Darren's death or even that he knew who was. But she did believe that by focusing on Bobby, she could pull enough threads to unravel his little tapestry. Had he believed that Darren's death was truly an accident? Or a suicide? She didn't believe that. Not for a minute.

But then again, the suicide angle had taken her by surprise. It always did. Suicide was something she just didn't get on any level.

Bobby might have concluded that there was no third party involved in Darren's death, but she hadn't. The more she thought about Darren and his lifestyle, the more convinced she was that Darren's death was no accident.

⅄

Kaitlin pulled into her driveway. As exhausted as she was, the thought of sleep was out of the question. Rachel was dead. Her hit-and-run had been planned and professionally executed. But why?

There was only one possible answer. Rachel's cooperation with Kaitlin's investigation had led to her death. Kaitlin felt a painful sadness ripple through her body. But her sadness soon became anger. An intense anger toward someone who had mercilessly run down a bright young woman in a parking lot. The violent impact of the incident reinforced Kaitlin's conviction that the hit-and-run was intentional.

According to the detective at the scene, the collision probably killed Rachel instantly. "Small comfort," Kaitlin thought.

Maybe Rachel's family would find solace in the fact that she didn't suffer.

"Oh, my God," Kaitlin suddenly said, feeling immediate shame at the thought that popped into her head. Rachel Weinstein was no longer a suspect in the death of Darren Park. She'd been absolved, at a terrible cost.

Kaitlin shook her head at her enslavement to her powerfully logical mind. She walked into the dimly-lit kitchen, ruling out coffee given her already heightened state. Instead, she brewed herself a cup of tea. Kaitlin focused on the mechanics of the task, precisely measuring the tea leaves, spooning them into the diffuser, carefully timing how long the tea steeped in hot water, and then finally squeezing in three drops of lemon juice. All this momentarily took her mind off the events of the evening. She walked into the living room and took up her usual, comfortable spot on the sofa, the sweet aroma of the chamomile soothing her jangled nerves. Taking a slow sip of tea, she began to clear her mind and piece together all that had transpired that night.

Step by step, she walked through what had happened. Her goal was to create a compelling narrative that would allow her to move forward with her investigation. She began with the assumption that what happened to Rachel wasn't an accident. That it had been a perfectly synchronized attack. One possibility was that the assailant had waited for Rachel to leave campus in her car, followed her to the Stanford Shopping Center, and then run her down as she walked across the parking lot.

Kaitlin mulled over this first scenario. Yes, it was possible but not probable. It didn't make sense to follow Rachel. If they wanted her dead, why not take care of it on the campus grounds? But if they hadn't followed her, then they would've had to have been at the shopping center waiting for her.

But how could they have already been at the shopping center if they didn't know where Rachel was going?

There seemed to be only one possible answer. Kaitlin considered it as candidly as possible: if they hadn't followed Rachel to the shopping center, then they had followed Kaitlin from the police station. She reflected back on her drive from downtown San Jose to the shopping center on the outskirts of Palo Alto. Perhaps she'd been the intended victim of the SUV's parking lot mayhem.

The possibility that she could have been the target unnerved her. But she forced herself to diligently review her day. She hadn't noticed anyone following her. Even tired, she would have spotted an enormous SUV on her tail. For now, she rejected the possibility they'd been gunning for her.

"Then, what happened?" Kaitlin wondered.

She had boxed herself into an A or B scenario where neither A nor B made sense.

She challenged herself to seek an Option C.

As she considered this question, she pushed past the idea that either of them had been followed. "If the SUV had been waiting in the lot for Rachel to arrive, how would they have known her plans," Kaitlin pondered. She began charting the conversations she'd need to have with Rachel's roommates and university contacts, when she stopped cold.

"The e-mail!" she yelled.

Somehow, some way, they'd intercepted the e-mail exchange between Rachel and Kaitlin that afternoon. But how was that possible?

She grabbed the cordless phone off the coffee table and, with trembling fingers, rapidly dialed Slim's number. The fact that it was the middle of the night was irrelevant. Time did not proceed in a conventional manner for hackers, as Slim verified when he answered the phone with a bright, "Yeah?"

"I didn't wake you, did I?" Kaitlin asked out of polite habit.

"Of course not. I'm awake. I'm in the Dungeon. I had a couple workstations blow up on me ... I'm just now getting them back online. What's going on with you?"

"It's been a bad night, Slim, really bad. Rachel Weinstein is dead."

Slim went silent. Kaitlin had previously mentioned Rachel to him; the fact that she'd been Darren's girlfriend, that she was a Ph.D. candidate on the Farm, and that Kaitlin had felt affinity for her from the moment they'd met. He was the only person who would know that Kaitlin was taking Rachel's death hard.

"I'm ... sorry to hear that Kaitlin. What happened?"

Kaitlin proceeded to fill him in on what had occurred, and on her new suspicion that either Rachel's, or perhaps Kaitlin's, e-mail account had been electronically surveilled. As she'd expected, Slim was in the know with respect to such things.

"It's a possibility," he conceded.

"But how?"

"Lots of different ways. And it's getting easier and easier to do. Hackers have been doing this for a long time, and now the government is getting into the action. Even the Department of Justice is pushing to get legislation enacted that'd legitimize bugging devices on suspects' computers ..."

Slim was a staunch civil libertarian. He had serious concerns when it came to the government's intervention in personal conduct. But this wasn't the time to have him go off on a screed about the government, privacy, and individual liberty. She needed information. She needed to know how someone could have read her e-mail.

"That's interesting Slim, but how is it that they manage to pull messages from the Internet? Through the Internet Service Provider?" she asked.

"They could do it that way … but that's the hard way," he noted with the distaste that a true hacker had for amateurs.

"Okay," Kaitlin said, sitting up straighter on the sofa. "Tell me about the easy way."

⅄

They talked until dawn, took a break, and Slim arrived at Kaitlin's house at seven a.m. This was no small gesture on Slim's part. Techies might have weird hours but they do sleep. Generally during the morning hours. So Slim was not a morning person, and Kaitlin knew he was operating on only two hours of sleep.

She opened the door, after checking first through the peephole –something she usually did haphazardly but now performed with true caution.

"Thanks," she said by way of greeting.

He waved his hand gently through the air, silently following her into the kitchen. He pulled out a chair and sat down at the table, crossing his arms on the tabletop and burying his head in them.

"How about some coffee?" Kaitlin asked, already pouring a prodigious amount of steaming black liquid into a large cup. She placed it in the center of the table.

"How could you tell?" he asked sarcastically, dragging the cup slowly toward himself. As the aroma of the aged Sumatra coffee hit his brain, he immediately began to feel and look more alive than he had when he'd rung the doorbell only a few minutes earlier. With Slim semi-revived, the two of them headed out for their morning activities.

"Which place first?" Slim asked, adjusting the Oakland A's baseball cap on his head and assuming his customary position in the car – slouched low with feet on the dashboard.

Slim explained to Kaitlin earlier that morning that if computer tapping *had* occurred, it had most likely occurred at Rachel's office or Kaitlin's squad room. The former locale seemed more likely, and more palatable to Kaitlin. The thought that her squad room had been infiltrated scared her to death.

"Let's check out Rachel's office first," she answered, turning the key in the ignition and rolling back out of the driveway.

"Kaitlin, remember that there are at least a couple of ways that your e-mail could have been intercepted without leaving any physical or electronic trace," Slim said.

"Yeah, I remember. What was it again that you described, *Van Nuys freaking*?

Slim laughed. "Close, it's called 'Van Eck phreaking'. It's a way of monitoring the electromagnetic waves generated by a computer while in use. They could do that through the window. Very James Bond. But also very unlikely."

"Well, we'll just have to hope they used a more conventional approach," Kaitlin said, her usual optimism barely discernable.

They arrived on the Stanford campus twenty minutes later. The campus police met them in front of the Allen Center for Integrated Systems, as Kaitlin had arranged by cell phone. The two uniformed campus cops escorted them upstairs, unlocked Rachel's office, and agreed to wait outside in the hallway.

"It looks exactly as it did when I met Rachel here," she said, surveying the small office. "Nothing's been moved." The dim space was illuminated in part by the glow of a large computer monitor. Swirling lines danced across a bright purple background, generated by the computer's screen saver program. Kaitlin and Slim both put on latex gloves.

Slim looked down at Rachel's nondescript office computer. "So, let me see what damage I can do," he said in his understated way.

He pulled out the black vinyl office chair and parked himself in front of the computer. He pressed the space bar with his gloved forefinger. Instantly, the swirling lines vanished and a small text box appeared on the monitor, prompting him to enter a password. "The screen-saver is password protected," he said.

"That's just great," Kaitlin said, disappointed.

He gave her a look as if to say, "Do you really believe it's a problem?" Ordinarily, Slim's first action would be to hack the screensaver's password. An easy exercise but potentially time-consuming. A different thought occurred to him.

"This should be interesting," he said as he grabbed the computer keyboard with both hands and raised it to a ninety-degree angle.

"What're you doing?" Kaitlin asked, pulling up a chair and moving as close to Slim as she could in the narrow confines of the office.

"You'll see soon, grasshopper ..."

Deftly, Slim extracted a small black tool case from his flannel shirt's front pocket. He removed a tiny Phillips-head screwdriver and quickly unscrewed the four diminutive chrome-plated screws that held the keyboard assembly together.

"If I'm right about this," he said, speaking mostly to himself, "then it'll be immediately apparent." Using an even tinier flat head screwdriver from his kit, he gently pried the top of the keyboard from its base.

"Well, well, well ... what do we have here?" Slim said contentedly. He carefully examined the base of the keyboard.

Kaitlin stood up, looking over Slim's narrow shoulders, her breath warm on his neck.

"What is that?" she asked rhetorically. "Some sort of a transmitter. And that looks like an antenna," she continued, before he could elaborate.

"Give the detective a Nobel prize," Slim said, nodding his head. "That's *exactly* what it is." He flipped the keyboard over to expose the keys. From his leather case, Slim pulled out a pair of small technician's pliers. Using them, Slim delicately pried up from underneath the keys a thin circuit board that Kaitlin could now see covering the entire face of the molded plastic keyboard.

"This circuit board is able to track each one of the user's key strokes," Slim said, holding it with the pliers in his left hand and pointing at it with his latex-gloved right one. "This lead wire attaches to the wireless transmitter inside the base. Right here, see? That allows someone tuned to the right frequency, within say a half-mile radius, to capture everything typed into this computer."

Kaitlin nodded. "So, on a computer monitor elsewhere, an exact transcription of everything typed here pops up."

"Right," Slim said, "The beauty of this is that even if the sender is using software to encrypt their messages before emailing them, you are getting the original text of their messages as they're being composed. In plain old English."

He carefully laid the keyboard tapping device on the desk.

"This, my friend, is the easy way," he said. And in an appreciative tone in honor of the ingenious device he'd just found, he remarked, "But it's also fabulous." He grinned proudly until he saw the serious look on Kaitlin's face.

His grin immediately evaporated. "Sorry," he said.

She nodded her head slowly. Someone had actively monitored Rachel Weinstein, that was clear.

"There's only one problem, Slim."

"What's that?"

"In my e-mail exchange with Rachel – the one intercepted – *I* was the one who typed the time and place of our meeting. In *my* e-mail. Whoever put this here couldn't have known where she was going by monitoring only her key strokes," Kaitlin said.

A certain degree of alarm showed in Slim's expression. "I see what you're getting at," he said, carefully tucking each of his tools into the little case and back in his pocket. "I guess we need to take a look at your keyboard too, don't we?"

"Yeah. I guess we do," Kaitlin said.

Had she not been bathed in the purple glow of Rachel's happy screen saver, Slim would have seen the color draining from her face.

# Chapter 24

They pulled into the SJPD parking lot at eight a.m. Parking at the far end of the lot, opposite the building, Kaitlin aired her worries.

"Slim," she said, her voice heavy with concern, "if my computer is tapped, it means that someone with access to the building – or even someone inside the department – is involved."

"Yeah," he conceded, already having considered the implications.

"I'm thinking," she went on slowly, "if my computer *is* tapped, we need to use that to our advantage."

"How so?"

"Whoever put it there doesn't know we know."

"Got it," Slim replied. "We need to be stealth. Here, take my screwdriver and pliers," he offered.

"Wait a second … I'd really like you in there with me," Kaitlin said, lacking her usual self-assurance.

"It doesn't make sense; it'll draw too much attention. Besides, you watched me disassemble Rachel's keyboard. It's a no-brainer." He motioned his arm toward the building. "You need to go in there and handle it yourself," Slim said, handing her his miniature toolkit. "I'll wait for you right here."

Kaitlin knew Slim was right. "Okay, I can do this," she said trying to convince herself. "Hell, I did my share of hardware work in the old days."

"Good girl," he said, gently egging her on.

"Here's my cell phone. I'll call you – ."

"No," he cut her off, "if your computer's tapped, it's likely they've got your phones tapped too. Put that thing away."

"Shit," she said, taking in the enormity of the situation.

"Better do this old-school," Slim said with confidence, making up for her shortfall. "If you find anything, just walk yourself back here. We'll go somewhere and think things through."

Kaitlin straightened her shoulders, took a deep breath and nodded agreeably. Slim's composed demeanor had helped her. She unlocked the car door and stepped out of the car.

"Let's hope I don't find anything in there." She gave Slim a weak smile as she shut the car door. She walked toward the ugly gray building without looking back, hoping for the best and preparing for the worst. She disappeared within.

Kaitlin had been fortunate enough to arrive at a time when only a few other detectives, namely Newmeyer, Holland, and Camhi, were in the office. They exchanged the usual morning pleasantries and went about their business. Kaitlin hid her nervousness as she sat down at her desk. She examined everything with fresh eyes, determining whether or not anything on her desk had been tampered with. The red light on her telephone was lit, indicating that she had one or more voice messages to retrieve. She had a strong urge to check her voicemail, but refrained.

Everything looked normal, including the computer keyboard. Kaitlin subtly turned around to make sure that the detectives seated a few desks away wouldn't see what she was about to do. She dismantled her keyboard, but not as quickly as Slim. Of course, he had done it without the fear of being caught in the act by someone else – like his boss. There was little chance that Torres would be strolling in this early in the morning, but Newmeyer, or any other detective, could very easily walk up on her. And she didn't want to deal with questions she couldn't or wouldn't answer.

She removed the final chrome screw and placed it in a tidy pile with the others. Emulating Slim, she pried the back off the keyboard.

And there it was.

Seeing the miniature transmitter, identical to the one they'd found in Rachel's office, Kaitlin became overwhelmed with a strange mix of emotions. She felt validated but also horribly betrayed and scared. Like Rachel, her every keystroke was being monitored.

She looked at the phone. "Was that tapped too?" she wondered. Kaitlin felt a sudden panic to leave. She knew she couldn't stay in this place.

Less than ten minutes after she'd entered, Kaitlin exited the building. Slim watched her cross the parking lot. As she approached her car, Slim knew that the troubled look on her face was bad news.

She hopped into the car and ran her fingers through her hair. He pulled his feet off the dashboard and leaned toward her.

"Well?"

"My keyboard was rigged exactly like Rachel's. I put it back together without damaging the setup, I think."

"Wow," said Slim.

"Yep," Kaitlin replied.

After a moment of joint silence, Kaitlin continued, "A couple of the guys were in, so I couldn't take apart my phone to see if it was tapped. That would've been too obvious." Kaitlin wished she didn't sound as paranoid as she was feeling.

She turned the key in the ignition. "Let's get out of here."

She quickly looked around – checking to see if they were being watched. Her paranoia put Slim on edge. And she knew he didn't like feeling that way. She backed the car rapidly out of the space and sped through the parking lot, glad that driving would keep her mind occupied. She considered asking Slim to drive, thinking it might help him settle down. But her needs prevailed.

The Lumina hurtled down West Mission Street toward the freeway.

⅄

Neither said a word on the entire drive to Slim's Oakland Hills house. Their combined IQ approached three hundred – and every milliamp of brain power they possessed was being utilized to contemplate the implications of what they'd just discovered. And to figure out how the hell to move forward from here.

Slim's best thinking space was his home, not the passenger seat of a car. His first inclination was to head down to the Dungeon and start hacking. But his best thinking happened on his outdoor patio. He looked over at Kaitlin and saw the tight set of her jaw. He believed that the patio would be a good place for Kaitlin too.

They arrived at his house an hour later and found themselves the beneficiaries of one of winter's few sunny days. The air beneath impossibly blue skies was clear, crisp, and invigorating. Wearing a brown wool knit sweater, Kaitlin plopped herself into the wooden deckchair and tilted her head towards the morning sun. She was wearing dark sunglasses and had pulled back her hair, fully revealing her face and neck.

Slim couldn't help thinking how beautiful she looked.

After sitting in silence for several minutes, Slim hesitantly asked, "Shall we get down to business, detective?"

Kaitlin sighed deeply. Reluctantly, she drew herself up into an upright position. She locked her eyes on Slim's. "Yes. I suppose we should," she said softly. "But first, let me call my office. I'm going to call in sick and check my voicemail messages."

"Okay, I'm just going to check on a few things downstairs," Slim said, uncharacteristically excusing himself. He thought she could use a little extra space.

The pleasant electronic voice told Kaitlin that there were two new voicemail messages. The first one caught her off guard. "Jeez," she sighed as she listened to it twice. The first time she wanted to make sure she'd captured every word and nuance. The second time … well, that one was just to hear it again. The message was from FBI Special Agent Renfro:

*"Detective Hall, I was calling to suggest that we meet. I think we should talk – first, about Bobby Park. And, if you like, Federal export controls – and Warren Harriman. Call me on my pager, 408-555-5928. Thanks."*

For the second time that morning, Kaitlin felt a strange mix of emotions. If finding her tapped keyboard hadn't validated her suspicions, Renfro's call certainly did. She also felt surprise, disbelief, and some relief.

But she couldn't shake her paranoia. Was she really on the right track? And given her bugged computer, could she trust Renfro?

Kaitlin was in deep, maybe in over her head. She needed help, but she didn't know whom to trust.

In this swirl of emotions, she advanced the voice mail and listened to her second message. This one was from Newmeyer:

> *"Kaitlin, you bolted out of here this morning before I could talk to you. Where are you? Anyway. Good news on the Comtak case. A bunch of those computer monitors are sitting in a warehouse in Fremont. A disgruntled warehouse employee called it in to the local P.D., and they called me. I want to roll on this. Call me ASAP."*

Kaitlin smiled. "That'll make Torres and his golf buddy, Art Berg, happy," Kaitlin thought, hanging up the phone. But Kaitlin wondered how she could assist Newmeyer, given the current circumstances. Anyway, she was far more intrigued by Renfro's message; she paged him from Slim's landline.

He called less than two minutes later. "It must be serious. No one answers a page that fast," Kaitlin thought.

"Is this a secure line?" he asked.

"Good morning to you, too," she said, hiding her surprise.

"Kaitlin, please. Answer the question."

"Yeah, I guess so," she said. "As secure as anything these days."

"Come again?" he said, quizzically.

"Nothing," she said, unprepared for a conversation about electronic bugging devices that she'd found in her and Rachel Weinstein's offices. She had a feeling there'd be time for that later.

"Well ... thanks for paging me."

"No problem. What's up?"

"About the Darren Park case," he said, very businesslike, "When it comes to his brother Bobby, you're chasing a dead end. But I'd rather not elaborate on the phone. Secure line or not. I'd prefer to have this conversation in person. Can we meet?"

Kaitlin paused. He certainly had grabbed her attention. How could he say so definitively that Bobby Park was a dead end? She looked at her watch and thought about everything she needed to get done. "I'm wrapped up in something right now ..."

But Renfro persisted. "Meet me for a quick lunch. I'll come down your way," he offered. "This is business, Kaitlin."

Kaitlin's curiosity was piqued.

"All right, a quick lunch. But I'm in the East Bay today."

"Even better. How about Jack London Square? Scott's Seafood."

"That'll work for me. Twelve o'clock?"

"I'll see you there, Detective," Renfro said. "And thanks – I think you'll find it worth your while."

"I hope so. Bye," Kaitlin said, hanging up the phone.

She picked up the phone again to return Newmeyer's call, but decided that she had too much on her mind. Comtak's computer monitors could wait a little while. She'd call him later.

Kaitlin walked inside Slim's house and down the narrow steps into the Dungeon. Slim was busy booting up the various computer systems and waiting patiently for her. He wanted her there when he launched the search. Even in its dim lighting, her look of concern was noticeable.

"Everything okay?" he asked.

"Yeah," she answered, unconvincingly. "I just got a call from that FBI agent – Renfro."

Slim's eyebrows arched. "You mean, Mr. Vegas?" Slim teased, knowing about her dalliance at DEF CON.

"Cute," she shot back with a menacing glance meant to hide her embarrassment.

"What did he want?" Slim asked plainly to get back on Kaitlin's good side.

"He says he wants to talk about the Darren Park case. I'm meeting him for lunch at noon."

"I see." Slim thought of the device he'd discovered embedded within Rachel's computer keyboard. It didn't look government grade, but it could've been. There was no way of knowing whether Renfro was a bad actor. He simply didn't know enough facts of the case, or about Renfro. He knew he didn't like him, that was for sure. "I hope he has something interesting to say," Slim said.

"You and me both," Kaitlin said. For a second, she sensed a tinge of jealousy in Slim's voice.

"Noon, huh?" Slim said, nodding his head toward the computer workstation, "Well, that gives us a couple of hours."

"Where do you want to go today?" Slim asked Kaitlin, cribbing one of Microsoft's better marketing slogans.

But Kaitlin had become lost in thought sorting through everything that had happened in the last couple of weeks, especially the last couple of days, including her brief conversation with Renfro.

"I'm sorry. What?"

Slim looked at her curiously. "Where to?"

"Ah," she said, looking into Slim's eyes. "Harriman & Co. I feel like we've barely scratched the surface. I want to know everything there is to know about them. And about our friend Warren Harriman." She vividly remembered Harriman's exact words, *"After all, knowledge is power,"* and took them to heart. And considering his smug tone when he said it, Kaitlin decided to also take it as a personal challenge.

"What about Bobby Park? You want me to run the search we discussed?" Slim asked.

"Um, let's put that one on hold for now," Kaitlin said casually. "I'd rather focus on Harriman."

Slim nodded, accepting the challenge with composure. He crackled his knuckles with a flourish and began typing away.

"How long will this take?" she asked.

Slim shook his head in disbelief at the timeworn question but kept typing. He expected more from Kaitlin. "Depends ... won't know 'til I get there," Slim said with a grin. "That's how I answer that question every time a client asks." He paused for effect. "Even to my *paying* clients," Slim said as he flashed a look at her.

Kaitlin laughed.

"Okay, okay. I'll try to be patient. But you know, in the movies, computer hacking looks quick and easy."

As soon as the words left her mouth, she realized how similar she sounded to Ms. Hammond, the old lady from Los Altos who had critiqued Kaitlin's work performance against *Murder She Wrote*. TV detectives always solved cases in the course of a single episode. And movie hackers always cracked passwords and breached firewalls within minutes.

Kaitlin recognized how naïve she must have sounded to Slim. She knew better. And she knew that Slim knew that she knew better.

Without another word, Kaitlin sat down at one of the other desks in the Dungeon and unpacked her laptop computer.

She'd stay out of Slim's way and make the most of the morning before her lunch with Renfro.

While Slim worked single-mindedly on the Harriman & Co. search, she outlined all the evidence and theories that she'd developed to date. She used a custom computer program that she'd developed for her Berkeley honors project, nicknamed 'Devil.'

Devil was designed to draw on Kaitlin's intellectual strengths and anticipate her weaknesses. She'd written it in such a way that it automatically applied multiple rules of thought to different types of data and displayed the results in a manner that best suited the way her mind worked. In other words, the program served as the quintessential devil's advocate; hence, the name. Devil examined data in ways that Kaitlin wouldn't, then organize and present it in a way most meaningful to her.

Devil was adaptive. As she used the program, it learned more about her thinking and how she arranged complex relationships, continuously improving its feedback. Not only did her creation earn her a computer science degree with high honors, it was awarded special recognition from the National Science Foundation and wrote Kaitlin's ticket to her choice of grad schools. She'd used Devil to her advantage frequently over the years, making Devil smarter and smarter. Kaitlin worried about using it too often because she felt relying on it was actually making *herself* dumber. Like using a calculator to do basic math rather than do it in your head.

Kaitlin was anxious to see how it would respond to everything she knew and believed about the Darren Park case. The project would also keep her occupied while Slim worked feverishly on his research task.

Devil was still processing the data when Kaitlin left at 11:40 a.m. She arrived at Scott's Seafood exactly at noon, knowing nothing more than when she'd hung up the phone with Renfro that morning.

Renfro was already there, waiting for her in a booth overlooking the waterfront.

"Hey. Thanks for agreeing to meet me," he said, standing up and shaking her hand awkwardly. He motioned for her to sit down.

"After all that cloak and dagger stuff on the phone, how could I resist?" she asked rhetorically. Truthfully, Kaitlin didn't think Renfro was a grandstander.

"I'm sorry about that," he said earnestly. "But after you hear what I'm going to tell you, I think you'll understand."

Renfro halted the conversation when the waiter came by to take their orders and when the busboy filled their water glasses.

Renfro leaned in closer. "It's about Darren Park …," he said in a voice inaudible to anyone nearby, "and about his brother, Bobby."

"Yeah, you mentioned that. What about them?"

"I know you suspect that what happened to Darren Park was not an accident, right?"

"Okay ..." Kaitlin answered evenly, unsure where Renfro was going.

"And you think Bobby Park is a suspect. Maybe the leading suspect. Right?"

"Possibly."

"He's not your guy," Renfro said, emotionlessly and unequivocally.

"And how do you know that?" Kaitlin responded, an eyebrow raised.

Renfro paused, as if deciding whether or not to go forward.

"Because he was meeting with me and my team in Marin County the night his brother died." Renfro looked in her eyes unflinchingly.

"*What?*" Kaitlin hissed, caught totally by surprise. "*What are you talking about?*"

"Bobby Park is a federal informant." Renfro paused. He took a big drink of ice water, giving Kaitlin a chance to absorb his news before beginning again. "Shortly after he started running his family business, the Great Fortune Trading Company, Bobby found an easy way to boost profitability."

"And what was that?" Kaitlin asked, still incredulous.

"The company business consisted almost exclusively of importing goods into the U.S. from Asia. After the stuff came into port, they'd unload the shipping containers and send the containers back to Asia – empty. Bobby realized that if he filled those containers with expensive items, like luxury cars, there was a large clientele waiting to receive them back in China. Those clients were willing and ready to pay hard currency."

"So, that's what he was doing with all those empty containers," Kaitlin said, remembering her suspicion when she'd driven past them leaving Great Fortune Trading Company's facility.

"By late last summer, we had a very strong case against Bobby Park. But rather than put him out of commission, we used his operation to collar a bunch of unsavory characters. Most of whom are tied to Asian organized crime."

"Like the people at Pacific Exotic Motors?"

"Exactly."

"Why the hell didn't you tell me this earlier?"

"I'm sorry. I can't emphasize enough how closely guarded this operation is." He looked down at his hands on the table. "Put it this way, remember the guy you spoke with at the Asian Criminal Enterprise task force? Chan? He doesn't even know about this. Our investigation is coming to a head within the next couple of weeks – I couldn't risk it all unraveling. When you started dabbling in the Darren Park case, I figured you'd poke around a bit, not find anything, and move on," Renfro explained.

"But then I started putting the squeeze on Bobby ..."

"Yeah," he said with a mixture of annoyance and respect in his voice. "He almost decided to walk. And when you planted the seed in his mind that what happened to Darren wasn't an accident, he took matters into his own hands."

"What does that mean?" Kaitlin asked nervously.

"Well, the first thing that occurred to him was that he was to blame. That one of his enemies had done it. Or that someone was on to him working with the Feds. He had his people hit the street trying to find out what really happened to Darren."

"I can't believe that ..." Kaitlin said, stunned that she'd been so wrong about Bobby.

"And that's not all ..."

"There's more?" she said aghast. "You're joking."

Renfro smiled apprehensively. "You aren't going to like this. But Bobby Park put a tail on you."

Kaitlin was silent. That silence was opportune as the waiter returned and placed large plates of broiled salmon and steamed vegetables in front of her and Renfro.

The waiter departed, and Kaitlin began stabbing at the piece of fish with her fork.

"He had someone tailing *me*?" she whispered, her eyes narrowing.

"Yes. Former Yakuza … a big Japanese mob guy. Drives a large Mercedes sedan."

"I know the guy," Kaitlin said, nodding her head. "He was following me while I was out jogging. And I caught him waiting for me in the parking lot in the Embarcadero. I almost took a shot at that guy! *Jesus.*"

"I talked to Bobby," Renfro said, apologetically. "He was only trying to find out what you knew. That guy had no intention of hurting you."

"Oh, that's reassuring," Kaitlin said sarcastically.

She'd already drawn several conclusions about her unknown stalker and Rachel's murder. Now with this new information, she tried erasing him from the picture she'd drawn.

"Would this Yakuza guy have entered my house? Or Darren Park's apartment?" Kaitlin asked.

Renfro thought about it for a minute. "No, I don't think so. According to Bobby, he was under strict orders not to have any direct contact with you. And I don't see why he'd enter

Darren's apartment. He was just supposed to follow you. See who you met with, where you went, that sort of thing."

Kaitlin wanted to know who had been breaking and entering into her business. "Well then, can you do me a favor?" she asked.

"Sure, what?"

"Have some of your counter-surveillance people check out my house. I had a break in, and I think my place might be bugged. I thought maybe it was the big guy in the black Mercedes. But now ..."

Renfro's eyes narrowed. He was going to say something about the break-in but decided to move forward. For now.

"No problem. It'll get done today," Renfro answered, pulling a notepad from his shirt pocket and scribbling a reminder. His handwriting was so poor it barely looked like English, Kaitlin thought. She was an expert at reading upside down, but this was beyond her talent.

As Renfro jotted down his note, Kaitlin considered her case and the obvious turn in direction.

"On your voicemail message, you mentioned Warren Harriman and export controls. Can you elaborate?" Kaitlin asked.

Renfro looked sheepish. "Well, not really. I just wanted to make sure you'd come meet me. I had a feeling mentioning that stuff would help."

Kaitlin smiled. While she didn't like being manipulated, she had to appreciate Renfro's ingenuity. But all that aside, she still had questions.

"Well, be that as it may, I'm still interested in exploring those topics," Kaitlin said. "Now that you've vindicated Bobby

Park from Darren's death, are you open to hearing an alternative theory?"

"What? Your Warren Harriman angle? Torres told me about that," Renfro said, dismissing her theory out of hand. "Come on Kaitlin, you don't really have anything supporting that theory, do you?"

Now she was annoyed. But she didn't feel like defending her theory to Renfro.

"I do. And within the next day or so I'll have more. Maybe I'll fill you in someday."

The busboy dutifully cleared the plates and she looked at her watch. It was one p.m., and she hoped by now that Slim had succeeded hacking into one of Harriman & Co.'s network servers. She was anxious to get back.

"Anyway, Alex, thanks for lunch. And thanks for the information on Bobby Park."

Before he could respond, she was already standing.

"I've got to run," she said, looking off in the direction of the restaurant's entrance.

"Listen," he said, "Torres really likes you. He thinks you're a good detective. Don't blow it by chasing a wild goose – especially one named Warren Harriman."

"Thanks for the advice, Alex," Kaitlin said condescendingly, "I'll see you around."

She'd heard enough out of Special Agent Renfro. And from what she'd just learned about Bobby Park, she was convinced more than ever that Warren Harriman was tied to Darren Park's death.

# Chapter 25

Slim was still in the Dungeon working away. Like most techies, he didn't feel the passage of time in a normal manner. He could sit in front of his monitor for hours on end without eating or drinking. Even amongst techies Slim's feats of endurance were legendary. His focus and intensity were awe-inspiring.

"How's it going?" Kaitlin asked pleasantly, not wanting to sound like a pest. "I picked you up a sandwich," she said, placing a brown paper bag on the desk.

"Thanks," he said, spotting the sandwich out of the corner of his eye. "I think we're almost there. Just a little patience, please!"

He was wearing headphones and couldn't hear a word she was saying.

He was obviously in a groove, and Kaitlin didn't want to disturb him. She was eager to fill him in on what Renfro had revealed, but she'd wait until he was ready.

A little less than an hour had passed when Slim stood from his chair and yanked off the headphones, blasting Metallica into the room.

Slim exclaimed breathlessly, "I've gotten past the front door!"

Kaitlin gave him a big high five. The "front door" was Harriman & Co.'s primary external security points. From here, he was free to explore its network's substructure, subject only to any internal security protocols. Usually, such protocols were far weaker than external security points. And Slim had easily gotten past those.

"That's fantastic!" Kaitlin exclaimed as she put her arm around his shoulder. "Next time, we'll have to find something a little more challenging for you ..."

"Don't let me fool you. It was challenging enough. But it's incredible how sophisticated companies protect such valuable information so poorly. All I had to do was blast their server with thousands of password attempts. I used a special password generator that can be downloaded for free off the Internet – thank you, Nomad Mobile Research Centre. Eventually it hit the right password, and I was in. Not an elegant hack – certainly one I wouldn't admit using to my friends."

Kaitlin smiled, she knew the friends that Slim was referring to. She was well aware of the hacker code of ethics and the huge egos in that community. They used lock picks, not sledge hammers and explosives to do their "work."

"Not the worst security system I've seen, but it's second-rate at best," Slim offered authoritatively.

"Okay, now that we're in," Kaitlin replied, "Let's look deeply through their financials. Like the stuff we found earlier on the portfolio companies. The info that isn't publicly available."

Slim looked concerned.

"What is it?" Kaitlin asked.

"Just wanted to make sure you know that whatever we find here won't be making any court appearances. You don't have a warrant, remember."

Kaitlin nodded. "Yeah, I remember. In a perfect world, I'd have a warrant and free reign to use whatever we discover. But in this world, my Captain doesn't believe I have a case and a judge wouldn't either."

"So, you still want to do this?" asked Slim.

She thought hard before answering; she'd excelled at constitutional law at the police academy and knew there were definitely right answers and wrong answers.

"Right now it's something of an archaeological expedition. We need to keep digging. Even if the information is inadmissible, it'll point me in the general direction and ensure that I'm not chasing a dead end. Ultimately, I'll be able to develop a case against Harriman without relying directly on what we find. I'm counting on that."

Slim shrugged. "You're the cop. Personally, I've never needed a warrant for any of my purposes," he said and smiled at Kaitlin reassuringly.

They sat down and began plumbing the depths of Harriman & Co.'s electronic data.

Five hours later, Kaitlin stood up from the computer. She raised her arms behind her head and arched her back, which emitted a loud crack.

"Ow," said Slim. "That didn't sound good."

"It didn't feel particularly good. Come on, let's get some air and go over what we've pulled. Besides, I still haven't told you about what happened at lunch," Kaitlin said, gently tugging Slim's t-shirt and pulling him out of the Dungeon and up to the patio.

Kaitlin swore Slim to secrecy before recounting what Renfro confessed about Bobby Park and the man that'd been following her.

"Very cool," Slim said with a grin, "being followed by Yakuza. Those guys are *bad ass*."

Kaitlin failed to see the coolness.

But both she and Slim were relieved to know that she would no longer be followed. With this common knowledge between them, they went over the work of the previous several hours. In that time, they had discovered a multitude of data points that supported their suspicions against Harriman & Co. Among other things, they'd successfully tapped into Harriman & Co.'s private internal telephone system – the PBX – that connected all of the individual phone systems to the public phone system. Through the PBX, they constructed a comprehensive employee list, as well as a record of the phone calls made by each Harriman & Co. employee.

"I think I'm closer to a strong motive," said Kaitlin.

Slim understood what she meant without further elaboration. The financial information they'd garnered about

Harriman & Co. showed a surprising yet unmistakable decline. Warren Harriman had built his reputation by investing in companies that had explosive growth during the tech boom, but his firm had been hit hard by the recession. Harriman & Co. was also burdened with several large lemons, companies with interesting technology concepts but no commercial potential. On paper, Harriman & Co.'s portfolio had lost more than half of its value.

Despite the massive downturn in his company's investment portfolio, Warren Harriman had personally achieved more wealth. He had gone to great lengths to keep this wealth hidden, but Slim's artistry brought those secrets into the light of day. A chain of numbered Swiss and Caribbean bank accounts all led back to Warren Harriman and his family. His wealth had doubled while his company's was halved. There were no clues as to other legitimate sources of income: no family inheritance, no big real estate transactions, and no huge stock sales.

Harriman & Co.'s current portfolio included substantial ownership interests in about twenty-five high-tech companies, most of which were located in the Silicon Valley. It included all nine companies that Slim previously identified as having lost employees over the past two years.

One thing in particular nagged at Kaitlin. It tied back to Devil's suggestions. She stared intently at Slim and asked, "If you factor in U.S. export controls, about half the portfolio companies operate under heavy restrictions. If you focus only on those companies, you find that they've been the biggest losers in the portfolio. The other ones have managed to keep their heads above water, even during the downturn, right?"

"Yeah ..." Slim agreed, recalling the Excel spreadsheets they'd examined in the file directory belonging to Harriman & Co.'s chief financial officer. Those records confirmed that the portfolio had lost close to eight hundred million dollars in value. During the same period, Warren Harriman had accumulated close to forty million in offshore accounts, and possibly more in accounts and investment vehicles yet to be discovered.

Kaitlin constructed a theory by connecting several dots churned out by Spock. Harriman was an active political donor, and Harriman & Co. was one of the few West Coast venture capital firms that retained the services of a white-shoe lobbyist in D.C. Not just any lobbyist, but Sid Alexander of the Blacktower Group. Although his name was unfamiliar to the vast majority of Americans, Sid Alexander carried more influence in Congress than half of its members – combined. His specialty was persuading the Pentagon to back big bets like multi-billion dollar jet fighter projects, "encouraging" the Department of Commerce to expand tariffs on foreign competitors, and other helpful decisions that directly benefitted his clients.

Kaitlin slowly and deliberately presented her theory to Slim: "So Harriman & Co. invests in companies with hot technology, even though they are tightly restricted from competing in global markets, and then hires Blacktower Group to lobby Washington to lift those restrictions. If Washington eases export laws, they win. If they don't, they lose."

Slim wasn't familiar with the world of D.C. lobbyists like Blacktower, but he knew well what little progress had been made in terms of liberalizing the export laws.

"Do you know that when they came out last year, the latest video games weren't lawful for export because the processors they used were too powerful?" Slim asked rhetorically. "Kaitlin, the Feds have made little progress updating those laws from the 20th Century."

"Right," she said, "Harriman gambled that the export laws would loosen or go away. But he was wrong, and his investment portfolio has suffered. So, what does he do? He exports the technology under the table. He funnels some of the proceeds back into the companies. And stashes the rest of it, most of it, into his personal offshore accounts."

"Possible. It sounds a little too tidy for me, Detective," Slim said with his characteristic cynicism. "If Harriman's pocketing most of the cash, the portfolio companies don't really stand to gain. And how would he get legitimate companies to participate in this?"

"He doesn't."

"Then, how – "

Kaitlin interjected, "I bet the management of these companies has no idea what's going on. Harriman chooses lesser-paid, non-management level employees who have access to the technology. He chooses them because they're easily manipulated. And they're hungry to cash in."

"Like Sys Admins," Slim concluded.

"Like Sys Admins," echoed Kaitlin.

"But why kill them?" Slim asked, thinking of the long list of fatalities connected to Harriman's portfolio.

Kaitlin stopped to consider the man she'd met. His cold blue eyes. His piercing look. Italian designer suit. She recalled the news articles she'd read. He had a reputation for being smart, and for being aggressive. Warren Harriman didn't get where he was by being a pushover.

"No loose ends," she said flatly.

Kaitlin continued, "He chose his operatives in the various companies because they were easily manipulated. But that same characteristic also made them liabilities. Think about it. Everything we found on the Harriman & Co. network offers only circumstantial evidence about what we suspect. No direct evidence."

Slim nodded in agreement.

Kaitlin was on a roll. "I have a feeling that Harriman lives his life without a trace. And without witnesses."

"Dead men tell no tales," Slim intoned gravely.

Kaitlin walked over to the deck's wooden railing. A dozen or more sailboats bobbed in the distant San Francisco Bay. Every few seconds, the lighthouse on Alcatraz pulsed out light through the thin blanket of fog that had crept over the rocky little island.

She turned toward Slim, resting her back on the railing, and spoke, "So, let's find out who's lined up as the next dead man."

# Chapter 26

Working quickly, Kaitlin and Slim defined a strategy for the next, crucial phase of the investigation. In silence and with efficiency they spent the better part of the afternoon on the deck, each working independently on laptop computers that were wired to Slim's home network via Ethernet, their thick blue cables snaking out from the patio door. Slim would have preferred working in the basement, but Kaitlin had vetoed that. There was only so much time Kaitlin could tolerate being locked in the Dungeon. She much preferred it out here.

After several hours Slim stood up, without explanation or apology, and engaged in a brief tai chi chuan session on the deck. Such sessions were part of his daily ritual. As much as Kaitlin needed Slim's expertise and friendship, she was sensitive to the intrusion she was making on his life. She was glad that her presence didn't disrupt his ritual. Just watching him relaxed her. He moved gracefully in a subtle display of body coordination, balance, and strength. He finished his routine and sat down cross-legged on the deck. After a few minutes of quiet meditation, he raised himself, sauntered over to the table, and took his seat.

"That was rejuvenating," Kaitlin said quietly, looking down at her computer screen with a wistful smile on her face.

"Tai chi isn't generally a spectator sport," he said lightly. "You should try it sometime." He gave her a quick wink and resumed work on his computer.

Kaitlin was too Type A for something so soothing, and Slim knew it.

Kaitlin returned her focus and efforts on analyzing the list of portfolio companies. She placed twelve of Harriman & Co.'s portfolio companies as the most likely targets for illegal technology transfer. The previous week, she'd briefed herself on the nine companies within that group that had lost employees through untimely accidental deaths. Today her goal was to learn as much as possible about the other five technology companies that were subject to tight export controls. Those companies had yet to lose any employees.

"Just a matter of time," she thought, with a mix of anticipation and regret. Kaitlin believed that if they existed, Harriman's inside pawns would still be operative. In order to focus her attention using some semblance of logic, she presumed that the less profitable the company, the more likely Harriman was seeking an illegal return from it.

Kaitlin studied the information on these five companies over and over. They specialized in encryption algorithms, integrated circuits, communications signaling and scanning equipment, high-energy batteries, digital video recorders, and lasers – a veritable cornucopia of technologies that the U.S. government tried fiercely to control from export. Black market sales of any of this technology would bring Warren Harriman tens of millions of dollars, dollars he might be desperate to recoup after a financial nosedive.

"LightWave Design," Kaitlin said out loud, breaking a long silence.

"Huh?" Slim replied, not lifting his head from his work.

"LightWave Design. Based in Milpitas. They develop design lasers. Cutting-edge stuff." She raised her eyes and smiled. "No pun intended."

"Lasers, huh? What did the PBX report give us on them?"

Kaitlin leaned to her left and flipped through the two-hundred-page printout that had been generated when Slim remotely activated Harriman & Co.'s PBX phone system diagnostic program.

"Lots of calls to them in the last few months. Particularly from one phone extension. Extension 2157."

"Well then," Slim said in a professorial tone, "why don't we check out who belongs to extension 2157?" Slim pulled up the PBX system's user log on his computer. "The log shows the extension belonging to one 's-calloway'." He shrugged his shoulders apologetically. "It doesn't give full names."

Kaitlin was already ahead of him. She'd pulled up Harriman & Co.'s corporate web site and clicked on the page with biographical information on each company executive.

"Calloway … Calloway …" she said softly as she scrolled down. If 's-calloway' were someone other than a member of the company's administrative staff, he or she would be described. She scrolled down to the C's in the bio page and found what she was looking for. "Shane Calloway." As she said it, she had an inexplicable feeling of déjà vu. "Shane, Shane, Shane ..." she repeated quietly to herself. "*SHANE!*" she shouted.

"Hey! What is it? Who is he?" Slim sputtered.

"Slim, Shane was one of the names in Darren Park's Palm Pilot calendar. Someone he was having regular meetings or calls or something with every couple of weeks."

"What does his bio say?" Slim asked.

Kaitlin read out loud from the web page:

> *Shane Calloway, 42, U.S.M.C. Lieutenant Col., ret., joined the firm as an associate in 1996. His background as an electronics engineer, with an emphasis in satellite and guidance systems, and over twenty years of armed forces experience, brings real-world expertise to Harriman & Co. and its portfolio companies, particularly in civilian and military global sales and marketing.*

"Jesus," Slim whistled.

"Jesus, is right," she said. "I'd bet you fifty bucks that Calloway is Harriman's resident spook. This guy definitely has the wherewithal to offload the technology. And I wouldn't be a bit surprised if he also supplies the muscle."

With an involuntary shudder, Kaitlin wondered whether it was Calloway himself who'd run down Rachel Weinstein as she walked across the shopping center parking lot.

"Slim, let's have Spock do a search on Shane Calloway. I want to know everything, especially about his military tenure. And maybe take a peek inside LightWave's computer network too?"

He gave Kaitlin another knowing look and shook his head, signaling his continued concern about the 4th Amendment and fruits of an illegal search being inadmissible in court. She remained silent, holding eye contact with Slim. He knew her silence gave him the green light.

"No problem, but to do that, I'd prefer to log in on a different system from downstairs," Slim said as he rose from the patio table.

Kaitlin watched Slim slowly descend into the darkness of the Dungeon and disappear.

For the next hour, Kaitlin worked outside until the sun faded below the horizon. It had been an incredibly productive day. She knew tomorrow would demand at least as much from both her and Slim. She anticipated that the pace would pick up. Along with the danger.

⅄

The following morning, Kaitlin woke up unusually early, as one does when sleeping in an unfamiliar place. She poured several spoonfuls of ground French Roast into the coffee maker, turned it on, and walked downstairs to the Dungeon while it brewed. Sometime late last night, after she and Slim had eaten pizza, watched a movie, and gone to sleep, Spock had returned the search results on Shane Calloway. A mountain of paper sat in front of the printer, all two hundred plus pages. She began thumbing through the stack as she headed up the steps to the kitchen.

Calloway's bio and picture were at the top of the heap. From a digitized photo taken during his Marine Corps days, Shane Calloway had the appearance of a tough-as-nails military officer. Squared-jawed. Salt-and-pepper hair closely cropped. He looked a little like Sergeant Carter from the Gomer Pyle TV show. Kaitlin smiled despite herself. But then she remembered that Calloway had likely been involved in killing any number of real people – civilians. She dropped his photo onto the table and delved into the stack of information.

Calloway had attended M.I.T. on a full ROTC scholarship. Most of his military career was during peacetime. Not that everyone regarded peace similarly. The time between the Vietnam War and the Gulf War rankled military die-hards. Instead of taking pride in serving their country they'd been forced to justify their existence and reduce their budgets. It was a time when large conventional armed forces looked less and less necessary. Especially when political poseurs demanded those dollars be spent on social programs and infrastructure.

Calloway was a dyed-in-the-wool military man. And real military men liked paying their dues out in the trenches, putting their skills to the test, fighting for their country, for freedom.

Men like Calloway embraced the Gulf War. A soldier without a war is not a soldier.

Calloway's military record was spotless. With his ROTC training, he'd entered the Marines with the rank of Captain. He soon had command of an elite force of infantry/special tactics troops that specialized in infiltrating and disabling command and control centers. At the time, that was as high-tech as the USMC got.

Calloway and his men were trained in every method of disrupting the enemy's military communications. From remote electronic jamming to the more conventional means like blowing up the enemy's radio transmitter.

As she pored through Calloway's history, Kaitlin was conscious of the brilliance of modern technology. Spock's prowess amazed her. Overnight, it had assembled an incredible amount of information on Calloway's Gulf War exploits. As a military history buff, she found herself intrigued by one of Calloway's missions. She'd watched enough *History Channel* documentaries to get a good flavor for what had gone on behind the scenes in Iraq.

On the ground early in theatre, Calloway had been supplied with a military goal, a suitcase full of cash, and CIA operatives in the region. His immediate goal had been to recruit Iraqis. Specifically, members of Saddam Hussein's "elite" Republican Guard. Men trusted by Hussein's regime. Men with reliable and immediate access to vital information and key facilities central to the Iraqi war machine. The pay was higher for a turned loyalist, more than the typical Iraqi infantryman, but they were far more valuable. The U.S. dollar was strong. And Calloway had no reservations spending lots of it in order to buy the cooperation that he and his men needed. Twice decorated, his efforts had contributed to the victory and to his own promotion.

It was an immaculate narrative, one that Kaitlin knew left out the unthinkable and unspeakable acts that often accompanied the pursuit of high-value targets and covert operations in a high-stakes war.

As she read through the pages, Kaitlin realized that the role she suspected Calloway of playing at Harriman & Company was entirely consistent with his military experience and training. A chill ran through her body.

Calloway was a dangerous man. He was getting paid handsomely. And he made sure everyone knew it. The research showed that he lived in San Francisco's tony Nob Hill. He leased two very expensive cars, a 1999 Range Rover and a 2000 BMW Seven Series. This was a lifestyle that could not be maintained on a military pension. And if that wasn't enough to suggest motive, Kaitlin now realized that Calloway was a soldier in search of a war.

Kaitlin wondered if there was a more dangerous creature on the face of the earth.

# Chapter 27

An hour or so after she'd brewed the coffee and began studying Calloway's file, Slim slowly made his way downstairs from his bedroom, pausing to yawn at each of the last couple of steps.

"How'd you sleep?" he asked her.

"Like a rock," she said. She rested the pile of papers on the table. "But not long enough. How about you?"

"Not bad." He breathed in deeply through his nostrils. "You found the coffee."

"You know me, I'm a divining rod when it comes to coffee," she said. "You want some?"

He shook his head. "No thanks, not yet. I think I'll just have some OJ. As for you, I'm not sure why you don't just inject it."

Kaitlin laughed. Slim knew that she'd been a coffee addict since college. Not a bad vice as far as vices go. Slim figured he'd wait until she was older and got the shakes before convincing her to cut down.

Slim pulled out a box of corn flakes, milk, bowls, and spoons and sat down at the table. He dipped his spoon into the bowl of cereal and looked up at Kaitlin. She had borrowed his pajamas the night before, and she was still wearing them. Even in the morning, having just rolled out of bed, she was strikingly beautiful. He was on the verge of complimenting her, but stopped himself. Instead he said, "Nice PJs."

She smiled. "Thanks."

He nodded at the neat piles of paper spanning the length of his kitchen table. "What have we here?" he asked.

"We have the fruits of Spock's labor. I must say, he delivered quite a work-up on Shane Calloway. You ready to hear about it?"

He held his hand up to stop her. Then he spooned a large spoon of corn flakes into his mouth. He chewed them considerately and then swallowed. He sipped some orange juice and smiled. "I'm ready now."

Kaitlin gave him an overview of Calloway's military record, and she explained her theories on what Calloway was doing for Harriman & Co. and why someone at LightWave Design would likely be his next pawn.

Based on the information Kaitlin gleaned from the Harriman & Co. PBX phone system, the numerous calls from s-calloway to LightWave Design piqued her interest. The company was located in the southernmost part of the Peninsula in Milpitas, the self-proclaimed "Gateway to Silicon Valley." To those developing silicon-based chips and circuits, LightWave held the key to that gateway.

Silicon Valley's high-tech industry had suffered economically, but strategically it was more important than ever. Companies and technologies that could meet that global strategic need would survive the economic downturn successfully. With investment capital drying up, everyone was more willing to go to extreme measures to gain competitive advantage.

Development of silicon microchips demands sophisticated equipment. Particularly the equipment necessary to etch complicated circuit designs, measuring mere micrometers in size, onto silicon wafers. And the U.S. was the leading developer of circuit design equipment.

Such information was well-known to both Slim and Kaitlin. It was the white noise of everything that happened in high tech. She quickly briefed Slim. "LightWave was founded only two years ago and has already developed extremely sophisticated laser design equipment. With LightWave's technology, microchips can be made to hold greater amounts of data and achieve faster processing speeds, making computers and networks significantly more powerful."

"Making Pentium chips look like Model Ts," Slim interjected.

"Right," Kaitlin said. "Huge business potential. But, due to the recession, LightWave's financial statements are bleeding red. The money they'd been counting on is drying up; every quarter their losses grow larger."

"I don't get it. Why wouldn't chip companies be salivating for their products? Weak economy or not, the world runs on silicon now," Slim observed.

"Big microchip companies like Intel and AMD, all of which are U.S. based, have a vested interest in selling chips they've already developed for as long as possible," Kaitlin explained. "As soon as they announce a new chip, the price of the old one drops. There's a calculated pace to how quickly, or rather how slowly, they release faster chips. I'm sure a foreign microchip manufacturer would hop on a faster chip design."

"Which is probably the *real* reason why export controls prohibit LightWave's technology from leaving the country. Damn protectionist government," Slim stated bluntly.

Kaitlin smiled. Slim always called a spade a spade. "I think the term is 'national security'," Kaitlin said with a laugh. "But if LightWave were free to sell globally, their financial picture would look a lot brighter. That's where Shane Calloway comes in. I think he's delivering Harriman a good return on his investment. Export controls be damned."

⅄

Kaitlin recalled Calloway's corporate bio and his '*real-world*' expertise. She worried how that expertise was being applied to one or more LightWave employees, and which one was in peril at this very moment.

The downloaded call record, when charted in a graphical format against a calendar, revealed a fascinating pattern of calls by Calloway to Entrex, Synergy Secure Computing, and each of the other Harriman & Co. portfolio companies whose employees had died. In each case, Calloway's call volume to the portfolio company peaked shortly before the employee's death and dropped off dramatically following the death.

"My God," Kaitlin sighed, studying the graphic analysis. Another intriguing theory in the case supported only by statistics and the creative application of logic. Digesting the disturbing correlation between Calloway's call volume and the deaths, Kaitlin whispered unconsciously, *"It's as easy to learn as your A-B-C . . ."*

"What's that?" Slim asked, his eyes still on his computer monitor.

*"Murder by numbers, 1-2-3 . . ."* she sang out loud. Then she smiled, hoping he wouldn't think she'd lost her mind. "It's a song, Slim. This pattern must have made me think of it ..."

Slim silently nodded.

It was an interesting pattern. Unfortunately, the PBX database from Harriman & Co. didn't show who Calloway was calling. Only that calls were made by him to the portfolio companies' main corporate phone number.

As difficult as the objective might be, Kaitlin realized that she was determined to stop Calloway before anyone else wound up dead. She wanted to protect the next victim. She also wanted to avenge the ones who had already been killed. And to do that, she would have to get Warren Harriman. Harriman was the real menace. Calloway was merely a tool. A frighteningly effective tool, but a tool nonetheless.

After a long silence, Kaitlin said, "We need to employ some low-tech means to figure out who Calloway is working with at LightWave."

Slim, now seated at the opposite end of his kitchen table reading through a stack on Calloway, looked up at her.

"Low-tech?" he asked, as if the term wasn't self-explanatory. "What do you have in mind?" asked Slim, his curiosity spurred. He was a techie. So he was as intrigued by a low-tech solution as he was by this beautiful young woman wearing his pajamas.

"We don't have nearly enough information on LightWave," Kaitlin said. "It's a small, privately-held company that doesn't even have much of a web site. We've struck out in trying to hack their network, right?"

"So far ..." Slim conceded begrudgingly.

"I suspect a little white lie will succeed where computers, algorithms, and brilliant hackers have 'so far' failed," she said. She picked up the cordless phone and started dialing.

"Ah," Slim sighed, beginning to understand.

"Watch this," she said, with a gleam in her eyes. Slim folded his arms and leaned back in his chair.

"Good morning, LightWave Design," the receptionist greeted politely over the phone.

Kaitlin's usual morning voice was replaced with an exaggerated silky smooth purr. "Yes, good morning. This is Paloma from Harriman & Co. in San Francisco."

Slim gave Kaitlin a quizzical look and silently mouthed, "*Paloma?*" He shook his head in disbelief.

"We've had a bit of a computer glitch here, and I'm trying to put Mr. Harriman's contact list back together. I hate to impose on you, but would you be able to help me out for a few minutes? I just need to confirm some names and phone extensions at LightWave."

The receptionist answered with just a hint of hesitation. "Umm, sure. Just let me answer this call coming in on the other line." The line went silent.

Kaitlin hoped the receptionist would buy her story without questioning it. For a few, heart-stopping seconds, she hoped that the receptionist was not on the other line informing her boss that she'd just received a strange call asking for confidential employee information.

Soon the line came back to life. The receptionist sounded cheerful and happy to help. "Thank you for holding. What can I get for you?"

"Well, I have the number for Mr. Chambers and Ms. Wong. But because of the system crash, I don't see a number for Bob Thornton or Victor Simons," said Kaitlin, beginning her bluff. She had simply recited the names of LightWave's President and their Chief Financial Officer that she'd found on LightWave's site.

The receptionist was oblivious to Kaitlin's ruse and answered efficiently: "Bob is at 2107 and, let me see, Victor is at 4116. Anything else?"

"Yes, come to think of it. Mr. Calloway had the same problem with his computer. And his assistant isn't the type to pick up the phone and actually do anything about it. You know what I mean?" Kaitlin said cattily.

"Oh yeah, I know *exactly* what you mean," the receptionist sympathized.

"Do you happen to know what extensions Shane would need?" There it was: the question on which Kaitlin's charade and some techie's life potentially hinged. Slim watched Kaitlin bite her lower lip.

"Oh, he always calls for Gary Tyler, our IT Manager. He's at extension 5100."

"Great. Thank you so much for your help."

"No problem. You have yourself a great day, Paloma."

"You too!" Kaitlin said exuberantly. After all, the day was just starting, and it already had all the earmarks of being great.

# Chapter 28

As she made progress in her investigation, Kaitlin knew she had to cover herself if she was ever going to see it through to its conclusion. She still hadn't responded to Newmeyer's days-old voicemail message. If she didn't call him now, she would have to face Torres' wrath. Considering the potential fallout of targeting Warren Harriman, closing the Comtak theft case would earn back some much-needed points.

"Hey Newmeyer, it's me," Kaitlin said. "Sorry it took so long getting back to you."

"Where have you been? Are you all right?" he asked, concerned.

"I'm fine. I've just been mired in this case – "

"Not *that* again?" he cut her off.

"Yeah, that again. Anyway, what's the word on those computer monitors?"

She knew that Newmeyer had a hard time being pissed off at her. He liked her too much, so Kaitlin managed to get away with pulling crap. She'd learned more than technology as a computer student.

As she expected, Newmeyer cooled down quickly and his mind turned back to Comtak. "The word is that the bust is about an hour away from going down."

"What? How'd you line that up so quickly?" Kaitlin said, impressed.

"I didn't. It's Fremont P.D.'s bust," Newmeyer said dejectedly. "The guy who blabbed about the stolen computer equipment put the finger on another guy working in the warehouse. He's an ex-con wanted in connection with a double homicide outside a Fremont pub. They're going in after him. And we, assuming you can fit it into your schedule, are simply going along for the ride."

She smiled, seductively responding, "For you Rob, I can certainly fit it in. I'll meet you at the Fremont station in a half hour. Oh, and I need to give you a different cell phone number in case you need to reach me."

"What happened to your cell phone?" he asked.

"It's a long story. But here's the new number ..." she said as she rattled it off, looking down at the little yellow LED screen on Slim's borrowed cell phone. After she'd found the computer tapped in her office, she'd ditched her old cell phone thinking that it too may have been compromised. She now knew the level of people she was playing with and wasn't interested in taking any chances going forward.

"Okay, see you in Fremont."

"Thanks, Rob. And I really am sorry about being flakey lately. Trust me, I have a good reason."

He didn't reply. She could picture him floundering for words. He was worried about her, and he didn't want to see her screw up her career. But he wasn't in a position to influence her decisions. She was simply too headstrong.

"Whatever you say, Detective," he said. "Just don't keep crossing the line with Torres ... that would be a *big* mistake."

"Yeah, I know," she said sincerely. "Thanks again. I owe you."

Throughout life, Kaitlin was always known as a do-gooder. She always did the right thing and got the job done. She never cut corners, did things by the book, and prided herself on her sense of responsibility.

However, in the past few weeks, she was aware she'd used up much of her good reputation and was becoming known instead as a screw-off, undoing the hard work that had established her credibility in the first place. She was determined to work the Harriman case without further tarnishing her professional reputation. She needed to do a better balancing act.

An hour later, armed and wearing a Kevlar vest, Kaitlin joined Newmeyer and a half dozen members of Fremont's S.W.A.T. team and stormed the mammoth warehouse off Stevenson Boulevard. The bust went off without a hitch.

Inside the warehouse, standing in plain view, were veritable mountains of cardboard boxes and crates. Attached to their sides were Comtak shipping labels and serial numbers, which matched the list from Newmeyer's investigation report. With the assistance of the Fremont police, they took the warehouse's owner and general manager into custody along with the murder suspect, a scrawny blond white guy with a mustache and numerous tattoos.

"I don't know what you're talking about … that stuff came from my distributor," the manager yelled angrily as they read him his Miranda rights.

"There's a shock," Kaitlin said sarcastically. A quick count suggested that fifty to seventy-five percent of the items stolen from Comtak were still there.

"I guess this stuff wasn't such a hot seller, after all," Newmeyer said, taking pictures of the cache of boxes with one of the department's new digital cameras to document the crime scene.

"This should make one of Torres' golf buddies happy," she said with a chuckle.

"You're so right," Newmeyer said, clicking away.

"And whatever makes his golf buddies happy, makes Torres happy," Kaitlin said with a smile, filling out the arrest report. She was perhaps happier than anyone to close the Comtak case. She could now focus on Darren Park's case undisturbed.

"I can't wait to see the look on Torres' face when I show him these pictures," Newmeyer said, turning off the camera.

"You'll have to bask in that glory alone."

"What do you mean?"

"Technically, I'm on a sick day today – so I'm not heading in," Kaitlin said, content to spend the afternoon in her own home.

They watched Fremont P.D. secure the warehouse, and then headed out to Newmeyer's car parked down the street.

Kaitlin noticed that Newmeyer seemed disappointed that he wasn't going to share the victory, such as it was, with her. But to the extent either of them deserved any credit on the Comtak case, it was him. They were quiet as they drove back to the Fremont P.D.'s main station, where she'd left her car.

"Well, I guess I'll see you tomorrow then," he said. There was no use in trying to convince her to head back to the squad room.

"Absolutely," Kaitlin replied. "Enjoy your moment with Torres," she said half-seriously, closing the car door behind her.

Newmeyer watched her as she walked away. He so admired Kaitlin's professionalism, and how she didn't take things too seriously. She exuded a self-confidence and sense of perspective that he lacked. If he'd expressed this opinion to Kaitlin, she would have laughed it off. Most people would never guess that Kaitlin was her own worst critic.

# Chapter 29

Traffic was light as Kaitlin traveled south on 880 to the Dumbarton Bridge and over to the other side of the bay. She'd missed being in her own house and looked forward to having some time to nest.

She resisted the urge to make calls on the drive home by cranking up the radio to fill the void. She glanced at the radio dial and debated whether to partake in a serious rockin' out or instead enjoy something deep and complex. Depth and complexity won out. Kaitlin tuned in the Bay Area's classical station, which treated her to a powerful rendition of Bizet's L'Arlésienne Suite No. 1 which transported her through Menlo Park as she thought through the day's events.

Once home and approaching her front door, she felt a wave of apprehension. The locks had been re-keyed, but Kaitlin felt uneasy as she stood in the entry way. Renfro had delivered as promised, but the FBI search of her house had turned up nothing.

She lowered her duffle bag to the floor, dropped her keys on the hallway table and pulled a pile of mail from the mail slot. It took a while to get through the pile of junk. She flipped past the J. Crew catalog, the duplicate Crate & Barrel catalogs, and the triplicate Victoria's Secret catalogs. She'd once purchased a pair of underwear at Victoria's Secret and now it seemed as if she was their most sought after customer.

She took her time refamiliarizing herself with her space, keeping herself mildly occupied with little tasks around the house. She opened the fridge and wrinkled her nose at its few pathetic contents. She threw out items that were suspect either due to abnormal color or expiration dates long since passed. Inconsequential things without a doubt, but ones that obviously needed tending.

She jumped when the phone rang and debated picking up the call.

"Hey," said the friendly voice. It was Cathy.

"Hey, yourself" Kaitlin said enthusiastically.

"Alex is working late again. Come on over, I don't want to be alone for dinner again."

Kaitlin thought about declining, but after being at Slim's for two days she was feeling a bit lonely. "You know, me neither," she agreed, "I would love the company."

"I was hoping you'd say that," Cathy said, pleased with herself.

After a day of domestic chores, Kaitlin drove to Cathy's for a pleasant and relaxing evening. They shared a bottle of Pinot noir and watched a Meg Ryan chick flick on pay-per-view.

When Cathy asked about work, Kaitlin shrugged and gave a non-committal answer, commenting about how frustrating it was to work with men who were convinced they were always right.

"Sorry to hear that," Cathy commiserated. "You should get married. Your odds of always being right get significantly better in that scenario."

Kaitlin laughed along with Cathy and thought to herself, "So this is how regular people are ... people who don't have to worry about murderers and tapped phone lines." The quiet, *normal* time Kaitlin spent at Cathy's went a long way towards easing her mind. She was home by eleven and slept like a rock.

When Kaitlin awoke the next morning, the impulse to call Slim seized her. Fresh from her day off and a night of restful sleep, her subconscious strung together all the pieces of information she'd so far gathered, in an immensely rational way. Not even Devil could have helped her do this.

It was late morning, still on the early side for Slim. He was probably asleep, but she dialed his number anyway. As it rang, she wondered how frequently her predisposition to logic had stunted her ability to think creatively.

"Hello?" Slim answered groggily after about ten rings.

Without bothering with a 'good morning' or 'sorry to wake you,' Kaitlin blurted, "You know what? Gary Tyler paints very much the same picture as Darren Park." She pushed several pillows behind herself and sat up against the headboard of her bed.

"Oh, hi Kaitlin – you miss me already?" Slim said jokingly, with a yawn.

She ignored the tinge of sarcasm in his voice. "And he's not a whole lot different than Dale Cho or Michael Owens for that matter."

"Except that he's still alive," Slim answered with a chuckle.

Kaitlin was not going away. Slim would just have to hear her out. "Cute. Very cute," she responded. "But I'm serious. Tyler is just another number in a sea of single, young, intelligent guys with ambitions of making a name and lots of money in Silicon Valley. Working for the machine."

Slim appreciated Kaitlin's insight. Computers didn't form the entire substance of techies' lives, but many spent ten or more hours in 8 by 8 foot cubicles at work, then spent the remaining waking hours in their small stucco apartments eating Domino's pizza, playing video games, or surfing the Internet. This techno-industrial path was comfortably taken by many of Kaitlin and Slim's classmates and colleagues. Although he had a genius for computers, working for the man was not a lifestyle option for Slim. Nor was it an option for every right-brained engineer.

Slim listened to Kaitlin with a personal understanding of what she was describing. Her assessment of Gary Tyler. The why and how of his involvement with Harriman. His helping in illegal foreign exports of LightWave's designs.

"This is what I'm thinking, Slim. Tyler is clever and somewhat cocky. He knows that he can get away with this. He'll send a few e-mails, make a few weekend trips, and then walk away with a lot of cash. In his mind, he'll be the last man standing in a collapsing economy. Not to mention the fact that he's getting in the good graces of one of Silicon Valley's most powerful men, Warren Harriman." Suddenly, Kaitlin came to a dead stop. "Oh, by the way, what have you got on Gary Tyler?"

"Oh, you know, the usual," Slim said coyly, walking downstairs into his kitchen in a faded Fight Club t-shirt and gray flannel boxer shorts.

"Slim! What've you got?" she pleaded.

"Well, aside from several weekend trips to Japan, Singapore, Korea, and Thailand, and a fast-growing numbered bank account in the Netherlands Antilles, Gary Tyler is just your average system administrator."

She leaned back in the chair amazed. She didn't know how Slim had done it. And to some degree she didn't *want* to know. "Wow," she whispered.

Kaitlin's brain went into overdrive figuring out what to do next. *Pay Gary Tyler a friendly visit? To what end? Bring him in for questioning? What sort of legitimate case could she mount? Should she tell him his life was in danger? Like he'd believe her ...*

Most, if not all, of what Slim had found wouldn't be admissible in court. Indeed, the mere collection of it could have her thrown off the force. So getting Tyler to turn state's evidence against Warren Harriman was a long shot. On the other hand, if confronted Tyler might run. After all, he'd already socked away enough cash to finance a life of leisure in the non-extradition country of his choice. Banishment to a tiny Latin

American country wasn't so bad, Kaitlin thought, when you have high-speed Internet access and digital satellite television.

"Confronting Tyler is too risky," Kaitlin concluded, "So it's time for you to make a phone call, Slim," she continued.

"*Me*? Who am I going to call?" Slim asked puzzled.

"It's not *who* you are going to call. It's who you're going to be when you call," she replied devilishly.

"Huh?"

"You pulled LightWave's TRW credit report, right?

"Yes ..." Slim answered cautiously.

"What were the names of LightWave's vendor references? Usually they list the biggest suppliers first."

Slim walked over to the kitchen table and shuffled through the accumulating pile of papers and folders regarding LightWave.

"Here it is. Let's see ... you got Milpitas Technology Park, that's most likely their landlord. Microtech, they're an electronic component supplier. Inacom, another equipment supplier. And Sun Microsystems, you know who they are. Overall, looks like they spend a lot of money and mostly pay their bills on time ..." Slim reported.

"Slim, remember what we saw with the other guys? Darren Park, Dale Cho, and Michael Owens? Their courier trips for Harriman were done as infrequent three-day weekends. The bag man flies out of SFO, usually on a Friday afternoon, departs from the foreign location Sunday night, and arrives back Monday morning at the latest."

"Keep going ..." Slim yawned.

"We need to find out when Gary Tyler's making his next trip!" Kaitlin nearly shouted.

"Right ... of course," Slim answered.

"But you aren't able to access airline reservation computers. So you can't tell me when his next flight will be, right?"

"That's right," Slim acknowledged sheepishly. He didn't like to admit there were computers out there that he wasn't able to crack. "But he may not even have an airline reservation."

"Which is why a low-tech solution is needed again. And you my friend, are *it*," Kaitlin said proudly.

"Thanks, I really like being referred to as low-tech," Slim said sarcastically. "What exactly am I supposed to do?"

"You, Mr. Yamazaki, are the new sales rep for Sun Microsystems. You call Gary Tyler's assistant to schedule a meeting with Gary, because 'Sun has some great new discounts on servers and workstations that LightWave might be interested in.' Unfortunately, for the next month, you can only meet on a Friday afternoon. So, you need to know which Fridays Gary is in the office, and which Fridays he's not. Got it?"

"That's it?" Slim asked skeptically.

"That's it," Kaitlin replied, smiling to herself. "There is beauty in its simplicity, don't you think?"

"Sure. It's almost as beautiful as you are, much more simple though. Anyway, let's hope Tyler has an assistant as clueless as the company receptionist. In fact, let's hope that he even *has* an assistant."

"That would certainly help," Kaitlin said, remaining optimistic.

Slim was puzzled over how he'd gotten roped in, but he always had a hard time saying no to her.

"I'll call now. Wish me luck," he said, surrendering to her will.

"Good luck! And call me as soon as you get off the phone!" Kaitlin said excitedly. She stopped short as she was about to hang up. "Slim, you know what you said a couple of seconds ago? It sounded like some sort of back-handed compliment."

Slim paused. "I'll talk to you later," he said softly and hung up the phone.

Over the years he'd made little comments like that to her. But never once had she acknowledged them. Kaitlin guessed that maybe she had left Slim to wonder whether she was clueless, awkward, or simply unwilling to acknowledge that he had feelings toward her beyond friendship. She didn't know why she'd chosen to acknowledge his compliment now. Nonetheless, she liked the slightly nervous feeling it inspired in her.

She pulled herself out of bed, brewed some coffee and quickly got ready for work. Officially, she'd been out sick for two and a half days. But Torres would know that was a bullshit excuse. Particularly in light of her participation in the warehouse seizure the day before.

She still hadn't decided whether, or how, she'd bring Torres into the loop on everything she had done. Informing Torres of her activities could easily bring her work on this case to a screeching halt. And possibly result in a demotion or suspension. On the other hand, not informing Torres at this critical juncture would pave the way for her professional suicide, as he would surely find out later.

These considerations occupied her as she scrambled through her mess of a closet and pulled an outfit that might help persuade Torres to support her investigation. Self-consciously, she realized she was using her gender and good lucks to her advantage. This was becoming a habit.

She stood naked in front of the mirror, holding up a pair of stylish black pants and tight-fitting periwinkle sweater that she'd never worn since buying it last Fall. The outfit tested the bounds of professional detective attire. But if she were to hit Torres with the full weight of her case against Warren Harriman, she may as well be artfully dressed. "Mom, you'd be *very* proud of me," Kaitlin remarked aloud.

Just as she was about to step into the shower, the phone chirped noisily in the living room. Kaitlin quickly wrapped a towel around her body and ran to the other room to find the cordless phone. She found the handset just before it went to voice mail, and picked it up, slightly out of breath.

"Hello, may I speak with Paloma please?" asked Slim jokingly.

She was thrown off for a half-beat. "Very funny," she recovered. "So?"

"I hate to admit it, but low-tech has its charms. Tyler's in the office every Friday for the next six weeks – except for this coming Friday. He's making it a three-day weekend."

"Excellent!" Kaitlin said.

"You're a genius," Slim said.

"I don't know about that," she said humbly. "Thanks for your help again, Slim. Nicely done."

"So, what now?" Slim asked, in part hoping for another assignment, in part dreading the possibility.

"Well, I'm heading into the office in a half hour."

"And ... what are you going to tell your captain?"

Kaitlin paused thoughtfully. "I don't know. I haven't decided yet."

"You gotta decide soon," Slim said.

"I know. Let's talk tonight after we've pulled together more information on Gary Tyler. I want to know everything about him and what this weekend will look like. In the meantime, I'll figure out what exactly I'm going to tell Torres."

"Later," Slim said, signing off.

Kaitlin swept into the bathroom and jumped in the shower. Under the pulse of hot water, Kaitlin methodically reviewed the timeline of all that had brought her to this place. From Sergeant Collins' initial phone call reporting Darren Park's car accident, to Slim's help in finding out Gary Tyler's travel plans, she had been rewarded with confirmation and luck for her assertiveness, her intuition, and her computer savvy.

She pulled a plush blue towel over the top of the shower and gently dried her hair. In the half-fogged mirror, the bathroom's bright ceiling light cast a muted halo around Kaitlin's reflection. As she wiped clear a spot on the mirror, she realized how critical the next forty-eight hours would be. Everything had to be cleanly executed in the next two days. Or else everything she had accomplished so far would be rendered meaningless.

# Chapter 30

Gary Tyler frowned. Three tech support e-mails and two voice-mails were waiting for him when he logged on in the morning. Not surprisingly, all of these requests were, in the minds of their senders, extremely urgent. He couldn't wait to be something other than a sys admin.

"Crybabies," he muttered softly to himself, not wanting to he heard by the guy in the neighboring cubicle. He was resigned to the fact that marketing and sales people couldn't keep their computers running properly by themselves but when so-called "software engineers" couldn't resolve simple glitches in Windows 98 he wanted to scream.

But not today. Today, he would take things in stride.

Six months earlier he'd just about had enough. He was ready to call it quits. He was sick of the routine at LightWave. But he felt trapped. With the economic downturn taking hold, panic had set in. People traded in dreams of BMWs for nightmares of losing their jobs. He'd gotten some stock options when he joined LightWave, but those options weren't worth much these days.

It was then that he'd met Shane Calloway. Calloway was part of a group visiting LightWave from Harriman & Co. All that Gary knew was that Harriman & Co. had sunk a lot of money into LightWave, and that they visited from time to time to look in on their investment. Water cooler whispers said they weren't too happy with LightWave because sales hadn't ramped up according to projections at the time they invested. A sense of gloom had descended on LightWave.

On that day, most of the Harriman & Co. executives spent the day in the conference room with LightWave's upper management, poring over the company's financial statements and sales forecasts.

Calloway had asked to meet with LightWave's IT department to better understand how systems were set up and to confirm that the company's security measures were up to par. Gary was given the task of babysitting Calloway. Whatever else he did, he wanted to come off as knowledgeable and helpful. If LightWave went down, Gary was smart enough to think that maybe these venture capital guys could help him find a new job.

Gary was introduced to Shane Calloway as LightWave's resident IT guru, the guy who kept everyone working. Gary had winced. He liked the credit but he wasn't anxious to be given responsibility for anything.

"Nice to meet you, Gary," Calloway said, shaking his hand firmly as he held a LightWave coffee mug in the other.

"Gary, if you can walk me through the network set-up, firewall protection, whether you use a sniffer, etc.... I really just want a ten thousand foot view of the system," Calloway said, raising his hand above his head like a high-flying jet aircraft.

"No problem," Gary said. The time he spent with Calloway would put him behind on his work, but at the moment he viewed it as an investment. "Ready to start?"

"I'm right behind you," Calloway said.

Together they walked down the hall and so began Shane Calloway's tour of LightWave. As they toured along, Gary quickly realized that Calloway knew his stuff when it came to networks and network security. His questions were exact, intelligent, and appropriate. It was apparent that this was not a cosmetic visit.

Soon, they were immersed in a discussion regarding the most obscure technical details of LightWave's computer systems. After a solid hour of discussion in the server room talking things through, Calloway brought the discussion to a dead stop.

"Gary, you've done quite a job setting up this network. And a great job keeping it going, day in and day out. This company couldn't keep business going for an hour if it weren't for you. Am I right?" Calloway said encouragingly.

Gary sensed that Calloway was not a man to mince words with. "Yeah, pretty much," Gary confided. "It's incredible how incompetent these guys are. I'm the only guy in the entire company on call 24/7," Gary seethed.

"I see the same situation in different companies," Calloway continued. "Executives are making *a ton* of money – we're talking private jet money – and the engineers making a shit-load too, but the IT guys like you get the shaft *every single time.* Guys are losing their jobs and stock options left and right. It's not right, if you ask me," Calloway said. He took a big final swig of black coffee. He placed the mug on the desk and stood up.

Gary didn't say anything. But Calloway knew what he was thinking. It wasn't hard to get into the heads of these guys.

"Sorry about going on like that," Calloway said, patting Gary on the shoulder in a fatherly way.

Tyler didn't shrug so much as shiver under Calloway's touch. "No. Don't be sorry. You're totally right," Gary said, not looking up from the computer monitor.

"Listen, let me give you my card. I know of a little side business you may want to consider. Weekends only. And you'll make a hell of a lot more dough than you're making here," Calloway offered.

He had Gary's interest. "Sounds great," Gary said, finally making eye contact with Calloway.

They walked out of the server room and into the corridor. Down the hall, the conference room doors were pushed opened and the occupants started spilling out.

"All right, Chief. I gotta go, call me next week," Calloway said. He checked his wristwatch, turned swiftly, and marched down the hallway. He'd been out of the Marine Corps for five years, but to anyone who encountered him, it was obvious that he still talked, walked, and thought like a Marine.

Calloway was no longer surprised that the same tactics that worked with Republican Guards in Baghdad also worked with IT personnel in Silicon Valley. Play on some dissatisfaction and wave a lot of money around. Done.

Gary called Calloway early the next week. They arranged to meet on Saturday.

Gary walked into the dilapidated coffee shop near the MacArthur BART station at eleven a.m. and immediately spotted Calloway seated alone at a red vinyl booth at the far end of the restaurant. The breakfast crowd had already cleared out. The place was deserted, and it smelled of bacon grease and burnt coffee.

Calloway smiled broadly as Tyler approached the table. "Good morning, son, glad you could make it," he said cheerfully. "I know this place doesn't look like much, but they've got the best corn beef hash that I've been able to find out here."

Calloway flagged down the matronly waitress, a large African-American woman. Gary ordered buttermilk pancakes and juice. They made small talk for a while until Gary's food was served, and then Calloway got serious.

"Gary, I served this country for over twenty years. I risked my life, and the lives of other fine American men and women, on three different continents. But now, I see all that I worked for placed in jeopardy. You know what I'm talking about, don't you Gary?" Calloway asked.

Tyler nodded, despite having *no idea* what he was talking about. It didn't seem necessary to understand. He viewed this meeting as a quasi-job interview. In other words, bullshit counts.

"Technology, Gary. It all comes down to technology. U.S. technology. Like what LightWave is working on ..." Calloway said, trailing off. He grabbed three packets of sugar from the small plastic holder in the center of the table, and in a single swift motion simultaneously tore all three open. Tyler noticed that while Calloway's fingernails were neatly manicured, his hands were tough and weathered. The backs of his fingers and hands bore old scars. Serious scars. Calloway poured the sugar into the cup, and stirred it gently with a dull metal teaspoon.

"What about it?" Gary asked when the silence became uncomfortable.

"It's a simple truth, really," Callahan finally said. "Technology represents the single most important factor in global politics. It alone will determine which countries make it through the next millennium. History tells us that those of our primitive ancestors that harnessed fire lived. Those that didn't perished."

Calloway studied the impact of his words on his subject. He could not yet discern Gary's receptiveness, so he continued measuredly, "The same lesson applies today. Right now, the U.S. holds far and away a significant technological advantage over the rest of the world."

Calloway stopped talking again to let this statement sink in and drank his coffee methodically. Gary had no idea what Calloway was getting at, and he was starting to worry that this would soon become obvious.

"Okay, so where do I fit in all this?" Gary asked, hoping Calloway would stop beating around the bush and tell him about the job offer.

"Are you familiar with the term 'export controls' Gary?" asked Calloway.

*Finally*, thought Gary, *a question I can actually answer.*

"Sure. Everyone in the Valley is," he answered confidently. He remembered the document he'd signed on his first day of work at LightWave, acknowledging that he would not export anything in violation of U.S. law.

Calloway nodded his head, "And do you know that because of those export controls, your company is pretty close to going out of business?"

"What?" Gary replied with surprise. "You've got to be kidding." He thought about the value of his stock options plummeting into nothingness.

"I tell you that in the strictest confidence, Gary. But I tell you because it goes right to the heart of the matter. And because it matters … in light of what I'm going to propose."

Gary had unconsciously shifted to the edge of the red vinyl seat.

"LightWave has the potential to revolutionize the entire semiconductor business. If it goes out of business, America loses a tremendous technological advantage and possibly an important sector of its economy. *That* is the singular impact of U.S. export controls."

"But isn't the whole point of the export controls to keep U.S. technology safe and prevent foreign countries from exploiting it?" Gary said, pleased with himself.

Calloway smiled. "That's the stated theory behind them, yes. But what politicians fail to realize is that if developing the technology in the first place isn't lucrative, it simply won't get developed. On top of that, other countries don't have the same export laws as we do here in the U.S. So countries like Japan and France are developing sophisticated technology – not as good as U.S. technology, but close. Very close. And they're gladly supplying it to all the places U.S. companies aren't allowed to."

It took Gary some time to soak in the words, but the impact of Calloway's earnestness was immediate. Calloway was rolling now. It was time to play the authority card.

"At the end of the day, only the U.S. suffers. That's why my friends at the CIA and I got scared. We realized that we were quickly losing our technological advantage, because of the ill-conceived laws designed to protect us."

The argument made sense to Gary. Calloway was a veteran military officer. And he had an excellent grasp of technology. He knew what he was talking about. Hell, even the CIA was involved. This was the real deal.

"This is where you can help, Gary," Calloway said, focusing his intense blues eyes on him. "Do you want to help your company? And your country?"

"Yeah, of course," he replied, with the confused uncertainty of a teenager signing up for military service after a long night of drinking.

"Good," Calloway said confidently, with a big friendly grin. "Let me pay the bill here. I'll fill you in on the details in the car."

They walked out into Oakland's gray haze together, and Gary's life was forever changed.

⅄

Since that breakfast meeting with Calloway, Tyler didn't mind dealing with tech support calls anymore. Working at LightWave was now a means to a very prosperous end. Working for Shane Calloway, Gary had amassed close to three hundred thousand dollars in a numbered bank account. That was some serious cash. And after only a half dozen weekend trips to Asia. Calloway had promised him a handful more of such trips during the upcoming year. And then he'd be finished, with an even million. Tax-free. Not bad for a sys admin at a startup. For a million bucks, he would clean the bathrooms at LightWave.

This coming weekend would make him another fifty thousand dollars richer. All he had to do was make it to SFO by one p.m. Friday and fly to Bangkok. *First class.* Free drinks. Inflight movies. Sleep. He'd meet some guy for five minutes, and then spend the rest of the weekend partying on the beach of Koh Samui. He'd fly back early Monday morning and, with the time difference, be back at work the same day.

In the unlikely event someone asked about his weekend, he'd offer up the usual stuff – mountain biking, surfing the web, watching videos. No one would ever doubt Gary's life was as boring as that. *Oh, I spent the weekend in Thailand.* Now that would shock the pants off people, Gary mused, smiling.

He spent the morning answering e-mail and putting out fires. He set up a new workstation for an incoming employee.

The new hire was a wet-nosed twenty-four-year-old engineer from South India getting paid almost twice as much as Gary. But that was all right. Gary consoled himself with the knowledge that unlike Sandeep, he'd be a millionaire in less than a year. He'd simply been at the right company at the right time, impressing the right people. *That* was what Silicon Valley was all about.

At noon, a couple of other guys in the IT department came by to collect Gary to go to lunch. It was one of those rare days when people in his department actually had enough time to walk down the street for a sandwich. They walked out the building's front door onto Calaveras Boulevard. They chatted about that morning's activities and the system upgrades that needed to be done that afternoon.

Parked across the street was a silver Chevy Lumina with an attractive brunette behind the wheel. From a grainy photo printed from the Internet, Detective Kaitlin Hall identified her subject exiting the building and studied Gary Tyler's every feature as he walked down the street.

# Chapter 31

Sitting across from LightWave's building, waiting for a glimpse of Gary Tyler, Kaitlin reflected on her most recent meeting with Torres. When she'd arrived at the squad room, Torres was in casual conversation with Newmeyer and a couple of the other detectives. As soon as she walked in, all conversation stopped and all eyes fell upon her as she shut the door, its frosted glass rattling loudly as the door struck the jamb.

"What?" she asked nonchalantly, staring back at them.

No one answered, so she shrugged off their strange silence. "Good morning gentlemen," she said.

That seemed to work. Torres acknowledged her entrance with a nod. They returned a trio of good mornings and went back to their discussion.

Kaitlin settled into her chair and logged onto the computer. She was acutely aware that someone was still monitoring her every keystroke. She looked at the phone, sitting useless on the desk. She still didn't know whether it too had been tapped. She continued to use Slim's cell phone to check her voicemail and make all her calls. She hated the feeling of being under a microscope. Of being watched. She felt violated. Her personal space, both her home and her office, had been intruded upon.

She had no intention of letting that go unanswered.

Torres and the others shared a big laugh over something, and then their discussion dissolved. The detectives each headed back to their desks. She couldn't tell what they'd been talking about, and it didn't much matter. Kaitlin worked in an institution that frequently seemed like a men's club. But she'd known that when she joined the police force. She was under no illusion that any of that was going to change anytime soon. Most of the time, she felt welcome and accepted. But there were other times, like this morning, when it seemed as if she was operating on the periphery.

Torres walked in Kaitlin's direction. As he passed Kaitlin's desk on the path towards his office he said without stopping, "Glad to see you're feeling better, Detective. I'd like to get the status on a few things when you have a minute ..." That was Torres' diplomatic way of saying, '*Into my office – now.*'

Kaitlin played it cool. She spent the next few minutes finished up her duty log for the last couple of days before rising to meet with Torres. He was on the phone when she rapped softly on the door and eased it open. She poked her head in, and he waved her in.

"It was terrible, an absolute bloodbath," Torres said to the person on the other end of the line. His tone was curiously out of sync with the content of speech. "Yeah, really pathetic," he continued.

Kaitlin considered the possibility that Torres was describing some mass murder or large-scale police shoot-out. She feared, for a second, that something major had gone down in her absence and that she was totally aware. She walked forward and sat down.

"Well, the back nine really helped me out. But the damage was pretty well done by then ..." Torres said, looking up at Kaitlin and holding his thumb about an inch away from his forefinger. The universal sign for 'it'll be just a second.'

Kaitlin felt stupid. Torres was describing a damned golf game, not a triple homicide. Men and golf. She would never get the level of emotional connection there.

"Okay, see you next week," Torres said, finally hanging up. "Sorry about that," he said, apologizing to Kaitlin.

"No problem," Kaitlin said. "It's your office, sir" she smiled genuinely.

She saw him look her over with great subtlety. Most men wouldn't have noticed that she was wearing a new outfit. But Torres was not most men. He believed that clothes made the man, or made the detective. Besides, Kaitlin was far more interesting to look at than guys out in the squad room.

Torres, of course, would never comment on Kaitlin's appearance. He'd never let on that he took any special notice of her. Successful careers had been ruined for lesser things, and even a trivial, off-handed remark could be easily misconstrued and used against him. He wasn't going to let that happen. Torres always acted carefully.

"You look like you've made a complete recovery. What'd you have? A cold? The flu?" he asked skeptically.

"Captain, I know that you know that I wasn't out due to illness."

"Good," he said as he clasped his hands together. "Now we can have a straight conversation." He chuckled and shifted his weight back in his chair. "I'm just hoping that you're not going to tell me that you've been doing anything pertaining to Warren Harriman. Or his alleged involvement in a homicide," Torres said blithely. "You wouldn't do that to me, would you?"

"Captain Torres, it's *funny* that you say that …" Kaitlin responded, in a measured tone similar to his. She crossed her legs casually and folded her hands on her lap. She hoped Torres wouldn't see them trembling.

"Christ, Detective …" Torres said, running his hand over his brow and wincing. It looked as if he was suffering a sudden migraine. "Are you hell bent on causing my political suicide?"

"Captain – "

"Listen up, Detective," Torres said, cutting her off. "This is how it's going to be. If you're going to risk the credibility of this department, not to mention my professional reputation, you're going to fill me in on every last detail. Every last suspicion that you have regarding this case."

It was not the statement she'd expected him to make. Torres looked at his gleaming silver diver's watch. "You have *exactly* one hour and seventeen minutes. At eleven thirty, I'm walking out that door for a lunch meeting. After I've heard you out, I'm going to make a final decision. Either to put you on paid leave or give you my full support."

Kaitlin gulped. This was it. Time to lay out the case against Warren Harriman, acquaint Torres with Shane Calloway, and convince him that a young systems engineer named Gary Tyler was engaged in federal crimes of the highest nature. She took a deep breath. She knew that her charisma and nice outfit would not get her through this. She would need to use her real gifts – sheer intellect and presence of mind.

⅄

Seventy minutes went by in the blink of the eye. Kaitlin had systematically taken Torres from start to finish. He'd asked but a handful of questions, listening intently throughout her monologue. He heard her start to build a case against Bobby Park. But just as soon, she tore it down and built a stronger, more compelling case against Warren Harriman. A man he respected. A man he considered above reproach.

As Kaitlin relayed only the facts of her case, she closely gauged Torres' every reaction to the information she imparted. Particularly the fact that both Rachel Weinstein's and Kaitlin's office keyboards had been bugged.

Before this morning, Kaitlin was not entirely sure that Torres was unaware or uninvolved in the tapping of her computer. So she had anticipated his reaction to that particular piece of news. His face went from pale to red as he rose from his desk. He looked down, wary of his own computer.

"Are you *sure*?" he asked in disbelief. "Jesus. If your computer is bugged, all of them might be!" he exclaimed.

"That's a possibility. But I think only mine," Kaitlin answered calmly, "... and maybe yours."

Kaitlin then walked Torres over to her desk, under the pretense of examining some paperwork. As he flipped through pages of a lengthy report, Torres intently watched Kaitlin as she, with improving skill, disassembled her keyboard. When she had pulled the major pieces of the keyboard apart, the bugging device was clearly visible to him. He was distraught to find that a computer within the police department – indeed, within his own squad room – had been compromised.

Without speaking, they walked back into his office. He immediately pointed at his keyboard, silently signaling Kaitlin to disassemble it. The shock on Torres' face was unmistakable when Kaitlin pried apart his keyboard to reveal a bugging device identical to the one found on hers. Someone had been monitoring his every keystroke. Kaitlin had not fully expected to find the bug. But now she was both relieved and scared. Relieved that Torres was absolved from any complicity with Harriman. But scared by the further realization that whomever was behind these activities would stop at nothing to accomplish their objectives.

Ashen-faced, he silently pointed to the door. Together they walked out of his office, through the squad room, and down the corridor to the building's exit. As soon as the glass doors of the station closed behind them, Torres angrily let out a forceful, "*Goddamn it!*"

Caught by surprise, Kaitlin suggested they go across the street to Denny's and talk.

Torres nodded, still furious but recognizing the need to rein in his emotions.

After a few minutes sitting in a corner booth stirring his coffee, Torres had calmed down. Finally, he broke the silence: "I've met Shane Calloway."

Kaitlin waited. She was curious to hear about Calloway from someone who actually knew him. When Torres remained silent she asked, "How? When?"

"Golfing," Torres said. She couldn't tell if he was angry or embarrassed. "Calloway had accompanied Warren Harriman a couple of times at the Olympic Club."

Kaitlin knew that golf was an almost-holy male bonding experience for guys like Torres. If Torres had golfed with Calloway, then he'd probably been friendly toward him, maybe even given him some regard. "So, what's he like?" she asked.

"Like a typical ex-Marine. And very smart and very polished."

Coming from Torres, who was as smooth as they got, that was quite a compliment.

Kaitlin had filled in Torres on Calloway's Gulf War activities and expertise in covert operations. The picture she painted was one of a patriot. But also one of an opportunist.

Kaitlin wondered whether Torres could reconcile her portrait with the man he had golfed with. Could Torres also work out the evidence that Kaitlin presented with what he knew of Warren Harriman, a man he'd interacted with for six years?

"I'm having a hard time understanding the motive here, Detective," he said. "What makes incredibly wealthy and reputable men violate export laws? And commit cold-blooded murder in support of that? Greed? Torres continued to shake his head in disbelief. Maybe it's part of a government-sponsored agenda that we're simply not aware of? Maybe Harriman doesn't know anything about Calloway – about what he's supposedly doing. Have you considered that?"

The question surprised Kaitlin and she didn't know quite how to respond.

"Captain, I don't know if Harriman and Calloway are doing this out of love of money, love of country, or some combination of both. What I know … what I suspect … is that they *are* doing these things. As for a government-sponsored operation, the systematic killings rule that out. And Calloway is no entrepreneur. He's definitely working for someone, and Harriman is the logical employer."

For Torres' sake, she continued expanding on his thoughts. "Captain, you know how hotly debated the export control laws are. People in Silicon Valley aren't lukewarm on the topic. They're either violently in favor of them or violently against them. With the money at stake, profit alone is a compelling motive. Even to a man like Warren Harriman.

"In reality, he's done a pretty bad job of picking investments over the last couple of years. And in Calloway's case, I presume he's in it for the money. I also think he might be acting on motives that he considers patriotic, not treasonous.

"But whatever their motives, young men are being murdered. And sensitive technology is leaving the U.S. every month."

Torres fell silent. He quietly contemplated what he'd heard over the past hour and a half. He looked at Kaitlin, but said nothing. The case she had sketched out was compelling. As far-fetched as the story seemed, the pieces did fall into place. That someone had the audacity to tap computers in *his* police department, shook him to the core. No one would do that unless they had a great deal to win, or lose. It was evidence he could not dismiss.

He could no longer ignore the possibility that this young, inexperienced detective had actually stumbled upon a plot of global proportions. He had no choice but to put his support behind her investigation – but on his terms.

Torres' grim silence had unnerved Kaitlin. She worried that Torres might not risk his well-established, powerful connections without something more concrete

"Okay," Torres said finally. "The investigation proceeds with my full support."

Kaitlin breathed a sigh of relief.

"The first order of business is calling in Renfro."

"What? Why?" Kaitlin replied with dismay.

"Because this is clearly a federal case, that's why. The FBI has the expertise with this sort of thing. Without their backing, I simply won't take the risk of going after Harriman ... and being wrong."

Kaitlin had convinced Torres to proceed, but that didn't mean he was going to be reckless and not cover his bases.

"You don't have a problem working with Renfro, do you?" Torres asked, sounding somewhat like a high school homeroom teacher.

"Please, Captain. Any reluctance doesn't have anything to do with Renfro personally." Kaitlin hoped to heaven that Torres knew nothing of her personal encounter with Renfro. "You know how it is working with the Feds. They always want to take over the case, even when they've been two steps behind, as is the situation here …"

"That may be. But no Feds, no case. Understood?" he replied decisively.

She knew he was right. The FBI had jurisdiction. And the political stakes for Torres were too high to go it alone. Perhaps, bringing in Renfro wouldn't be all bad. The case clearly was taking on an international flavor, and the FBI's resources could be helpful in arranging foreign surveillance.

"Understood. Will you do me the favor of guaranteeing that I'll remain involved in all facets of this case on behalf of the department?"

Torres decided to entrust his future to the hands of the most junior detective on the squad. He nodded silently in agreement.

She handed him Slim's cell phone. "Let's call Renfro," she said.

# Chapter 32

It had only been a few days earlier that FBI Special Agent Alex Renfro had perfunctorily dismissed Kaitlin's suspicions that Warren Harriman was engaged in illegal conduct. But at the urgent request of Captain Torres, he agreed to immediately meet them at the FBI Field Office in San Francisco. Sitting in the 13th Floor conference room overlooking Golden Gate Avenue, Renfro sat through the same presentation that Torres had only hours earlier. Her theory of the case now bolstered by the fact that SJPD's own Captain Torres had been surveilled, and with Torres himself supporting her, things were different. Kaitlin also brought along two file boxes filled to capacity with computer printouts that she and Slim had culled over the past two weeks.

Renfro was not dismissing her theory now.

His task force had been closely monitoring several Silicon Valley companies for the past twenty-four months. They were certain that illegal technology exports were occurring but, because of the nature of the crime and the sophistication of the participants, the FBI had been unable to establish a single case during that period. The evidence Kaitlin had produced, while certainly not free from doubt, was better than anything his people had managed to obtain. In light of the pressure his office was getting Renfro needed to act.

The FBI's reputation was suffering an all-time low. They'd botched several high-profile cases, and their once esteemed Director had just resigned in frustration. Moreover, the federal government was fighting tooth and nail to preserve export controls in the face of growing, and more vocal, complaints by the U.S. business community. Washington had made it clear that the FBI needed to make some high-profile busts. Like catching sales of missile components, nerve gas, or supercomputers to hostile enemy countries like Sudan, Syria, Iraq, or North Korea. Anything to convince American voters that export controls were reasonable, indeed necessary, to protect national security interests. Otherwise, the relentless drumbeat of business could carry the day.

Renfro sat silently for some time after Kaitlin finished. He looked at Torres, then Kaitlin.

"Detective Hall," Renfro said after a quick but sober deliberation, "shall we keep a close eye on Gary Tyler?"

Kaitlin had convinced both Torres and Renfro of the merits of her investigation. The stakes had now been raised to the highest level. She hoped, to the core of her existence, that she was right.

Unbeknownst to her, Renfro indulged in a long look at Kaitlin as she left the conference room. "There is no doubt about it," he thought. "That is a nice sweater."

# CHAPTER 33

Eighteen hours later, Kaitlin found herself in the security office at San Francisco International Airport. She stood next to Renfro and the FBI's resident agent, Max Wallace, who was permanently assigned to the airport detail. On Renfro's orders, and with Wallace's oversight, over a dozen plain clothes FBI special agents were scattered throughout the airport's international departure terminal and its exterior.

It was Friday. The start of Gary Tyler's scheduled three-day weekend. The FBI had requested reservation information on Gary Tyler from international airlines servicing Asia. As it turned out, none of them held a reservation in his name. Kaitlin was not surprised. She suspected that Mr. Tyler was instructed to travel without a reservation, purchasing a first class ticket only a few hours before departure time. At $8,000 for a full fare ticket, the first class cabin to Asia was never sold out. But she didn't know *which* airline Mr. Tyler would be taking.

That's what all the FBI special agents were there to find out.

Renfro turned away from the bank of video monitors and looked at Kaitlin. Inside the confines of the security office, they stood uncomfortably close to each other. Like it or not, she'd be spending the next forty-eight hours with him.

"Deal with it," she whispered to herself.

Having slept with Renfro wasn't what bothered her. It was the impersonal way that she had – that they both had – ignored what happened between them in Vegas that made their close quarters awkward. Their lunch last week had been painfully short and casual. However, the business at hand required their undivided attention, as well as their total cooperation.

Suddenly, Renfro's walkie-talkie crackled and squawked to life. *"He's driving past the car rental return. Blue Nissan Maxima, license plate 492TKG3. He's pulled into the short-term parking lot. Pick him up, Hamilton."*

The walkie-talkie squawked again as Special Agent Hamilton stationed in the parking structure reported, *"I've got him. He's heading to the third level."*

Wallace spoke into his walkie-talkie, "He'll probably walk across the pedestrian sky-bridge into the terminal. Follow him in."

Kaitlin compulsively chimed in, practically shouting into her walkie-talkie, "Not too close! We don't want to spook him!"

"Relax," Renfro said to her, gently pulling the walkie-talkie away from her face. "These guys are on our national security surveillance team. They aren't going to blow it." Wallace and Renfro exchanged looks.

"Sorry," she said apologetically.

"No need to apologize," he said, letting go of her forearm. "So far, so good. Now we just watch him buy his ticket. Are you ready?"

"I'm ready, but not excited for a fifteen-hour flight. Too bad it's a weekend jaunt," she answered, immediately regretting the possible implication of her words.

He nodded his head in agreement. He switched channels on the walkie-talkie and spoke to the FBI agent who, posing as an airline reservation agent, stood inside the terminal next to the ticketing counters. "Anything, Travis?" Renfro asked.

*"He's in the main terminal. Suspect is wearing a navy blue polo shirt and khaki pants. Carrying one article of luggage and a laptop computer bag. He's looking at departure monitors now,"* the agent replied with a whisper. *"Okay, he's walking toward the ticket counters. Give me a few seconds …"*

Spontaneously, Kaitlin lifted her travel bag to her shoulder, readying herself to go. Out of the corner of his eye, Renfro saw her do this and smiled. She realized that she was getting ahead of herself and dropped her bag to the floor. They had at least two hours before any flight carrying Gary Tyler left the airport. They had a lot to do before they themselves could board that plane.

*"Thai Airways. He's at the Thai Airways counter."*

Kaitlin quickly flipped through the pages attached to a clipboard that contained that day's airline departure schedules.

"They've got one flight left today," she said excitedly. "Two-forty p.m. to Bangkok. Flight number TG5635." She fought the urge to again pick up her bag.

"Okay, good work, Travis," Renfro said. "Hang back until he's been ticketed. Gonzalez, pick him up after he leaves the counter. Let's get Tyler's ticket info from Thai Airways," he said, looking at Wallace.

"I'm calling their floor supervisor now," Wallace said authoritatively, hitting a pre-programmed button on his cell phone, contacting Thai Airways on an inside line.

"You have your frequent flyer number handy?" Renfro asked playfully, turning to Kaitlin. He laughed softly. "I always wanted to go to Thailand, just never thought it would be for work."

⅄

Captain Ramal Thitikatjatham of the Thai Royal Police was an extremely busy man. That was the message delivered by the Captain's secretary, and it was received loud and clear by Renfro and Kaitlin over a less than perfect phone connection.

"Hold please!" she said abruptly as she slammed the phone on the desk, not bothering to actually put the call on hold. In the background, the secretary's voice could be heard. She spoke frenetically to one or two other people in Thai. That neither Renfro nor Kaitlin could speak a word of Thai did not keep them from understanding that an argument was ensuing in the offices of the Thai Royal Police. The voices crested and were followed by a brief silence.

Footsteps grew louder, and the telephone receiver was lifted from the tabletop with a clatter.

A calm voice came through on the speakerphone. "Good day, this is Captain Thitikatjatham. To whom am I speaking?" said the man in perfect Oxford English.

Renfro cordially introduced himself and Kaitlin.

"Very well, it is a pleasure to receive your call. You may call me Captain Ramal. It's much easier to pronounce than *Thitikatjatham*," he said with a gentle laugh. "How may I be of service to you?"

Renfro was poised to respond, but before he could, Kaitlin interjected.

"Captain Ramal, this call is of the utmost importance. Both Thai and U.S. national security are at stake. Please confirm that this is a secure connection, and that no one else is in the room with you."

Ramal let out a hearty laugh, but then stopped short. "Detective Hall, please be assured that we are very security-conscious here. Especially within the Thai Royal Police. The phone lines are clear, and there is no one else present in my office or on this phone line."

Immediately following this statement, Kaitlin heard muted voices in Captain Ramal's office, as he held the palm of his hand over the telephone mouthpiece, followed by the dim sound of a door closing.

"At least no one else is there *now*," she whispered out loud. Renfro shot her a warning look.

The scientist in her wanted desperately to control all variables. Kaitlin was suspicious and on-edge. But she quickly realized that she'd just have to take a leap of faith and trust this man. "Very well, thank you for your confirmation, Captain." She allowed Renfro to continue.

Renfro resumed the discussion, unfazed by her outburst. In clear terms, he detailed the circumstances regarding the young engineer who would be arriving in Bangkok the following day. And that one male FBI agent and one female police detective would be surveilling the suspect non-stop until his return to San Francisco a day later.

"We suspect that this individual is traveling to Thailand in order to consummate an illegal transfer of U.S. technology. I'm not in a position to say more than that," Renfro said, not disclosing the fact that Tyler could be carrying information strategic to the entire semiconductor business.

"And who, per chance, do we think this young man will be doing business with here in Thailand?" asked Captain Ramal.

"We don't know. It doesn't really matter," Renfro said.

Captain Ramal sounded alarmed by his terse reply. "Pardon me?" he said rhetorically.

Kaitlin bent towards the speakerphone, about to say something to maintain a rapport with Ramal. But, unfortunately, Renfro continued.

"At this point in time it isn't critical that we apprehend the contact person in Thailand. It is imperative that Gary Tyler returns to U.S. soil. It's his employer that we are really after, and we'll need a solid case against Mr. Tyler in order to get his assistance and cooperation. Following his return to the U.S., you'll be free to apprehend individuals in Thailand, as you see fit."

"I see …" Captain Ramal responded with uncertainty in his voice.

"So, can we count on your support once we hit the ground in Bangkok?" Renfro inquired.

Captain Ramal's silence was disconcerting. Finally, he cleared his throat to respond. "Regrettably, due to the short notice, making the necessary arrangements for this weekend will be quite difficult. And, while this is a matter of some importance to U.S. interests, I am having difficulty seeing how it possibly involves Thailand's national interest."

Renfro had blown it. He'd told Captain Ramal that he'd walk away from the weekend without an arrest. *Why would he invest his department's resources, and perhaps his own personal time, without even the prospect of an arrest?* Kaitlin lamented silently. She was surprised at how little Renfro knew about what motivated people. She'd have to say the right thing now, or Ramal would walk away.

"Captain Ramal, I agree that we've put you in a difficult position," she said, feigning regret. "We'll make do with the assistance of a private investigator in Thailand. That's probably better anyway. It'll be easier to have him travel to California for his testimony. And for all the media appearances ..."

Renfro gave her a look, but Captain Ramal immediately bit at the carrot. "To which media appearances are you referring, Detective?"

She smiled knowingly at Renfro. "Well, this is a high-profile case. It'll probably get picked up on CNN International, the BBC, and others …" Kaitlin drew a mental picture of Ramal wearing an exotic navy blue dress uniform as a guest on *Larry King Live.*

Ramal spoke in a conciliatory tone, "Well ... *perhaps* I can offer you some assistance. The Thai Royal Police is always ready to assist our colleagues in the West. But I can't promise you ten men or anything!"

"That will be fine," Renfro said. "Thanks for your cooperation, Captain Ramal. Detective Hall and I look forward to meeting you tomorrow. In the meantime, we'll e-mail you photos of the suspect, and of our credentials. He'll be on the same flight with us, so please keep a very low profile at the airport."

"Understood," Captain Ramal said sincerely. "I will have a car waiting for you, with our best driver behind the wheel. I'll be in plain clothes. But I'll wear a colorful flower in my lapel, so that you'll recognize me," Ramal said proudly.

Kaitlin thought that he'd perhaps seen one too many American detective films. Ones from the 1950s that had made their way to Thailand in his youth.

In any event, Kaitlin was excited for her first international investigation. She was bound for Thailand to meet the head of the Thai Royal Police. Wearing an orchid in his lapel.

# Chapter 34

The pre-boarding announcement for Thai Airways flight TG5635 echoed throughout the departure terminal, sounding simultaneously muffled and insistent. Kaitlin looked up, as if searching for the source of the voice and reflexively powered down her laptop. As she shut the clamshell cover, she raised her eyes and gazed across the length of the terminal to where Gary Tyler had been quietly sitting for the past forty-five minutes.

Tyler was booked in first class – seat 3A – a window seat on the Boeing 747-400. As such, he'd pre-board and be treated with the utmost care and respect, unlike the cattle-car handling that she and Renfro would receive. They would be waiting in the terminal for a good while longer. Their seats were in row 62, in the rear of the plane. By request.

She was looking forward to walking right past Tyler on the way to her seat, excited for such a close brush with her suspect. But that would be as close as she'd want to get during this trip.

Kaitlin looked over at Renfro sitting next to her. He was also watching Tyler. She shivered with a mild case of goose bumps. She couldn't believe that she'd be spending the next forty-eight hours with Renfro. Her feelings about *that* part of the case were complicated. She told herself that everything would be fine as long as he did his job and didn't get in her way. However, she was prepared for the possibility that he'd pull the typical macho "I'm in charge" routine. She'd deal with that if and when it happened. Mostly, she tried not to think about anything more personal occurring. But vivid memories of Vegas kept popping up, much to her chagrin.

Gary Tyler took a last look at his watch. He gathered up his personal effects, a black leather laptop computer case and a large green daypack, and stood up. Kaitlin felt a jolt of nostalgia. The daypack reminded her of a similar bag that she had buried somewhere in her bedroom closet, a bag she used to bring along on day hikes with her friends in Marin.

She enjoyed a pleasant memory of fresh air, rugged mountain trails, well-made sandwiches, and plastic cups filled with Napa Chardonnay, imbibed at the summit of Mt. Tam. She couldn't even remember the last time that she'd passed a Saturday doing that. She pledged to treat herself to a day in the mountains as soon as this case wrapped up. She added that to the Giants game she'd previously promised herself.

Kaitlin began to think about Gary Tyler a bit differently. He was a pawn – just like Darren Park and the others. He was still alive, but life as he knew it was over.

Tyler handed the Thai Airways counter person his boarding pass. Despite the modest nature of his luggage, he had the regal demeanor of one flying first class on a full fare ticket as he sauntered down the jetway toward the airplane.

Renfro stood and swung his overnight bag over his shoulder. Pulling out two boarding passes from an exterior pocket of the bag, he held one in his outstretched hand and offered it to Kaitlin.

"Are you ready to go, Mrs. Renfro?" he asked.

She flinched. She looked at the ticket as he handed it over. By agreement, they both had dressed in travel-appropriate casual clothes, hoping to look as inconspicuous as possible, but they hadn't formally agreed to any aliases.

"You have *got* to be kidding," she said, annoyed and amused. "Kaitlin *Renfro?* I guess if you want me to play the role of your mother during this gig, I'll have to go along with it," she said drolly.

"You're supposed to be my wife," he said, stating the obvious.

Kaitlin ignored him. "Son, do you need to use the bathroom to make a wee wee before we get on the big airplane?" she asked in her most maternal tone.

"Cute. Let's go honey," Renfro replied light-heartedly.

As they boarded the airplane, Kaitlin deliberately walked down the left-handed aisle, so as to pass right by Tyler's seat. The plane was already two–thirds full, but only a handful of passengers were seated sparsely about the first class cabin.

Tyler and the rest of his first class companions had already been served drinks. He was sipping a Bloody Mary and watching a DVD on the airplane's personal entertainment system. He was so ensconced in the lap of first class luxury that he was oblivious to the shapely young woman slowly walking past him, checking him out from head to toe.

⅄

*Please make sure your seat and tray tables are in an upright position ….*

She'd heard it a million times. She pressed the button on the armrest that sprung forward her seat then closed her eyes for take-off. When she was younger, she loved the sensation of lifting up into the air. Now she just prayed that some Canadian geese didn't fly into the jet's engines.

The flight was long and uneventful. After a brief stop-over in Taipei, the jet continued on and was on its final approach into Bangkok. Renfro had offered Kaitlin the window seat, which she had accepted gratefully. From the window, she gazed down upon the bustling Asian cosmopolis of eight million people, skyscrapers, crisscrossing expressways, and the Chao Praya river undulating like a taupe-colored snake.

As the plane prepared for landing, Kaitlin and Renfro had come to a tricky part of their plan. "We need to get up there," she said, keenly aware that they couldn't risk being caught behind a herd of deplaning people rummaging through overhead bins and under seats, while their suspect dashed through the airport into a waiting car.

"I know," Renfro agreed. "I've been trying to figure that out for the past few hours . . ." He gently elbowed her and whispered. "Come on."

Just before the captain requested the flight attendants to secure the cabin for arrival, they grabbed their bags and bolted forward to two open seats near the front of the plane. They padded down the carpeted aisle and swiftly sat down in the executive class. They were now in the row just behind the first class cabin. The handful of people in that cabin, mostly businessmen, looked at them disdainfully. An exotic looking flight attendant sauntered pass them. She briskly pulled open the velveteen curtain that separated the first class and executive class cabins. As she did, the passenger in seat 3A turned around.

Kaitlin and Renfro found themselves staring eyeball to eyeball with Gary Tyler.

Spontaneously, Kaitlin turned towards Renfro, nuzzling her face in his neck. She had no reason to believe that Tyler would recognize her, but the moment was unsettling nonetheless.

"*Just great ...*" she whispered softly into Renfro's ear. Renfro played along, running his fingers through Kaitlin's hair. Unable to resist, he kissed her softly on the forehead. And then he kissed her again, on the lips.

Kaitlin was startled by the intimacy of the moment. Renfro was playing along a little too well. "All right, Romeo, try not to draw too much attention to us ..." she said, adding a little diplomacy into her words.

"Don't worry honey, he's already turned around," Renfro said, whispering in her ear.

With that, she pulled her head away and gave a firm push off his chest. She was relieved that Tyler had turned completely around; she could only see the back of his leather wrapped seat. She crossed her arms and refused to look at Renfro. She could feel the next thirty hours stretching out before her like an interminable trial. She was determined not to allow what just happened to repeat itself. She'd have to keep things under control.

A few seconds later, the immense jet aircraft landed on the tarmac with a bouncing thud. The whine of the engines and air brakes grew into a loud crescendo. They'd been smart to move up toward the front of the plane. Yet, by the time they exited the plane onto the jetway, Tyler had vanished.

"Let's go!" Kaitlin said, flustered that she couldn't spot Tyler as they entered the interior of the main terminal. Kaitlin and Renfro broke into a slow run, again trying to catch up to Tyler without looking horribly obvious in the process.

They were surprised to see that Tyler had already been cleared through customs by the time they'd gotten there. There were two lines of people waiting to go through, each about fifteen people deep. Kaitlin and Renfro bypassed the line, pulling out their credentials, and discreetly explaining their situation to a Thai customs inspector.

The inspector surreptitiously raced them forward and through the double doors past the checkpoint. Once through the heavy steel double doors, Kaitlin sighed a huge sigh of relief. Tyler was only a hundred feet ahead, near the exit door.

Without warning, a thin man with dark, pockmarked skin darted out from behind a bank of pay telephones, stepping right in front of Kaitlin and Renfro. Kaitlin stiffened, ready for anything. The slender man smiled.

"Welcome to Thailand, detectives," he said courteously. "I'm officer Sung, come right this way," he said, turning around and shepherding them to the curb.

Kaitlin's shoulders relaxed slightly.

Moments later, they were seated in the back seat of an unmarked police car quickly departing Bangkok International Airport and hurtling down Vibhavadi Rangsit Road at breakneck speed. Next to them, Captain Ramal sat grinning. In the dim light of the car, Kaitlin noticed a vibrant purple blossom tucked into his suit lapel.

# Chapter 35

It was near midnight.

Gary Tyler stood several hundred yards in the distance, presenting a ghostly red image through the lenses of the high-powered night vision binoculars that Kaitlin pressed tightly against her face. They'd been watching him stand on the riverbank for about twenty minutes. He'd come here, straight from the airport, through town, and onto Rattanakosin Island, Bangkok's ancient inner city. Bustling during the daytime, the island was now almost deserted.

As they followed from a careful distance, Renfro and Kaitlin determinedly tracked the car in front of them. Captain Ramal played tour guide as if he hadn't a care in the world, or as if he was auditioning for a part in a movie. He excitedly described in great detail the various cultural and historic sites that they passed.

From the car window, Kaitlin had scant time to appreciate sites like the Grand Palace, the National Museum, and Bangkok's famous Floating Market.

"You will have to return when you have time for a proper visit," Captain Ramal said hospitably.

She didn't give much thought to coming back. A true vacation? In Bangkok? She'd love it but … she'd just have to add it to the growing wish list of things to do and places to go.

She pushed thoughts of her wish list aside. All she wanted to concentrate on was Gary Tyler. He paced nervously along the brass railing that separated the palisade from the riverbank and the dark water below. Parked in the shadows, their car was cloaked in darkness. Renfro mounted a camcorder on the car's back door frame. Like Kaitlin's binoculars, the camcorder was equipped with a special night vision lens and circuitry that allowed it to film in exceedingly low light.

In begrudging acknowledgement that maybe Renfro wasn't a complete ass, she was impressed at how many devices he had managed to stuff in that backpack of his. He was, if nothing else, industrious, Kaitlin thought. Captain Ramal and his assistant were also impressed by Renfro's gadgetry, and they praised him exuberantly.

Renfro sighed, as he lifted his head away from the camera viewfinder and rubbed his eyes. "I've got twenty minutes of this guy walking back and forth. Hardly Oscar material."

"Ah, the Academy Awards ..." said Captain Ramal ponderously. "I'm quite a fan of American motion pictures. Let's see, *Titanic* ... *Sleepless in Seattle* ... *Beaches* ... All very good films!"

Kaitlin glanced at Captain Ramal and raised her eyebrows. She had correctly pegged him for an American film buff. But she found it surprising that he was partial to tear-jerker, chick flicks.

"How interesting," she said, returning her binoculars. "Those are *my* favorite movies." Her sarcasm was lost on Ramal.

"They are? Why, we have something in common, then!" Ramal said gleefully.

Renfro just shook his head in disbelief. He could tell Kaitlin was pulling Ramal's leg.

Suddenly, Ramal's assistant, the sprightly, dark-skinned Sung became agitated and began speaking rapidly, in a low voice.

"What? What's he saying?" Kaitlin asked Ramal.

"Behind us, a car is coming. Its lights are turned off. Look!"

The four of them simultaneously cocked their heads and looked out the small car's back window.

From a distance, a sedan was slowly approaching the waterfront from the dimness of the access road that cut through the park.

"This is it!" Kaitlin said. "Keep the camera rolling," she directed Renfro unnecessarily.

"Yes, Mr. Spielberg," he said.

The car slowly pulled to a stop at the curb about twenty feet from where Tyler was standing. Nothing happened.

Twenty seconds later, the car's headlights turned on, and a man stepped out of the driver's side door, in a curious reversal of normal sequence. The man approached Tyler, a dark object in his left hand. Through the binoculars, she could see no one else in the car, an old dilapidated Malaysian import.

"What's he holding?" Renfro asked.

"It looks like they are both holding something," Kaitlin responded. "Tyler has something really small in his right hand. It looks like a Zip Disk," Kaitlin said, knowing that the popular brand of high-density portable computer disk could hold a tremendous amount of data. "And the other guy is holding a bag. Looks like a knapsack."

"Damn ... I wish we had a little more light," Renfro said.

The two men stood an arm's length away from each other. In a single fluid motion, Tyler stretched out his right arm and dropped his item into the knapsack as the other man simultaneously handed Tyler something smaller that glinted in the weak light of the distant street lamp.

"They've made the transfer. It appears that Gary Tyler has been handed a metallic object. It's tiny, a key perhaps," Renfro narrated for the benefit of the videotape.

Kaitlin expected the two to go their separate ways. But rather than return to his car with the bag, the man who had come to make the exchange suddenly climbed onto the middle rung of the brass railing and began waving his hand above his head in a big sweeping motion.

"He's waving to someone. It's a signal!" Ramal said excitedly. "To someone on the other side of the river … or to a boat!"

Kaitlin cranked down her window halfway and listened intently. In the silence of the park she could clearly distinguish the rumble of a motorboat emanating from the river below.

"Captain Ramal's right. It's a boat!" she said.

Suddenly, the man on the railing clutched the top rung with his left hand. He leaned back, and with a heave, hurled the knapsack forward into the darkness.

"I'll be damned!" Renfro exclaimed.

The man hopped off the railing and, without another look at Tyler, walked to his car and drove off. Tyler slipped the metallic object that he'd been handed into his pants pocket and started walking in the opposite direction. He walked toward the main street, heading back into Bangkok's modern downtown.

The rumble of the motorboat peaked, its engine gunning, speeding away into the darkness of the Chao Praya river. Kaitlin knew that the Zip Disk and its priceless contents would never be seen again. Its buyer would never be known.

With the physical evidence gone, all that Kaitlin and Renfro had was Tyler's surreptitious travel to Thailand. And videotape footage of him exchanging some kind of disk with an unidentifiable man. It certainly looked suspicious. But it wasn't anywhere near enough to indict Warren Harriman. For all Kaitlin knew, the computer disk was a bootleg copy of Microsoft Office. She had no proof that the Zip Disk tossed into a waiting speedboat contained LightWave's export-controlled technology. To prove that, they'd need to get Tyler's cooperation.

The police car remained in a humble silence. As Gary Tyler neared the periphery of the waterfront park, Kaitlin finally spoke. "Tyler's going to get into a cab. Let's start moving, otherwise we'll lose him." Her voice was urgent, bordering on frantic.

Tyler was all that they had left. To put together a legitimate case against Harriman, they'd have to follow Tyler all the way back to his source. Back to Calloway. Ideally, back to Warren Harriman. All the dots would need to be connected.

# Chapter 36

Kaitlin and Renfro followed Tyler to the Shangri-La Hotel where he checked into a business suite. He instructed the desk that he would like a five a.m. wakeup call and asked the concierge to make arrangements for the six twenty a.m. flight to Koh Samui island. When Kaitlin questioned the pretty, and very helpful, Thai concierge, she learned that Tyler had asked her to schedule his return from Koh Samui on a five a.m. Monday flight so that he could catch the eight a.m. flight out of Bangkok International Airport.

The Bangkok Air flight to Koh Samui was aboard a puddle jumper – a plane holding at most twenty passengers. Kaitlin and Renfro decided not to risk being spotted by Tyler. Instead, they agreed that Captain Ramal and Mr. Sung should make the excursion – making sure Tyler didn't drink too many Mai Tais. They needed him back on that jet to San Francisco in one piece.

"But my family …" Ramal had protested, not at all pleased to work on a Sunday instead of spending time with his wife and children.

But Kaitlin, fond of exercising her low-tech skills related to human nature and the manipulation thereof, reminded Captain Ramal of his upcoming appearance on American television, and suggested that he try to relax and get a little sun.

Captain Ramal sighed deeply. “I suppose you are right,” he said, quietly agreeing to spend Sunday on Koh Samui’s white sand beaches.

Kaitlin and Renfro checked into separate, but adjacent, rooms. Riding in the elevator, Kaitlin noticed how tired Renfro looked. Jetlag had kicked in full bore. For the first time since they’d left, she viewed him with some sympathy. She was tired herself. The stress of the day’s events had wiped out both of them.

They got out of the elevator and walked down the hall, coming upon Kaitlin’s room first. Renfro’s was the next door down.

“Well, I guess this is good night,” she said with a yawn. “I had no idea that you were an aspiring filmmaker.” She inserted the plastic keycard into the door lock. “Good work out there tonight,” she said, remembering how adeptly Renfro had set up the whole surveillance despite being fifteen hours and 8,000 miles from home.

The tiny green LED flashed, and the door lock clicked with its release.

Renfro smiled despite his exhaustion. “Coming from you, that’s high praise indeed,” he said. Kaitlin was relieved; the air had been cleared.

"I think we got pretty damn lucky, seeing what we saw. And no matter what … this trip was worth taking," Renfro reflected. Unlike Kaitlin, he was less confident that they'd laid a foundation for a winnable case. But they had seen something significant.

She smiled slightly, wearily.

"Sleep well," he said, adjusting the weight of his backpack on his shoulder, walking sluggishly toward his room.

Their mutual exhaustion had saved them from any awkward moment before they went into their respective rooms. Kaitlin had worried there would be some weird tension. But there wasn't. Not much.

The hotel's turn-down service had lowered the lighting, fluffed the pillows, and closed the window curtains. The sound of traditional Thai instrumental music lilted gently through the room. As she admired the ambience, Kaitlin was disappointed that her short stay coupled with jetlag would compromise her enjoyment of the opulent hotel. She dropped her bags, undressed, and tumbled onto the amazingly comfortable bed.

As her naked body melted into the cocoon of her enormous bed, she deeply inhaled the fragrance of lotus flowers on the nightstand while her analytical mind wondered *how high is the thread-count on these bed sheets?* They were impossibly soft. Then Kaitlin's mind drifted automatically into her common bedtime pattern from childhood: counting to a million in prime numbers. By the time she got to 37, she was asleep.

⅄

The following day, which Tyler spent tanning and drinking on Lamai Beach as Kaitlin had predicted, Kaitlin and Renfro worked at a furious pace. They set up operations in Renfro's room. Both of their computers were set up on the small, ornate, wooden desk near the window. The task at hand was to succinctly summarize the factual case against Gary Tyler, down to the events of the previous evening. While Kaitlin began to type, Renfro got on the telephone and called the Federal Courthouse in San Francisco.

"I need to get a hold of Brad Field," Renfro barked to the courthouse operator. Field was the Federal Prosecutor with whom Renfro had spoken briefly about this case before they'd departed for Bangkok. Unfortunately, in his haste, Renfro had not made a definitive plan to contact him from Thailand, and so he didn't have Field's cell phone or home number.

"I know it's Saturday night," he said to the operator who clearly was uninterested in his demands, "but I need to get in touch with him. *Now.*"

Renfro felt the urgency and sense of panic more than Kaitlin. This wasn't San Jose anymore. This was the Big League. If he could provide Field with sufficient evidence by Sunday in California, and if he could convince Field to buy in on what they produced, Field could put the case in front of the federal Grand Jury as early as Monday morning. All the planets had to align.

If all of that happened, a multiple-count indictment would be waiting for Gary Tyler when his plane hit the runway back at SFO.

"I'm sorry, I *cannot* provide you his home telephone number," the operator said testily. "However, if you leave me a message, I can page him for you."

"Fine. Page him and tell him to check his office voicemail and his office e-mail *exactly* at midnight tonight. This can't wait until tomorrow."

"Thank you," the operator said hastily, hanging up.

"You think he'll actually get the message on time?" Kaitlin asked.

"I don't know," Renfro said, leaning back and rubbing his eyes. "We won't know until midnight California time."

That meant that they had a little over six hours to completely assemble their case. Kaitlin felt the comfortable rush of adrenaline. She performed best against a deadline – she had survived a countless number of them during ten years of higher education. Of course, this was different than anything she'd ever tackled before. And that knowledge led to a tightening of the muscles in her stomach.

Turning from her computer, she picked up Renfro's camcorder off the desk.

"What are you doing?" he asked.

"High-tech," she said with a smile. Her work with Slim over the past few days inspired her to apply all of her talents at just the right time and in the right measure.

Renfro gave her a quizzical look.

"I've got a high throughput video input cable with my laptop," Kaitlin said, beaming. "I can digitize your videotape, at least ten to fifteen minutes of it, and put it into a computer file. Using a compression program, I can squeeze that file into something small enough to e-mail. The Grand Jury will be able to see exactly what we saw last night."

"Excellent," Renfro said, genuinely impressed. Although he was no Luddite, he wasn't nearly as proficient as she was when it came to computer stuff. "You computer geeks really surprise me sometimes," he said.

"I'll take that as a compliment," Kaitlin said, initiating the download sequence.

Around two thirty p.m., Kaitlin hit the send button on her e-mail program, transmitting the fifty-page investigation report and the video file to Brad Field. Even with her 56k dialup modem, Kaitlin knew it would take a while. And if the connection dropped, she'd have to start from the beginning. So when the "file transfer completed" message finally flashed on her computer monitor, Kaitlin slumped in her chair with fatigue and relief.

"Nicely done, detective," Renfro said, patting her on the shoulder. "Can I buy you lunch?"

"Sure, I'm starving," Kaitlin said. She stood up and stretched her arms toward the ceiling, looking out the picture window at the spectacular city below. She'd been so focused on work that she hadn't so much as glanced out the window the entire day. Her eyes settled on the glittering blue water of the pool several floors below them.

"Hey, is there any way we can forward the phone calls to this room out to the pool and order lunch out there? I *really* need to get outside."

Renfro grinned. "Even I know that that technology exists," he said. "I don't know why I didn't think of it," he added, picking up the phone and calling the operator.

Ten minutes later, they were basking in the sun in the hotel's luxuriant tropical pool area and savoring the Thai joy of lemongrass noodles, mangos, and spicy curry, beautifully prepared and presented. Courtesy of the Federal government. Kaitlin was pleased to see her tax dollars at work.

⅄

"That was delicious," Kaitlin said, delicately wiping the corner of her mouth with a cloth napkin. An armada of tuxedo-wearing waiters cleared the dishes when the phone rang, startling them both. There was a brief second of inaction before they both reached for the phone at the center of the patio table.

Renfro got there first. "Renfro," he said.

"Renfro, Brad Field here."

"Brad, good to hear from you," Renfro said deliberately, so Kaitlin knew that they had succeeded in making contact. "We were concerned that we might not be able to reach you. You get the e-mail?"

Listening to the conversation, Kaitlin sat upright in her chair, and pulled off her sunglasses, observing Renfro intently.

"I received it."

After a very long pause Field continued, "I'll grant that you and Detective Hall have laid out an interesting set of facts. But I'll tell you quite candidly, we've got some serious 4$^{th}$ amendment problems here."

Renfro expected that.

"Is Detective Hall there with you?" Field asked.

"Yeah, she's here." Renfro glanced sidewise at her. He still couldn't believe he'd found himself 8,000 miles away from California with perhaps the most beautiful genius on the planet.

Kaitlin's ears perked up, and she went around to Renfro's side of the table. She put her ear up to his ear, allowing herself to hear the Federal Prosecutor. The line was crystal clear.

"You might suggest to her that she reread the police manual on searches and seizures. Apparently, she wouldn't know a lawful one if it came up and bit her on the ass," Field said jokingly. Kaitlin smiled.

"I'll let her know. But all things considered, do you think we have what it takes?"

Field paused again.

"As far as Gary Tyler goes, I think so. That videotape is key. Looks like there's enough documented history behind Tyler's weekend travel to Thailand and other foreign countries. Coupled with his unbridled access to his LightWave's technology – I think there might be enough to indict him. I'm not confident we'll win a conviction, but I never am at this stage …"

"Then you'll move forward and seek an indictment?" Renfro asked, trying not to sound too pushy.

"Sure … it's worth a shot to get one against Tyler. But I've got to warn you, Renfro. Before we go after *anyone* at Harriman & Co. or LightWave, we're going to need concrete evidence. Concrete and taint-free evidence."

"Understood. That's great, Brad," Renfro said cheerfully.

"Listen," Field continued, "police manual or no, after all that Detective Hall has done, we owe her the opportunity to get this in front of the Grand Jury."

Renfro raised his eyes to Kaitlin's. She was smiling ebulliently. "Good job," he mouthed silently.

"We'll be looking for you as soon as we hit the ground at SFO," Renfro said. "I hope you'll have a nice long piece of paper signed by the Grand Jury waiting for us …"

"I hope so too, Special Agent Renfro. Have a safe trip back," Field said, hanging up.

Renfro turned to Kaitlin. "Congratulations."

They hugged warmly, without any awkwardness. Kaitlin was happy. Happier than she ever remembered being. In a strange way, she was pleased that Renfro was there sharing it with her.

They spent the rest of the day making sure that they had all their "t's" crossed and their "i's" dotted. Before leaving, they said their good-byes to Captain Ramal and Mr. Sung at Bangkok's international airport. Gary Tyler had already boarded Thai Airways flight TG634 and was comfortably tucked into first-class; tanned and rested but nursing a moderate hangover.

With the time difference and their passage over the International Date Line, their flight would arrive first thing Monday morning in San Francisco.

"Have a safe flight," Captain Ramal said.

"Thank you for everything," Renfro replied.

"We look forward to seeing you again very soon," Kaitlin said, in an oblique reference to the captain's hopes of being on television.

The return flight to SFO was uneventful. She was not a woman that demanded luxuries, but flying sixteen hours in coach-class was no fun. The whole time she squirmed and stretched trying to minimize the aches and pains in her back and shoulders. She was mindful that Gary Tyler, on the other hand, spent the whole trip pampered by the fineries of the first-class cabin.

"He'd better be enjoying himself up there," Kaitlin said to Renfro halfway through the flight. She picked away unhappily at the less-than-appetizing economy-class meal. They'd served a small mosaic of Thai cuisine that didn't quite match her appetite.

"Don't worry," Renfro said. "He'll be missing many creature comforts for at least the next couple of years – or longer if he decides not to cooperate."

Kaitlin looked at her watch. Six hours to go. Six hours and they'd be at SFO, and one step closer to nabbing Warren Harriman.

# Chapter 37

"What the hell?" Gary Tyler stammered when the gaunt customs agent directed him into a secondary inspection room. He'd smoked a little bit of weed on Koh Samui, but he sure as hell wasn't stupid enough to bring any back with him. There wasn't anything to be found in his bag. How many times had he flown in and out of SFO to Asia? He'd never once been questioned by U.S. Customs, much less undergone a secondary inspection.

He felt a strange, fearful emotion rising up within him. Something had gone wrong, but he had no idea what it was. "Shit," he sighed. Even though his trip went off without a hitch, similar to every other trip, he had a bad feeling about this.

Tyler expected to be led to a small, sterile, windowless inspection room, where he'd be asked to unpack his suitcase. Maybe even asked to strip off all his clothes. But instead, his eyes widened in shock as he walked into a conference room filled with people. Very serious-looking people. None of whom he immediately recognized. There were several men wearing suits. One of them was a tall guy with dark hair and dressed in casual clothing. Tyler's eyes settled on him for a moment. He looked vaguely familiar. Tyler quickly placed the face; the guy had been on his flight to Thailand. In fact, so had the good-looking woman next to him. *They were the couple making out on the plane ... what the hell?*

The casually-dressed man stepped forward.

"Mr. Tyler, I'm Special Agent Alex Renfro of the Federal Bureau of Investigation, and this is Federal Prosecutor Brad Field," he said, introducing the man at his side. Field nodded at Tyler and then extended his hand towards him. Gary robotically reached forward, half-expecting a handshake. Instead, the prosecutor presented him with a lengthy document.

Before Gary read the title page, the FBI agent started speaking eerily familiar words. Time stood still. "*Gary Tyler, you have the right to remain silent, anything you say or do can be used against you in a court of law. You have the right to an attorney. If you cannot afford an attorney ....*"

The words trailed off into the background as Gary Tyler read the first few sentences from the document now in his possession. It was from the Federal Grand Jury. It stated that Gary Tyler was being indicted under charges of violation of Sections 736, 738, 742, 774, Categories 3 and 6 of the U.S. Export Administration Regulation and the Economic Espionage Act of 1996. As he read, his pulse raced, and he could feel his heart pounding. His throat went dry, and he had a vague feeling that he might vomit.

The FBI agent introduced the rest of the people in the room as if Gary Tyler was a late arrival to a dinner party. His mind still spinning, Tyler struggled to follow the introductions; there were a bunch of FBI guys, the woman detective from the San Jose Police Department, a guy from the Department of Commerce, and another Federal prosecutor.

"Why don't you have a seat?" Renfro said, gesturing to a metal folding chair. "This is going to take some time. You want something to drink?"

Tyler was in a daze. He swallowed hard. Then, with his voice cracking, all he could say was, "I want to call a lawyer."

Renfro nodded his head and handed him his cell phone. "That's a good idea, Mr. Tyler. You're in serious trouble here."

Gary stared at the cell phone blankly, trying to figure out whom exactly to call. LightWave had an in-house lawyer, but under the circumstances he knew he couldn't call him.

It was at that time that the woman detective's cell phone rang. She excused herself and stepped out into the back corridor.

"Detective Hall," she answered.

"Welcome home!" Even through the choppy wireless connection, the sound of Slim's voice was pleasantly reassuring. "How'd it go?" he asked cheerfully.

"It went great!" she said, unable to contain her pleasure at how things had turned out. "In fact, I'm at SFO and Gary

Tyler's in the next room. He was just handed a Grand Jury indictment. I thought he might lose his lunch when he read it."

"Excellent! You did it, Kaitlin. We have to celebrate. I want to hear all about Thailand."

Kaitlin smiled. "I'll be up for a celebration in a few days, I hope. As for Thailand, I can tell you all about the amazing interiors of the Shangri La hotel," Kaitlin said sarcastically.

"I know. It was a working weekend for you. But tell me – did you work as hard as Gary Tyler?" Slim asked mysteriously.

Kaitlin paused before answering, thinking of the guy in the next room having the screws applied. She didn't know what Slim was getting at. "Slim, I'm a little tired. What're you talking about?"

"Well, Gary Tyler returned to SFO this morning $50,000 richer. A certain numbered bank account in Barbados just received the funds this morning. The balance of that account now stands at 375,000 U.S. dollars."

"Slim, you never fail to amaze me. I'm glad you are one of the good guys," Kaitlin said admiringly.

"Hey, no need to hurl insults. One day I may put my talents towards doing the work of evil. My mom always said I wasn't ambitious enough."

"Very funny. Thanks for the scoop on our friend Tyler. The timing of that funds transfer certainly helps corroborate the fact that he was paid for making the trip to Thailand."

"Listen, let me know if tomorrow night works for you. I want to take you out for a big night of sushi and sake," Slim offered happily.

"That's sounds great. If there is any way I can do it, I will. Talk to you later, Slim."

When Kaitlin returned to the room, the crowd had thinned out. Gary Tyler sat at the table, looking catatonic as he stared blankly at the wall. Renfro came over to her and whispered, "His family's lawyer is on the way down here. We're moving him to one of the private conference rooms now." Kaitlin nodded in agreement.

"Let's go, Tyler," she said. "We're going to take a little walk and wait for your lawyer to get here."

He rose obediently from the table and followed them down the hall without uttering a word. He sat silently in the conference room for another hour, until his lawyer arrived. They met privately for a half-hour then Kaitlin, Renfro, Field, and the other Federal Prosecutor joined them in the conference room.

"It's a pretty heavy indictment," Field said coldly. "We have videotape of the exchange, and we just got confirmation this morning of $50,000 transferred to an account held by Gary Tyler in Barbados."

Tyler and his lawyer said nothing for several seconds. Finally, the lawyer, a stout balding man in a crumpled suit, asked Field, "What are you prepared to offer?"

"In exchange for your client's full cooperation, we're willing to recommend a substantially reduced sentence. Five years in a minimum-security facility."

"*Five years*?" Gary Tyler blurted out, before his lawyer could silence him.

Field turned the screws further. "Mr. Tyler, if the technology you helped export went to a hostile foreign government, you could face treason charges. That's a capital offense."

The lawyer interceded. "Respectfully, you know you aren't going to get a treason charge, Mr. Field, much less a conviction. As you have pointed out, this is serious business. I would appreciate you not playing games. That said, by my client's cooperation, what exactly do you mean?"

"Testimony. We want to know every detail about his activity and everything about the people involved in this scheme. Both inside and outside of LightWave. And we want him to wear a wire."

"*Forget it!*" Tyler blurted out again.

"Gary, please!" his lawyer said in frustration, trying to keep him silent.

Kaitlin spoke up. "Mr. Tyler, there's something you should know before you make a decision." She walked forward and sat in the seat next to him at the conference room table. "The men who set this up – and we know that includes Warren Harriman and Shane Calloway – have worked this deal with other young men like you. Several of them are now dead."

Tyler's face went white. He was about to speak, but his lawyer beat him to it. "What are you talking about?"

"In the last two years, at least ten guys working at Harriman & Co. portfolio companies have died. Their deaths were made to look like accidents, but they weren't.

Five of those guys were in system administration. Just like Gary. Shane Calloway convinced all of them to steal and illegally export sensitive technology from their companies. Each one received lots of cash, but the ones who profited most from this scheme were Shane Calloway and Warren Harriman.

"And I can tell you that those other guys didn't get to enjoy a fraction of their money before they were murdered." She paused and let the message sink in.

"Gary, you may not believe this," she continued, "but if not for us, you would have been killed within the next few months. They don't like loose ends. And if you don't help us, it's likely that several more guys, just like you, will die doing exactly what you were trying to do – chasing a fantasy."

Gary shook his head in disbelief. He thought of all his meetings with Shane Calloway. He respected him. He was a straight shooter. He was war hero. A torrent of questions followed: Had he really been misled? Was his life really in jeopardy? Was he really going to prison? Tyler's face screwed up in fear and pain.

He didn't want to believe it, but he quickly came to realize that these people were telling the truth. He'd been duped by Shane Calloway. A man who planned to have him killed as soon as he'd served his purpose. He felt stupid and bitter.

The pudgy lawyer put his hand on his client's shoulder. "My client is going to need some time to weigh the offer."

But before he could finish, Tyler cut him off and pushed his hand away. "I don't need more time. I'll wear the fucking wire," he said, looking right at Kaitlin and then Renfro.

"I'll draw up the paperwork for a cooperation agreement and a plea bargain right away," Field said, addressing his comment to Gary Tyler's lawyer.

Tyler's lawyer looked away, somewhat dejected. He knew his client was doing the right thing, but he certainly didn't have many options. His client had dug a deep hole, all he could do was throw him a rope.

Only a few hours later, the papers were signed. Renfro and Kaitlin returned to the conference room where they met members of the FBI's Special Operations Group, one of whom was a Technically Trained Agent.

"When are you planning to see Shane Calloway?" Kaitlin asked.

"Wednesday night," Gary answered with some difficulty, still uncomfortable discussing the subject.

"What's the purpose of the meeting?" Renfro asked. "You've already done your job and been paid, right?"

"After each trip, I meet with him."

"Alone?" Kaitlin asked.

"Yeah. Always alone. We go to a really fancy restaurant. He buys me a big dinner, and I give him one of these," Tyler said, reaching into his front pants pocket. He pulled out a large gold coin.

Renfro and Kaitlin examined the coin carefully. The coin looked very old. It had a small square in the center, and one side was covered with engravings of men and various animals; the reverse bore an inscription in Chinese characters.

"This is what you were handed in Bangkok, when you handed over the Zip Disk?" Kaitlin asked, remembering the scene captured on videotape.

"Yeah."

"And each time you hand off a delivery to someone, you get handed one of these coins?" she asked.

"Not the same coin. Each time they're different."

Renfro and Kaitlin looked at each other. "It's a code," Kaitlin said. "It confirms that Gary made the delivery. And it tells Calloway something."

"Like payment instructions?" asked Renfro

"Maybe," Kaitlin said. "We need to get someone to translate the inscription. But Gary needs to hold on to the coin. He can't show up at dinner Wednesday night without it. We'll x-ray and photocopy both sides of it."

"When and where are you having dinner with Calloway?" Renfro asked.

"In the City," Tyler concentrated, trying to remember the restaurant's name. "A place called La Folly. On Polk Street. Wednesday night at eight o'clock."

"I know the place," Kaitlin said. "La Folie" was the restaurant that Tyler was referring to. She'd read a write-up on it in a magazine a few months ago. It was one of San Francisco's most exclusive French restaurants. Needless to say, Kaitlin had not had the pleasure of dining there.

The SOG agents stepped forward. The TTA placed a shiny silver hard-sided briefcase onto the table. With his thumbs, he clicked the double locks open. He lifted the top to reveal a black plastic device nestled in a cushion of thick gray foam. It was a little larger than a pager. A couple of long stringy wires extended from it. It was a sound recorder. One wire led to a microphone, the other to an on/off switch.

"This is how it works," the TTA explained, his demeanor clinical and his words clear. "Wednesday night, by six p.m. at the latest, you'll want to strap the mechanism to the inside of your underwear. Wrap it several times with this medical tape. Use the tape to string this wire up the side of your chest, so that the microphone comes up to just below your armpit," he demonstrated, lifting his arm. "The other wire should come up inside your pants to just inside your waistline. Use the switch to turn it off and on.

"Wear a thick shirt. Heavy cotton. Or, better yet, a wool sweater. Turn the switch on no more than ten minutes before you go into the restaurant. It has a limited battery life. That's it – that's all you need to do.

"Any questions?"

Tyler shook his head despondently.

Renfro leaned forward, his hands clasped on the edge of the conference room table. "What we need on the recording is Calloway stating clearly that he knew what sort of information was on the Zip Disk that you took to Thailand. And it's got to be clear that *he* put you up to making that trip. We'll be right outside the restaurant, Gary," Renfro said.

Tyler remained mute.

"You have nothing to worry about," he said, trying his best to be sincere and convincing.

The TTA gently put the recording device into a black plastic case and handed it to Gary Tyler.

"Okay, Gary," said Renfro calmly. "It looks like we're set."

"Easy for you to say," Tyler said uneasily.

Kaitlin walked over to Gary and put her hand on his shoulder. "Listen, I'm sorry things played out this way for you. What you did was illegal, and you knew it. But right now, you need to do what you can to protect yourself. Signing the cooperation agreement was the right thing to do. You just need to get through the next couple of days like nothing's happened."

"*Like nothing's happened? Are you crazy?*" Tyler said, excitedly. "Calloway will kill me if he finds out what's happened. Or if he catches me wearing this thing," Tyler said, holding up the recorder. Beads of sweat glistened on his forehead.

"Frankly, Calloway was already prepared to kill you – to protect himself. You've got to keep your cool. It's business as usual." She handed him a business card. "Here's my cell phone number," she said. "If anything comes up, or if you just want to talk, feel free to call me." Kaitlin looked at her watch. "You need to get to work. You're already a couple hours late."

Gary Tyler dreaded the idea of going in to the office. His expectation of soon becoming a millionaire had kept him going the last several months. Now, rather than looking forward to a life of leisure on a tropical island, he was facing several years in prison. He was ruined.

*It's so goddamn unfair*, he thought. He picked up his bag and walked out the conference room door.

# Chapter 38

Torres was beaming. "Kaitlin, that was remarkable detective work. Really impressive," he said, nodding measuredly. She'd never seen Torres so ecstatic before – and the sight spooked her as much as pleased her. She knew he was relieved as well as pleased. His judgment and faith in her had proved correct. "I want you to take the rest of the day. Comp time. Go home and relax. You must be dog tired."

As soon as Torres said it, Kaitlin realized that she'd been running on sheer adrenaline – and coffee. She *was* tired. Beat. She'd never adjusted to Thailand time. And she wasn't yet on California time. Her internal clock was totally screwed up. The thought of going home, taking a hot shower, and sleeping in her own bed for the next eight hours seemed absolutely divine.

"Boss, I'm going to take you up on that offer," she said. She had meant the comment to be appreciative but, in her exhaustion, it came out as matter-of-fact.

"Good," he said, smiling.

While she'd been in Thailand, a team of San Jose police officers and FBI technicians had done a thorough sweep of the entire squad room. The only bugging devices found were the ones that she and Torres had discovered on their respective computers. The rest of the squad room was clean.

Over the course of the coming days and weeks, the FBI's Engineering Resource Facility in Quantico would be conducting a detailed analysis, trying to determine the source of the bugging equipment. Kaitlin didn't need their report to know that those devices had been placed in her office by operatives of Harriman & Co. If she'd had any doubts before, they had vanished in Thailand.

⅄

When Kaitlin returned to the office the following day, she felt like a new woman. That day was the best day she'd had in the office in months. The first part was spent chatting with Newmeyer, Camhi, and a couple of the other detectives, filling them in on the case that had occupied her time and thoughts over the past several weeks. She didn't worry about Torres busting her chops. She was in his good graces. For now.

Around noon she remembered Slim's offer of the prior morning. "Oh shit," she said, regretting that she hadn't called him back yet. She picked up the phone and was happy to hear his voice again.

"Can I take you up on that sushi offer?" she asked.

"Absolutely. Tonight?"

"Tonight would be great," she said.

"Seven o'clock – let's go to Ebisu. I know one of the sushi men behind the counter – we can skip the line," he said.

"You are too good to me, Slim," Kaitlin said. "See you there."

The next few hours at work she spent catching up on paperwork and other things that on any other day would have driven her crazy. But she was one day away from busting Warren Harriman and Shane Calloway. Life was good and she was loving it.

She left the office early, giving her time to go home, change into a celebratory outfit, and drive up to San Francisco for dinner with the one guy who had helped her make the investigation a reality.

⅄

"God, you look great," Slim said, giving her a big hug in front of the restaurant. Night descended and a light drizzle fell on the city. Gently illuminated by the restaurant's outdoor light, Kaitlin looked particularly beautiful. Indeed, compared to how she'd looked the last few times they'd been together, she seemed rejuvenated and confident; in other words, his old Kaitlin was back.

"So do you," Kaitlin replied sincerely. Slim had actually put on a midnight blue, long-sleeved knit shirt and khaki slacks for the occasion. She couldn't remember the last time she'd seen him wear anything other than shorts or jeans and a faded tee.

As usual, Ebisu was packed. Kaitlin and Slim squeezed through the crowd in the restaurant's main room. Ebisu had the best sushi in town, but the place was nothing much to look at. Over the years, Slim and Kaitlin had treated themselves to a few fabulous meals together here, even as students, when neither of them could really afford it.

Slim was greeted with a boisterous call of "Suminasen!" from behind the sushi counter, and his friend waved them forward to two empty seats at the center of the sushi bar. Soon Slim was pouring two shot glasses of hot sake and two tall glasses of Sapporo. He raised a glass of beer and offered a toast to his friend. "Here's to you, Kaitlin. On a job well done. And on risking everything to pursue the things that you truly believe in."

She smiled and clinked glasses with him. Then she leaned over and gave him a hug. "That's very sweet."

As they enjoyed their drinks, Slim thought about his toast to Kaitlin. It was true; she was the sort of person who risked everything in pursuit of her goals. And in that moment, Slim realized that he was not. And it greatly bothered him.

He was absolutely crazy about Kaitlin. But there was no way he could say anything to her. He'd invested too much in their friendship. And he didn't want to jeopardize what they had in pursuit of a relationship beyond that. They had a great thing between them, and as strong as his attraction was for her, he just wouldn't risk it.

"Damn," he thought, pushing his disappointment back.

A few minutes later, the sushi master presented them with the evening's first sampling of rolls, sushi, and sashimi. It was such a dazzling offering that it took the sushi chef some time to identify each by name. Kaitlin and Slim were especially impressed with a marvel of a roll called the "Pink Cadillac."

"Enjoy!" said the sushi chef.

Before they could take that first delectable bite, dinner was interrupted by the ring of Kaitlin's cell phone. Slim knew that she hated answering calls inside restaurants. She hesitated, wrinkling her face in mental debate about whether to answer it. She looked worried.

"Go ahead – answer it," Slim said with understanding.

"Hello?" she said.

"Detective Hall, it's me, Gary Tyler," he blurted.

"Yes, Gary, what is it?"

"Calloway just called, he changed the plan, I'm meeting him *tonight* at the restaurant, not tomorrow." Somewhat panicked, his words ran together.

"Exactly what time?" she demanded sharply, looking at her watch as her pulse raced.

"*Right now*, I'm on my way, north on 101. I'm supposed to be there by eight."

It was seven-thirty. She'd have to act fast. "Okay, Gary. Don't worry. I'll be there. Same plan as before?" she said, reassuringly.

"I guess so – " He paused in mid-sentence.

"What is it, Gary," Kaitlin asked.

"Calloway said that tonight I was going to meet someone. Someone very important … I think it might be Warren Harriman."

"Even better," she said with calm confidence. She worked hard to mask the panic in her voice. She didn't want to unnerve him. "Just do exactly as we planned. We'll talk to you after dinner. As soon as you're alone," she said before hanging up.

"Slim, we've got to go – now!" She practically shouted at him as she leapt from the bar stool.

"You've got to be kidding!" Slim said, pulling out his wallet and throwing several bills onto the counter. The next thing he knew, they were in Kaitlin's car racing towards Van Ness. As soon as they pulled away from the curb, she dialed Renfro's cell phone number, praying he would answer. It rang three times before he picked up.

"Renfro," he answered, his voice quiet and tense.

"Renfro, it's me, Kaitlin. We've got a problem!"

"What do you mean?" he asked.

"Gary Tyler just called. His dinner with Calloway is happening tonight. They changed the plan on him. We've got less than a half hour to get there!"

"Shit!" he snapped. "You're damned right we have a problem. I'm in the Port of Oakland right now with my entire team. The Bobby Park car shipment is happening here tonight. Everyone is in position for a major seizure and multiple arrests. I can't move them now."

"Well, I'm on my way to La Folie now. I don't want to go this alone. You had *better* get me some help soon."

"I'll do what I can, as soon as I can. Keep me posted," Renfro said. "Shit …"

"Shit!" Kaitlin agreed as she tossed the cell phone to Slim.

Slim didn't like the sound of the conversation, but he didn't see the sense in pursuing it. Not when Kaitlin was running stoplights at speeds upward of fifty. Maybe it was the hot sake, but he found himself thinking of the old saying that Native American warriors said before entering battle: '*It's a good day to die.*' He closed his eyes and gripped the dashboard.

⅄

Kaitlin's mind was occupied with driving at top speed and thoughts of what might happen to Gary Tyler tonight. He had never met Warren Harriman. It made perfect sense that Shane Calloway limited Gary Tyler's contacts with other people in their organization. The less Tyler knew, the better. But now, Kaitlin surmised, it was time for him to meet the boss. Naturally, at the City's most sumptuous restaurant. The type of meeting that makes a jet-lagged techie drive from Sunnyvale to Half Moon Bay on a rainy night, she thought, remembering Darren Park's so-called accident.

How many young men in Silicon Valley, Kaitlin wondered, were willing to illegally sell their company's – their country's – cutting-edge technology in exchange for a million dollars? *Too many*, she concluded. There seemed to be enough dissatisfied guys that would jump at an opportunity of a seven-digit Caribbean bank account and earning financial rewards sooner rather than later.

These were not people driven in desperation to desperate acts. They were talented but flawed young men with a sense of entitlement, trying to beat the system, cut to the front of the line, and go on to the next big thing.

Kaitlin pondered these leanings. What she was willing to do for money didn't even come close to what many of her contemporaries would do. Nevertheless, guys like Darren Park, Dale Cho, Michael Owens, and Gary Tyler didn't deserve to be murdered by the likes of Shane Calloway and Warren Harriman. She was determined to make their grim temptation come to a stop. She'd done all the calculations and was well ahead of Harriman. His number was up. This was Kaitlin Hall's *next big thing.*

# Chapter 39

The gray fog billowed in large clouds across Polk Street, driven by a light wind, casting shadows as it passed through the yellow glare of the streetlights. Small beads of water clung to the windshield of Kaitlin's car. Every so often, the beads would reach a critical mass and stream down toward the hood of the car.

Slim was much more relaxed now that the car was parked. He was fixated on the windshield, entranced by the geometry and randomness of the streaming droplets. *Maybe this wasn't going to be a good day to die.*

Kaitlin kept her attention fixed on the elegant front door of La Folie, diagonally across the street. They'd arrived at five minutes to eight. A few minutes later, a mammoth black Range Rover pulled up to the valet attendants. Shane Calloway stepped out from the driver's seat, and Warren Harriman practically leaped from the passenger seat to the curb below. With her window down, Kaitlin could just make out Harriman complaining.

"I hate these SUVs! Whatever happened to a nice sedan?" Harriman asked rhetorically, adjusting his suit jacket and tie. Calloway smiled and Harriman finished his complaint. "In every possible way, these vehicles are annoying."

As the valet took the driver's seat, Calloway accompanied Harriman into the ambient lighting of the restaurant. They were followed by a brief procession of Mercedes, Lexus, and Beemer owners who had a similar dress and demeanor of Calloway and Harriman. Ten minutes later, Gary Tyler pulled up in his blue Nissan Maxima, wearing a respectable blue suit. He stepped nervously from his car and onto the street.

Caught in profile in the headlights of traffic rolling down Polk Street, Kaitlin discerned the reddened cheeks and forehead that Gary had earned after a few hours on Koh Samui. He was sunburned and scared. She hoped Tyler was keeping his composure and wearing a nice cologne – and a lot of it. Calloway was trained to smell danger.

During the next two hours, Kaitlin and Slim waited anxiously for any sign of activity. A faint aroma emanated from La Folie's kitchen and wafted out over the sidewalk, across the street and in through the narrow crack of her car window. She was hungry, and her stomach growled with discontent. Kaitlin's slight sake buzz was a distant memory.

"Man, what's taking so long? Do you think they ordered the soufflé?" Slim asked impatiently.

"Well, as much as I'd like them to come out of there quickly, I prefer they take their time." Kaitlin checked the time on her watch. "The longer they're in there, the more time we have for the FBI to show up. Nothing I'd like more than to have the cavalry here." But in an attempt to hide her concern from Slim, she faced him and said, "Besides, fine meals are to be savored, enjoyed, indulged in. In a restaurant like this, every action is perfectly orchestrated. Timing of the meal is everything ..." Kaitlin rambled on, rubbing the sleeve of her coat against the inside of the window to wipe away the thin layer of condensation that had begun to impair her view of the restaurant's façade.

Her arm froze in mid-motion as the restaurant's dapper *maître d'* opened the door to La Folie. Two or three shadowy figures emerged. Slim instinctively slumped in his seat, avoiding any possibility of being seen. Kaitlin continued to stare out her window.

Harriman and Calloway were laughing heartily. But there was something wrong. Calloway stood too closely to Tyler. Tyler walked with a strange gait. His arm was propped around Calloway's shoulder. To the El Salvadorian valet parking attendants, Tyler looked like a small percentage of the expensive restaurant's patrons that imbibed too much Château Lafite Rothschild 1972. *Un poco borracho.*

But Kaitlin knew better. Watching them carefully load Tyler into the backseat of the Range Rover, it was obvious to her what had happened. "Jesus, they've drugged him!" she exclaimed.

Another valet parking attendant pulled up in Gary Tyler's Nissan Maxima. Two men that Kaitlin did not recognize exited from the restaurant. One presented the valet with the claim ticket for Gary Tyler's car and the other presented the ticket for another car, a Mercedes, which was brought up seconds later. Rather than get into the Range Rover, in which he had arrived at the restaurant, Warren Harriman got into the Mercedes, and sped away.

"Oh my God, they're going to kill him," Kaitlin said, certain about what was going to happen. "Tonight's the night!"

# Chapter 40

Kaitlin had the engine running by the time Calloway pulled the Range Rover away from the curb. The flow of traffic on Polk Street had now subsided, and she managed to pull in just two cars behind the Range Rover and the Maxima.

"Get on the phone, Slim. Call Renfro!" she instructed.

While Slim made the call, Kaitlin drove with agility, keeping up with her target. The procession led by the Range Rover had, within a couple of turns, hit Van Ness and was heading towards the waterfront. Kaitlin wracked her brain. She considered all the possible places they could be going: *the Marina, the Presidio ...*

"The Bridge!" Her shout startled Slim. "They're heading toward the Golden Gate Bridge!"

"Renfro," the weary voice came through on the cell phone.

Slim didn't particularly care for Feds and even less for Renfro, but in his adrenaline charged state, he wasn't the least bit focused on his personal feelings. "Yes, this is Slim

Yamazaki. I'm in the car with Kaitlin Hall and she asked me to call you. Where the fuck are you guys?"

"Who? What are you talking about?" Renfro responded befuddled.

"I'm Kaitlin's friend. We are in the Marina and heading toward the Golden Gate Bridge. We're following Shane Calloway. He's got Gary Tyler. We – Kaitlin – thinks he's been drugged or something." Slim was panting slightly. As they made the dogleg turn on Lombard and he saw the blue U.S. Highway 101 sign, it became clearer that the Golden Gate Bridge was indeed their destination.

Kaitlin grew impatient with Slim's conversation with Renfro. She needed backup, and fast.

She yelled in Slim's direction, projecting her voice so that Renfro could easily hear her. "Where are those agents, Renfro?"

"I cut them loose about twenty minutes ago," not sure if he was talking to her or to the Slim character. "But they called, they're stuck in a traffic jam on the Oakland-Bay Bridge. There's been an accident and a couple of lanes are closed."

"Well get someone out here now!" Kaitlin yelled. "We're heading north on the Golden Gate. Move!"

"I'll do what I can," Renfro snapped, frustrated by his inability to be there himself.

The fog grew dense and rain showered the windshield as they approached the edge of the Bay. In the darkness, Alcatraz's beacon light swept over Crissy Field with a momentary metallic flash and was gone. To the passing cargo ships and barges, that same light had steered them clear of the island's perilous rocks for decades. To the felons inside Alcatraz, perhaps it had been their SOS to the outside world.

But as they approached the toll gates at the southernmost end of the bridge's orange superstructure, Slim's mind was on the impending death of the felon-to-be in the car ahead. The bridge's majestic orange spires, illuminated by high-pressure sodium spotlights pierced the thick blanket of fog. Its cable spans stretched over the turbulent waters and into nothingness.

Without the soothing influence of Japanese sake, Slim was struck by the bizarreness of the situation. How had he been drawn out of the comfort and security of his Dungeon and put into a perilous cop chase? He looked over at Kaitlin, whose demeanor was composed, her eyes focused in perfect concentration on the cars in front of them.

"Do you think they're going to throw him off the bridge?" Slim asked. "Try to make it look like a suicide?"

Kaitlin shook her head. "Too many cars," she answered. "They can't stop on the bridge." She had considered the very same possibility; indeed, she had feared it. But forcing herself to think rationally amidst chaos, she knew that wasn't their goal. At this time of night, there was no way to stop one car, much less two, on the bridge without causing a traffic jam within a matter of moments. Besides, they had been traveling across the bridge's serrated surface for several minutes now and were passing the bridge's mid-point. They were crossing over into Marin County.

"Slim, call Renfro again. I think I know where they're going," Kaitlin said confidently.

At the northern boundary of the bridge, where its structure became brick and concrete and earth, Kaitlin remembered a small parking area. She'd passed it on many a Sunday afternoon, smiling at the hordes of starry-eyed Asian and Midwestern tourists standing astride their rental cars and tour buses. Cameras clicking away at the postcard-perfect view of the City by the Bay. As anticipated, they passed a blue "Scenic Viewpoint" road sign, a water-soaked blur, and the Range Rover's right turn signal sent out a yellow glimmer ahead.

Slim handed her the cell phone. "It's ringing."

"Renfro. It's the viewpoint at the Northeast end of the bridge! Tell me your people are coming!" She could barely hear him over the siren now blaring in his car.

"I'm on my way. Another team of agents is in the Presidio. Stay back. They'll be there in ten minutes. Fifteen at the most!"

"I don't *have* ten minutes!" Kaitlin yelled, and to Slim it sounded like she was losing her composure. "And before you get onto the bridge turn off that siren, or we'll all be dead!" She hung up and threw the phone into Slim's lap.

"Damn, damn, damn," she muttered to herself. She now faced a difficult decision. The viewpoint's parking area would most likely be deserted now. Which was, no doubt, why it had been chosen. But in the absence of other cars, could she risk pulling into that area? Only a hundred yards wide, the area was too confined.

She slowed her car to twenty-five and put on her hazard lights. Instead of turning into the viewpoint, she rolled by the entrance. Slim was confused.

"Kaitlin, they're in there. Where are we going?

She was taking the opportunity of a drive-by to carefully reconnoiter the area. At the far end of the vista point, two cars sat with their lights off. The fog and drizzle minimized what little ambient light existed. But Kaitlin could tell that the viewpoint area was completely devoid of people. In these weather conditions, there wouldn't be much for a tourist to admire, except the City's twinkling lights off in the distance.

A hundred feet past the viewpoint's exit, Kaitlin rolled to a stop on the shoulder of the road and turned off the engine. The only sound was the squeaking of the windshield wiper on the glass and the occasional car whooshing by.

"Lift the hood, Slim. We want to look like motorists in distress waiting for the Auto Club."

Kaitlin removed her Glock from her shoulder holster. In a fluid motion, she popped the magazine, checked it, and reinserted it.

"Wait a second, you're not going out there alone," Slim said.

"No worries, Slim. Renfro will be here in a minute with a team of FBI in tow," Kaitlin said matter-of-factly. Although she said it more for Slim's sake.

Before he could refute that statement, Kaitlin was standing on the asphalt and shutting the car door behind her. Slim didn't know what he liked less – her being out there alone or him being left alone. Helpless by the side of the road. Right now he really missed the Dungeon and the comforting hum of CPUs and electric fans.

Kaitlin pulled something out of her trunk and jogged into the darkness. In her right hand, she carried a pump-action shotgun, which she'd removed from its locked mount in the trunk. *Just in case*, Kaitlin thought. The damp, cold night air enveloped her, heightening the sensation of blood coursing through her veins.

Her fashion decisions for the evening had not anticipated these events, but fortunately her dark clothing helped camouflage her as she skulked through the shrubs that lined the northern boundary of the parking area. Her choice to wear boots rather than heels was fortuitous. A low rock wall circumscribed the parking lot; she hopped over it onto the narrow pathway, which followed it from north to south. At the southernmost point of the parking lot, where the two cars were parked, she saw no movement. Using the wall as a screen, she quietly approached the cars. About one hundred feet away she paused and crouched behind the wall. A car door thudded closed.

Slowly, she peered over the wall. Behind the Range Rover, stood the shapes of two men astride a figure lying on the ground. A third man stood next to the Maxima.

As they lifted the body from the ground, Kaitlin quickly realized it was Gary Tyler. Each man grabbed either of Gary's arms and hoisted them around their shoulders. It still looked very much like two guys assisting their drunk friend after a night of partying. The men ambled off ungracefully into the bushes.

Kaitlin was well aware that the lot sat upon a rocky bluff several hundred feet high above the churning white water of the

Golden Gate – the mouth of the great San Francisco Bay from which the bridge derived its name. Many people had jumped to their deaths from here. Chinese immigrants who'd tired of lives eking out a meager existence in the laundries. Young gay men who'd been jilted by their lovers, or who'd received the HIV test results they so desperately feared. Depressed, Mercedes-driving housewives from Belvedere Island. Gary Tyler would be just another statistic. It wouldn't even make the pages of the *Chronicle.* Only celebrity deaths made the pages of the City's second-rate newspaper.

Kaitlin had to act now.

One man had stayed behind to attend to Gary Tyler's car. She stealthily rolled her body over the wall, and jogged quickly but quietly toward the far side of Range Rover, using it as cover. She was now only about ten feet away, her back resting against the Range Rover's left rear tire. She carefully rested the shotgun underneath the Range Rover, pulled the nine millimeter pistol out of its holster and brought it up to her chest.

As she spun around the tail end of the Range Rover, she soon realized that the man had been carefully wiping off the various surfaces of Gary Tyler's car. Removing fingerprints and stray fibers. On the front seat of the car, sat a crisp white envelope. A suicide note, Kaitlin surmised. Quietly, she put the pistol back in her holster.

So occupied with his task, the man inside Tyler's car didn't notice the tall woman approaching from behind. He was leaning into the backseat when Kaitlin swiftly reached her right arm around his neck in a sleeper hold, crushing his carotid and jugular arteries between her bicep and forearm. The intense pressure silenced him, the blood flow to his brain almost entirely diminished. A formerly common police practice, the sleeper hold was banned in the San Jose police force. Kaitlin didn't care; going solo required some improvisation.

After ten seconds of continual pressure, he collapsed into unconsciousness on the backseat without making a sound. Kaitlin's heart pounded. Getting to this point had been easier than she expected. But there was no time to relax. From the dark hillside below, Gary Tyler's body was about to be heaved into the abyss. Rain began to fall. Kaitlin brushed her hair away from her eyes, blotted her wet face with her shirtsleeve, and pushed through the bushes lining the parking lot.

She moved as quietly and quickly as possible down the muddy trail. From the parking lot, she couldn't determine how far Calloway and his victim would trek. Fifty yards down the slippery hillside, the trail opened up on a clearing. Kaitlin stopped in her tracks. Only weak moonlight and the distant lights of the bridge offered any illumination.

In the clearing, which served to offer hikers a majestic view of the bay, one of the men was standing and the other, maybe Calloway, was crouching over Gary Tyler. Like the guy stationed at the car, Kaitlin speculated that they were going to begin cleaning up the victim. Ensuring that Gary's death looked like nothing other than a suicide.

In the event that Tyler's body was even found. The Golden Gate's surging currents and the fact that the water was a great white shark habitat lessened the probability that his body would be recovered. But Shane Calloway didn't take chances when it came to such things. To the world, Gary Tyler would be another computer nerd who got tired of chasing cybersex and the elusive IPO payday.

When Calloway pulled Tyler up from the wet ground by his lapel, Kaitlin took action. As Calloway stood upright, Kaitlin darted up from the bushes and crouched at the opening of the trail. The rustling of the bushes immediately caught the men's attention. They knew someone was there.

"Freeze! Police Department! Put your hands in the air where we can see them!" Kaitlin yelled forcefully. She trained the barrel of her pistol first on Calloway and then on the other man. They stood there motionless, staring at her. The quietness of the salty air was broken by the rumble of the sea crashing on the rocks below.

"I said, *hands up*!"

Slowly, one man raised his hands, looking at Calloway for further guidance.

Trying to provoke a response from Calloway, Kaitlin yelled again. "Calloway – Shane Calloway – put your hands up! Do you hear me soldier?" She was doing her best drill sergeant impersonation. The rumble of the sea punctuated her command.

Calloway smiled and loudly replied, "I hear you. But I'm a Marine, not a soldier!"

Suddenly, in a swift continuous motion, he drew his arm to his chest, pulling a revolver out of his jacket pocket, wheeling

Gary Tyler's slumped body in front of him. He was using Tyler's body as a human shield. Kaitlin's stomach dropped.

Before figuring out her next move, Kaitlin heard a rustling in the bushes behind her. As she spun around, she found herself face to face with the man she'd left unconscious in the back seat of Gary's car. His left hand was applying pressure to the back of his neck, trying to restore his circulation. In his right hand was a .44 Magnum. *The most powerful handgun on earth*, as Clint Eastwood's "Dirty Harry" would say. His face bore the mask of anger. Great, she'd let a very pissed off murderer get the jump on her.

She could hear the laughter in Calloway's voice when he called out from the distance. "Now, drop your weapon, *soldier*."

Kaitlin had no choice but to comply. She lowered her arm and let her Glock fall onto the muddy brown soil.

"You bitch," the man with the Magnum said, in a low, hostile voice. "You've got some nerve. Sneaking up on a guy like that."

"Sorry about that," Kaitlin said. "Hope I didn't hurt you. I tried to be gentle."

She was attuned to footsteps approaching her from behind. If this guy was pissed off, Shane Calloway was going to be beyond furious. It was then that she noticed something in the shadowy bushes behind the thug with the .44 – a slight movement and a brief reflection of light on metal.

With Ninja-like precision, Slim jumped out of the bushes and onto the trail. The Magnum-toting goon spun around, taken by surprise again.

Slim wielded the Mossberg Model 500 shotgun, leveled chest high. And if he was at all uncomfortable, it certainly didn't show.

The Magnum fired first and the deafening report of the shotgun followed an instant later, almost like an echo. With a scream, Slim was spun around and thrown to the ground. The guy with the Magnum was hit squarely in the chest by the 12-gauge cartridge. The impact kicked him backward five feet.

Kaitlin didn't wait for his body to hit the ground before grabbing for her own gun. She'd trained this move a thousand times. But this wasn't a drill. This was for real. Her life, Slim's life, Gary's life were all in jeopardy.

She gripped the wet gun, rolled over on her right shoulder, crouched and fired repeatedly into the clearing now in front of her. A half dozen shots later, Shane Calloway was lying on the ground, bleeding from his head and chest.

Silence. Then the roar of waves crashing onto the rocky outcroppings below the bridge. Behind her Kaitlin could hear Slim moaning softly.

The other man stood in the same place where he'd been all along. He raised his hands high above his head, standing over Gary Tyler's crumpled body.

Without taking her eyes or her aim off the guy, Kaitlin called out to Slim, "Slim, how are you doing? Are you okay?" Having been shot with a Magnum at close range, Kaitlin feared the worst.

Slim coughed and then cleared his throat. "I'm bleeding. It's my arm. Hurts like hell."

"You stay still. If you can, try to apply direct pressure to the wound with your other hand," Kaitlin called out. She was relieved to hear his voice. But they were a long way from being out of the woods.

She rose from the ground, her clothes completely soaked in cold mud, the wet wind chilling her to the bone. She approached the man and ordered him away from Gary Tyler. He complied and laid down on the ground with his hands behind his back, as she directed.

She carefully rolled Gary Tyler over. His face was pale; she quickly placed her index and middle fingers on the side of his neck. She was relieved to find that he was still alive. She pulled his shirttails out of his pants and frantically reached inside his waistband. He was wearing the FBI recorder. The green LED was still flashing. He had taped everything.

From the hillside above, Kaitlin could hear men's voices. Turning quickly, she saw a multitude of flashlight beams bouncing down the trail.

The cavalry had finally arrived.

# Chapter 41

Slim's arm was wrapped tightly in bandages and raised awkwardly by a series of cables. The large caliber bullet had grazed his humerus and had done some serious damage to his left deltoid muscle. "What muscle?" he would later joke.

Slim was going to make a quick recovery.

Sitting by the side of his bed, Kaitlin stroked his head as he drifted in and out of a morphine-induced haze. "I can't believe you almost got me blown away," Slim said, looking into her eyes.

"I thought I told you to wait in the car," Kaitlin responded gently. Then she smiled. "Thanks for ignoring me though. Guess you've been keeping your trips to the shooting range a secret. If it wasn't for you, I'd be swimming around the Bay right now with Gary Tyler."

"How's he doing?" Slim asked.

"He's doing fine. But still totally out of it from the massive dose of Rohypnol that Team Calloway gave him," Kaitlin said. "You see the *Chronicle* yet?"

He blinked his eyes. "Do I look like I'm in any shape to get to the newsstand?" Slim asked rhetorically.

"Front page, my friend," Kaitlin said, holding the paper a few inches from his face.

The large words appeared blurry but slowly came into focus: "*Venture Capitalist Warren Harriman Arrested.*"

She pulled the paper back and read the article aloud.

> *'Well-known San Francisco venture capitalist and principal of the Harriman & Co. firm, Warren Harriman, was arrested last night at his San Francisco residence shortly before eleven p.m. Harriman has been the subject of a joint FBI-San Jose Police Department Task Force investigation. According to FBI Special Agent Alex* Renfro, *Harriman is the lead suspect in a series of unlawful technology exports and a string of related homicides. A Grand Jury indictment is expected within the next few days. Two other men associated with Harriman, and also suspects in connection with his activities, were killed by officers of San Jose Police Department's elite High Tech Crimes Detail. One other man was taken into custody. In a public statement issued early this morning by Harriman & Co., the firm's spokesperson vehemently denied any wrongdoing. According to the FBI, no further information will be released until a full investigation has been completed and the Grand Jury has been convened.'*

Just as she finished reading, the door opened and Torres poked his head in. "How's your friend doing?"

Kaitlin answered with a big smile. Torres walked in, carrying a large potted plant looking curiously out of place in his arms.

"This is for you," he said to Slim, putting the gift on the bedside table. "Thanks for saving my detective," Torres said. "I really appreciate it … and I'm sorry you got hurt in the process."

"Ah, it's nothing. Just a flesh wound," Slim said weakly, borrowing a line from *Monty Python and the Holy Grail.* The movie reference was lost on Torres but much appreciated by Kaitlin, who winked at Slim.

Watching Torres in that moment of sympathizing, Kaitlin had no problem picturing him as Governor or a U.S. Senator. He was a good man.

Torres turned to Kaitlin, still holding the newspaper. "May I have a word with you, Detective? Outside?" he said, motioning toward the door.

When they'd closed the door to Slim's room, Torres pointed at the newspaper. "Nice story," he said. "Don't you think?"

"Yeah, not bad. I'm not sure why they had to quote Renfro. Or why it said *officers* of our elite unit rather than *outstanding female officer.*"

Torres smiled and nodded. "Agreed," he said. "Still, we look pretty good. The Chief *really* liked the story. He's called me twice today."

"That's phenomenal, Captain," Kaitlin said genuinely. It was. Especially given the way that things could have – and almost had – gone wrong. She was happy for herself. And she was happy for Torres, as well.

"The Chief asked me to pass on his compliments for a job well done. Also, he told me that he's authorizing a budget increase for the High Tech Crimes Detail. Enough to cover two more detectives," Torres said, grinning from ear to ear. "That means you'll have some help covering some of the less interesting cases."

Kaitlin knew exactly what he was saying. She would no longer be the low cop on the totem pole.

"That's excellent," she said. "They can start with Mrs. Hammond in Los Gatos. With all that was going on, I never returned the poor lady's calls," Kaitlin said apologetically.

Torres laughed. He and Kaitlin turned and walked down the hallway together, seeking out a cup of hot coffee.

Made in the USA
Coppell, TX
22 July 2021